OPUS 2019

ANTHOLOGY

WALTER E. LEDWITH

Opus 2019

ISBN: 978-1-970153-15-6

Cover Image shutterstock - 190267145

La Maison Publishing, Inc.
Vero Beach, Florida
The Hibiscus City
lamaisonpublishing@gmail.com

STORIES

Acknowlegements

A big thanks to Janet Sierzant from La Maison Publishing for her help each step of the way to publication. A special thanks to Judith Konitzer and L.H. Davis for their editing expertise.

Acknowledg...

STORIES

TIKAL

"This is taking a long time!"

The pressure she placed on my hand had been slowly increasing since we took our seats.

"It's been over an hour. . . . Where is he? I thought you said the Maya were obsessed with keeping time? This is not my idea of keeping time or of a vacation!"

I took another swig at my Corona; it was best to let Myselda run through her litany of complainants. It was a necessary coping mechanism for both of us.

"The Airport looks as though children painted it!" she

said, scanning the tarmac and terminal through the window for the hundredth time.

Myselda didn't like flying to begin with. The twelve-seat plane, although a jet, didn't exactly inspire confidence in her. Not compared to the 747, we flew into Guatemala City on.

"This is like a toy!"

I took another swig on my beer as the pressure on my hand increased. At this rate, I would be flying before we took off.

The stewardess passed by and asked the people behind us if they wanted to refresh their drinks. They were the only other people on the flight. The wife reordered, and the husband asked how much longer it would be before take-off.

"Our pilot has just arrived at the airport, and we should be leaving shortly," she said, feigning a smile.

I raised my beer to indicate that I'd like another.

Not looking at the stewardess, Myselda shook her head. "No, thank you." She scanned the tarmac through the window.

"Maybe we should switch seats for this flight?" Myselda always sat at the window.

"No thanks . . . but thank you!" Scanning the tarmac, "That must be his co-pilot. . . . Very young."

"Finally!" I said as she let go of my hand. "Ah . . . the co-pilot is here." I smiled.

She took my beer and downed half of it. "Maybe I should have ordered one," she said in a deep, raspy voice.

I could hear the co-pilot climbing the ramp. He appeared in the cabin, opened the cockpit door, and put his bag inside. The lady behind us called out to him.

"Excuse me. . . . Hello! Can you tell me when the pilot will be here and when we will leave?"

The stewardess and the young man smiled haplessly at each other and shrugged their shoulders as if to say, "Here we go."

"Good evening ladies and gentlemen. . . . My name is Louis Felipe de la Cruz. . . . I will be your pilot today for our flight to Flores Guatemala on beautiful Lake Petén. On behalf of Aviateca Airlines, the crew and I would like to welcome you aboard. We hope your flight will be a pleasant one so that we will see you many times in the future. It is a relatively short flight to Flores from Guatemala City, so sit back, settle in and enjoy."

The pilot did a 180-degree turn and entered the cockpit. The ground crew removed the blocks from the wheels and cleared the area for our departure. The gangway was removed, and the engines started with a whine, slowly working their way to a hum. Another whine and the engines revved higher, the lights became brighter and the air conditioning blew at full force.

Myselda, having grabbed my hand again, did not miss a beat and the pressure increased with each event. The pilot spoke on the intercom.

"Ladies and gentlemen, please fasten your seat belts and prepare for takeoff. Our stewardess will be available to assist you in any way. Please enjoy the flight and I will let you know when we are approaching Flores."

Myselda, already strapped in, leaned back into her seat, applying constant pressure. "How do we know that he's not some kid who took his father's uniform and wants to play pilot for a day!" Myselda said sarcastically.

She had a very fanciful imagination. "Can I borrow that? . . . I mean, can I write it down?" taking a pen and note pad from my shirt pocket.

3

"Stop making fun of me. This is what's happening. This is reality!"

"No, this is where you imagine something, convince yourself it's true, and spin a foreboding, detailed, apocalyptic scenario."

"Can I write that down?" she said with a laugh.

I raised my Corona saluting her. "Touché!"

The jet backed away from the terminal and taxied to the runway. The stewardess picked up our trays, stowed everything away and took her seat in the front of the plane. The engines reached a higher pitch, and we rolled down the runway. The pilot lifted the aircraft into the air, and we were off, as perfect a take-off as I'd ever experienced. Despite the perfect takeoff, Myselda's nails dug into my flesh.

I let out a yelp. "Hey . . . easy girl," I said, rubbing my hand.

"Oh, I'm sorry. I get so nervous." She leaned further back into her seat.

Thank God her piano playing kept her fingernails short, or I would have been in need of medical attention.

"You push any harder on the back of that seat, you're going to wind up in the bathroom," I said, frustrated and annoyed. "I really would like to switch seats. I wanna' look for pyramid combs in the canopy. It would be so surreal to see some. What do you say?" I rubbed my sore hand to add some guilt to the request. During the months of planning, I always saw myself flying over the jungle, looking for lost cities. It was big on my itinerary.

"Well, I guess so, since you put it like that. I'm sorry about your hand. I didn't even realize I was doing it. How can I refuse? Come on, let's switch." She unbuckled her seatbelt and stood. I slipped underneath her and buckled up. The

4

stewardess signaled Myselda to return to her seat, which she did so grumbling, "Isn't she bossy." She buckled her seatbelt just as the fasten your seatbelt light turned off.

"Hope they have a decent car for us at the rental," I said, making conversation.

"I didn't even think of that! . . . Ahh," she groaned.

"We could wind up with a nineteen seventy-eight Impala or something."

"Don't get me started, Seth!"

The stewardess came over and told us all to feel free to move about the cabin. "Can I get you anything?"

"Scotch and soda, please," the man behind us said.

"Ditto," chimed his wife.

"I'll have another corona."

"White wine for me please," Myselda said smiling, then turned to me with her 'serious face'. "Don't forget, we still have to drive to who knows where later." She turned away, then back again, "And I sure hope you remember how to handle La Grande Impala."

Myselda could get pretty salty when she was upset. But this was better than her getting nervous, frightening herself. I probably should have edited myself and not mentioned the car rental at all, but I had not mastered that skill. Didn't want to. The truth was that I didn't give a shit. Myselda would spin a cocoon and pull down the clouds. She could darken the earth with hours-long eclipses. That was the part of her life I didn't want to share. I was more than happy to wait for her 'same-ole-use-to-be' to return so we could move on. The couple behind us saved the day by standing over our seats and introducing themselves.

"Hi," the man said putting out his hand. "My name is Albert, and this is my wife Doris." We stood to greet them.

"Glad to meet you," followed Doris, waving.

Why is she waving? I am only three feet away and she's waving as though we were across the Alps.

"Doris and I are here on business for a few days. Looking at some potential development opportunities. Archio-tourism is becoming increasingly popular, and we want to get in on the ground floor." He spoke as though he had rehearsed his lines and was practicing on us. "We will be staying at the Ramada Tikal Inn, in Flores."

"Hi," I said, feigning enthusiasm, putting out my hand. Everyone shook hands again for the second time, round and round. "I'm Seth, and this is Myselda. We're from New York and we're here to visit the ruins."

There are times when the mundane is as welcome and as captivating as novelty; and this was one of them. That couple, in their country club clothes were a Godsend. Their friendliness and enthusiasm were as real and authentic as it could get. They brought a smile to Myselda's face. Their energy was contagious. *Perfect!*

The stewardess came back with our drinks. We raised our glasses to toast, which didn't get very far.

"Watch out for the water . . . and the salads!" Doris meant well. "And there's also been a couple of cases of cholera reported."

"The company keeps us informed of what's happening in the area," Albert said interrupting Doris. "They've had a lot of rain here lately, and things can get kind of backed up if you know what I mean," he explained almost apologetically before changing the subject. "Are you going straight to the ruins? I was just telling Doris you two looked like an adventuresome couple."

"Yes, he did," said Doris, nodding.

"No, we're going to spend the night in Flores. . . . Honey, what's the name of the hotel that we'll be staying at in Flores?"

"Hotel La Lancha."

"That's it; Hotel La Lancha."

"I've seen that one in the brochures. Looks very nice," Doris said approvingly.

"I hope so," sighed Myselda.

"And then we will get a fresh start in the morning." I knew he wanted details, so I filled him in. "When we get there, we'll be staying at the Jaguar Inn, on site."

"Sounds really interesting."

"It's going to be an adventure that's for sure. We'll be kinda' roughing it."

"That's an understatement," Myselda sniped.

I ignored her. "With local food from the cantina and a general store on site, who could ask for more? The generators are turned off at nine o'clock though, so we'll be in the jungle at night without power . . . and in the dark." Eyeing Myselda I added, "But we've packed some good flashlights, so we'll be fine."

"Thank God they have indoor plumbing," Myselda said turning to Doris. "I told him I would not go on this trip if they didn't have bathrooms."

"We've been on camping trips where we've had less." I was getting annoyed. Myselda was knocking our adventure before it even began.

Albert came to the rescue once again, raising his glass, "To finish our toast, here's to good weather, good business and good luck for our intrepid travelers. Cheers!"

"Cheers!" We all clinked our glasses and wished each other good luck.

The stewardess came by again asking if we wanted anything. Myselda and I declined, and Albert and Doris returned to their seats to wait for their drinks. Finally, I could get back to my jungle canopy.

There it was, rolling along like a carpeted conveyer, pulling us forward through a sea of green, with only an occasional clearing. *What would a Mayan think if he were here? Would he even be able to conceive of travelling at five-hundred fifty miles an hour through space? Would he think he was travelling with the Gods? Heading for the stars?*

Or maybe he would not be all impressed at all. Thinking about the sarcophagus of Pacal Votan, the John Glen of Palenque, my Mayan friend might already be familiar with extraordinary methods of travel. Their whole concept of time was a high-speed railway through Baktuns, Tikkuns and Ages; the beginnings and ends of worlds — in the past and in the future. Ask a shaman who has conjured the vision serpent, if they have ever traveled through space and different dimensions, and they will tell you, "To the end of time."

We were beginning our descent. The elevators were lowered, the engines voices deepened and the ground below moved a little bit faster. Just minutes before, at cruising speed, the landscape conveyer had rolled along at a slow but steady pace. The closer we got to the earth, the faster the conveyer turned. I saw pyramid combs in the distance. They jutted through the canopy, almost waving, beckoning us to them. I was familiar with the design of the tallest of the pyramid combs.

That must be Tikal!

The pilot came on the intercom. "Ladies and gentlemen, welcome to beautiful Lake Petén. We have begun our descent, and you will be on your way to your hotels very shortly. Please fasten your seatbelts. Stewardess, please prepare for landing."

It was a very smooth descent. In even, measured increments, he brought the jet to the ground as though he were kissing a baby. I clapped enthusiastically, with Albert joining in, giving the pilot a resounding round of applause. I had been worried myself about this guy's acumen. He did look awfully young. I taunted myself thinking that I would have been the world's biggest asshole if we'd crash in the jungle, and I hadn't spoken up, not wanting to hurt someone's feelings. But I dismissed it. It didn't matter because there I was, removing my bags from the overhead and everything was fine.

"I guess I overreacted," Myselda said apologetically.

I didn't let on that I had been concerned as well. "We all get a little nervous flying luv, not to worry. By this time tomorrow we'll be walking the sacred sacbe into downtown Yax Mutal." I thanked the pilot and stewardess on the way out and told them we hoped to see them on the return flight.

"What's a Yax Mutal?" asked Myselda, bouncing down the gangplank. "I know a sacbe is a Mayan road."

The gangplank was like a trampoline; you had to hold the railing to keep steady.

"That was what the Maya called their city. It translates First Mutal or First City. Kinda' like calling Rome the 'Caput Mundi'.[1] Tikal is the name given by locals who had long forgotten the language and culture of their ancestors. The Spanish conquerors beat it out of them. Tikal means 'at the well' or watering hole."

---

[1] Head of the world

* * * *

The terminal was modern, glass enclosed, with a variety of vendors strewn about in colorful kiosks. We crossed the terminal carrying our backpacks to the information desk. We asked where the luggage carousel and car rentals were. A very pretty young woman, who spoke excellent American English, told us the luggage carousel was to the left and the car rental was just outside. I asked her where she had learned to speak English so well. She told us she learned English in school, and that she had family in San Francisco who she loved to visit and would practice when she was there.

"They lost their whole culture?" asked Myselda on the way to the baggage claim.

"Just about," I said, "for a long time all they had was what the shamans remembered."

"Wow, cultural genocide."

"The conquistadors and the good friars destroyed their temples, burned their books and forced their religion and language upon them."

"Bastards! . . . Ferdinand and his religious police were a bunch of freaking sociopaths!" Myselda loved a good 'somebody done somebody wrong song'. She had an entire litany of crimes against humanity going back to Cain and Abel. "You just can't erase people's memory though . . . Can you?"

"Well, in the time of Plato, if you were to ask an Egyptian who had built the temples and the pyramids and why, they wouldn't have been able to tell you. It was a complete mystery to them. Only the priests had an inkling, due to their rituals and hieroglyphs. They had always lived in the shadow

10

of the colossal monuments, which only *the gods* could have built. The pyramids had always been there and life is about the day to day stuff. They were built so long ago . . . and living memory is so short. Lasts a couple of generations maybe."

Our bags were waiting for us at the carousel. We gave the attendant our tickets and we were off to the car rental. It was right across the street. The rental agent had the paperwork ready for us. We signed them and followed him to the lot.

Not a single Impala.

There were mostly Jeeps, a few town cars and a couple of compact Toyotas. The attendant showed us the main features of the Wrangler-- how to put the top up and down and how to use the four-wheel drive. The whole transaction took about twenty minutes. We threw our bags in the back, buckled up and we were on our way. Driving out of the lot, we saw Albert and Doris getting into a hotel van. I hit the horn and we waved goodbye. Doris waved, and Albert gave us a big thumbs up.

The rental agent had given us directions to the hotel and to Tikal. It was pretty simple. Not as though there were a lot of places to go in the area. The main road was a new highway, well-kept and a nice introduction to the roads in Guatemala. I could sense that the people of the area were very proud of their modern sacbe.

The turnoff for the hotel was about six miles up the federal highway. This would be the same road we would take to Tikal in the morning. We drove with the top down soaking up the forest. Quite a contrast to what we left in New York. The thatched roofed huts clustered along the highway appeared to be small villages.

Maybe for the workers?

I saw men sitting on their haunches, smoking cigarettes and talking. The women carried water jugs and bundles of firewood. The children followed, carrying as much as their little arms could hold. Smoke rose lazily from the roof tops. Chickens ran about chasing each other or running away from the occasional pig. This was a snapshot of *life* in central America.

"The men sit around while the women work." shouted Myselda. "It's the same all over the world."

"Not a lot to do around here Sel. These men are not lazy, it's just that there's little for them to do."

Between the engine and the wind flowing around the Jeep, we had to yell at each other.

"Look! Look! . . . I can see the blue light from a TV flashing in that hut," Myselda shouted. "Wow! Now it's orange. Must be a commercial."

"That's is so cool. Maybe they're watching Kojak," I shouted back.

We both noticed the road sign for our hotel at the same time. "La Lancha Hotel!"

"Great! I need a nap and a shower," Myselda said as I turned off the highway onto the hotel road. It was a good road for the first quarter mile or so, but, after that, as we headed back towards the lake, the road began to fill with water. I put the Jeep in four-wheel drive and slowly probed the road before us. I couldn't see through the muddy water. My tires would find a pothole now and then, nothing too deep, but soon the water was up to the middle of the wheels.

"Pick it up! Let's go." Myselda was getting nervous. "Come on. Move it! I don't want to get stuck here. Let's go!"

"The potholes aren't going away if I drive fast, ya know."

"Well you're gonna' get stuck in the mud at this rate, and

then we'll really be up shit creek."

"You want to drive?" I asked, figuring that would put an end to her complaints.

"Okay. Better than getting stuck out here!"

"All right then, let's see how well you do."

I pulled off the road at the first dry patch. We unbuckled, got out and walked around the back of the Jeep silently; sticking our tongues at each other as we passed. I figured that a few minutes of navigating that road would put an end to her complaints. Hopefully, it would put an end to that kind of thing for the rest of the trip. We buckled up, she put the Jeep in gear and hit the gas. She turned onto the road gunning the engine and flew through the next pool of water. We got soaked from the spray. The road rose, and we were on dry land again.

Okay, I thought, *let's see how she does with the next bad patch of road.*

There was no next bad patch of road. She drove about fifty yards and the road turned to the right, and soon we were passing through the stucco gates of the hacienda.

Aw shit! I knew I would never hear the end of it. The story would be retold a hundred times over the coming year. *Of course, she'll leave out the part where I got us two thirds of the way and concentrate on her prowess.* I could hear her at holiday dinners giving a minute-by-minute account of her success with her "difficult challenge."

She pulled under the canopy at the hotel entrance. We looked at each other and burst out laughing.

"You're covered with mud!" Myselda said.

"So are you!"

"We're a mess!" she said laughing.

I unfolded my handkerchief, wiped my face and passed it

on to Myselda. The Jeep was covered in mud. Looking around, so were all the other vehicles. The concierge arrived holding back a smile. He offered to hose off our luggage and have our bags brought to our room. We thanked him and followed him to the front desk. A worker in a jumpsuit parked the Jeep alongside the other muddy vehicles and brought the keys to the desk. A young man and woman, who did not hold back their smiles, stood behind the front desk. Myselda and I looked at each other, understood why, and enjoyed the scenario as well.

"We would like to hold your keys, with your permission, so that we may give your vehicle a wash," said the young woman.

"Complements of the house," said the young man.

Their sculpted looks told us that they were the descendants of conquistadors. The woman was exquisite, with jet black hair and dark oval eyes that held your attention captive. The young man looked like a bull fighter, exuding confidence and swagger.

"You will be staying in cottage number twelve. Enrique will show you the way, and your bags will be along shortly. We thank you for choosing the La Lancha Hotel for your stay at beautiful, Lake Petén."

"Thank you," we said and followed Enrique to our cottage.

It truly was an enchanting place. A meandering road connected all of the thatch roofed cottages. They were bright and airy, each made complete with a hammock on the front porch.

Every cottage had a view of the lake, and the colorful floral plantings along the road were like impressionist brush strokes. The concierge opened the door and gave me the key.

14

He said he would deliver our baggage shortly. I thanked him, asked for more towels and gave him a tip.

Just as the door clicked close, Myselda let out a yelp from the bathroom. I went in and found her in front of the mirror with her hands covering her face.

"My God . . .the mud has dried like a mud pack!"

I saw myself in the mirror. She was right. "Won't it come off in the shower?"

"I guess so . . . but suppose Mayan mud is different and doesn't come off. Then what? We might look like this for the rest of our lives!"

"Stop it."

"Just kidding! Lighten up, Seth. You can stay and watch me shower if you like." Myselda played an excellent coquette. "Might fulfill some of those mudwrestling fantasies you have."

I grabbed a beer from the frig and took my seat on the toilet to watch the show. Myselda was very theatrical and enjoyed every minute when she was "on." With her elixir, i.e. the water, she transformed herself from a clay statue into a marble Aphrodite. She beckoned me to the shower, and I immediately removed my, by then, very stiff clothing and joined her.

By the time I finished shaving and brushing my teeth, Myselda was out like a light, snoring away. I figured her ears were still stopped up from the flight as Myselda didn't snore. At least not that I knew of. Maybe she did, and I was always asleep. I opened my backpack, took out a tee shirt, a pair of boxers and my laptop. Luckily our backpacks were underneath our luggage and didn't get muddy. *Hope our other clothes didn't get soaked.*

I set up my laptop on the desk, opened a Corona and

began filling my journal with the day's events. There was a knock at the door, and the concierge dropped off our bags. *Okay, back to work!* It had been a full day and there was a lot to write about. The hotel checkout and taxi ride to the airport in Guatemala City had been uneventful, so I decided to start with the flight to Flores. I made notes, with descriptions of Albert and Doris, the stewardess and the pilot. My thoughts and impressions were the commentary. I must have been at it for hours, only returning to the present when my stomach growled and there was the smell perfume in the air. Myselda came out of the bathroom dressed, ready to go to dinner.

"How's the journal coming?"

"Okay. I had a lot of ground to cover," I said, yawning and stretching.

"Why don't you take a break? We can take a walk before dinner," she said holding out a neckless she had bought at a Bazaar in Guatemala City.

Taking the neckless I slipped it around her neck. "As soon as we get back home, I'm going to order Windows 95. It comes with Microsoft Office and I'll be able to get a lot more things done with it. This Word Pad I'm using is for the birds. Sorry I lost track of time, but I'll be right with you," I said searching my suitcase for something to wear. I was relieved that everything was dry, and I was ready in minutes.

Walking out the door, we entered a tropical paradise. We took the path down to Lake Peten soaking up the atmosphere, stopping to admire the exotic plants and sculptures along the way. The air was heavy with the scents of vegetation. It was a perfect, seventy degrees. When we left New York, it had been ten degrees and about to snow. This was definitely the right time of year to travel in Central America.

We came upon a bench and sat down to take in the vast

lake. It was dark and mysterious. *How many generations have lived along these shores?* The lake was a life-giving well that had sustained people for thousands of years. I noticed two middle aged women coming down the road. As they got closer, I recognized one of them as Linda Schele. She was my idol, an icon, a living monument in Mayan archeology. Her work with deciphering the glyphs, describing the Mayan cosmos, challenging Eric Thompson and the entrenched academic oligarchs, made her a Quixote-like heroine. They passed by, and I gave Myselda a shake.

"Do you know who that was?"

"No, should I?"

"*Forrest of Kings*? . . . *The Maya Cosmos*? . . . Linda Schele? . . . That's her!"

"Oh yeah, you've talked a lot about her. Who's the other woman? They must have come from dinner." Myselda's eyes followed them down the road. She loved celebrities.

"This is great!" I said getting up. "I hope we see her at Tikal. It would be great to talk to her. Are you ready for dinner?"

The restaurant was very nice with tables lakeside and in little alcoves. The menu was a full one, but I opted for the safety of steak and fries. Myselda had the oven-baked fish. We decided earlier that we would only eat food that had been cooked to the point where no living thing could survive. Coffee, Lipton iced tea, Pepsi, bottled water and beer would carry us for the most part, until we got back home to more familiar bacteria.

The beef was gamey, but the fries were fries. Myselda scarfed down her fish, saying it was delicious. We turned down the coffee and dessert, paid the bill and headed back to our cottage.

Once we left the bright lights of the restaurant, the night sky exploded with stars. They were like diamonds scattered upon dark blue velvet. The milky way was right over our heads and looked as though you could almost touch it. Little mystery as to why the Maya were obsessed with astronomy.

"You really found a gem here Sel. This place is great! We should take lots of pictures in the morning."

"I know, the hotel in Guatemala City wasn't bad either. If I ever need a career change, it will be to a travel agent. Just leave the booking to me, and a good time will be had by all!"

"You've got my business lady," I said, locking arms, savoring the night air.

* * * *

When I awoke, Myselda was already gone. I jumped in the shower, shaved and put on some fresh clothes. I packed my bags and got everything ready for checkout. I mentally walked through the morning's itinerary. Tikal was a short drive, about forty-five minutes. I hoped the hotel I booked at the site was decent. The pictures looked good, but I knew from experience that the advertising was often deceptive. Myselda came back looking as though she'd just had a massage and sauna.

"I took three rolls of film," she said putting her suitcase on the bed. "I couldn't stop myself. This was a perfect morning for taking pictures! I picked up five more rolls from the gift shop. I'll be right along."

"I'm all packed," I said putting my laptop into my backpack. "I just need to get something to eat and I'm good to go. I slept like a baby last night. The jungle air seems to agree with me. I'll be waiting outside for you."

18

We walked the same path we took the night before. The sun was glimmering on the lake, complementing the reflections of the clouds. The restaurant was very busy. The waiter showed us to a table in one of the alcoves. It was nice, cozy and private, with a view of the tables along the lake. Great for people watching. We both ordered huevos rancheros and washed it down with iced tea. It was very good and we both finished our plates without saying a word. Linda Schele and her entourage were by the lake, apparently discussing things over breakfast. I would have loved to be within earshot of that conversation. Perhaps some new finding was being discussed, the details of which were now being sorted out. *Maybe I'll see her at the site and get the skinny before it goes into print.*

We walked back to our cottage and picked up our bags. The young woman checked us out and held out the keys to the Jeep. "All clean, and ready to go."

I immediately snatched them and thanked her. I asked about the availability of rooms during the week, thinking that if the hotel at Tikal was a wash, we could come back. We would just have to make the drive every day. She indicated that it was likely we could get a room, but to call in advance to be sure.

Outside, the Jeep and all the other cars had been washed and were waiting. We loaded our bags into the back and were ready to go.

"To Tikal!" I said, leaning over to give Myselda a kiss.

"To Yax Mutal, driver!"

I backed out and entered the road that would take us to the federal highway. Most of the water had receded, so the road was pitted but passable. I was glad when we reached the open highway, which we had all to ourselves. It was a fine morning, crisp and clear. Columns of smoke rose from the houses along the road. The last of the breakfast fires were sending everyone off to the business of the day.

We didn't say much along the way. Absorbed in where we were, a glance and a smile were enough. The drive time was shorter than I figured, and only took us thirty-five minutes. I turned off the highway, drove a short way down the Tikal road and entered the parking lot. We had arrived!

There were two other cars in the parking lot-- a lemon-lime VW bug and a grey Chevy van. It was very quiet. There was not a soul around, so we decided one of us should stay with the baggage. Fortunately, a lady, obviously a tourist, came walking down the road. She was the owner of the VW and had driven with her husband from Guatemala City. They had come from Vancouver. I told Myselda I would check out where everything was located, leaving her with our new friend to chat.

I passed a building with a pickup truck backed up to it, loaded with kitchen trash. Walking around to the front, the sign over the door read, "Cantimplora y tienda Regalos (Canteen and Gift Shop)." It was screened on all four sides with tables along the perimeter. To the left was another building with a porch, rocking chairs and large wooden totem carvings on either side of the door. The sign above the entryway read, "Tienda General (General Store)."

The buildings sat at the intersection of three roads. In the center of a roundabout was a signpost. To the right was the road to Tikal, to the left Uaxactun and the third brought you back to the Auto Federal. The Jaguar Inn was on the far side. That would be our home for the next five days. I crossed over and passed through an adobe gateway with a Jaguar painted on the crown of the arch. It was fierce looking, painted in gold and black, blood red and tan. Now peeling and in need of attention, it must have looked nice in its day. I followed the arrow signs with "Oficina" written on them. The desk clerk looked happy to see someone. I introduced myself and told him we had reservations. He spoke English and said he was expecting us.

"Welcome to the Jaguar Inn. My name is Miguel and I will be very happy to assist you during your stay with us. The maid service has your room ready, so we are 'good to go'."

I thought it best to look at the room before checking in and asked if I could see it. It would save us a lot of trouble should it not be acceptable. We could just drive back to La Lancha and become commuters for the rest of the trip.

"Of course, sir. Right this way."

We followed a pathway that ran alongside the pool. It was in terrible shape. The paint was peeling and there were a thousand shades of green growing along its walls.

So far . . . not so good.

"We apologize for the pool. We are waiting for the rainy season to end before we begin our repairs. If you come back in the summer, it will be beautiful!" He said it as though their intentions to have the pool repaired was enough, and that made its present condition acceptable. The pool area was nothing like I'd seen on the internet. Gone was the lounge furniture and the tables shaded with colorful umbrellas. The waiter serving guests poolside in the pictures was nowhere to be found.

We won't be having cocktails here, that's for sure.

On a small hill, beyond the pool, was a building with four units. It stood two stories high and in front of each unit was a screened porch, with a bistro table and chairs.

"Here is Building A and since you are the first to arrive, you can choose from any of the rooms, the one you like."

Geez, we get the deluxe accommodations.

The first room I looked at was large, with a queen-size bed. The floors were tiled, and the walls were plastered with a stucco finish and painted in pastel colors. The bathroom was completely tiled white, and had an antiseptic look, simple and clean.

The adjacent room was the mirror image of the first. The stairs to the second floor creaked and sounded like a bass drum while walking up. The layout on the second floor was the same, except there were twin beds instead of the queen-sized. Each room had a small closet, a dresser, a desk, and chairs. The view was terrible. It looked down on the pool, which was an anachronistic aberration in contrast to the surrounding forest. The roundabout, the general store and canteen lay in the distance. I tried to imagine seeing this clearing from thirty-thousand feet, a bald spot in the forest.

There were quite a few birds flying about, darting from canopy to canopy, chirping on their way. Some of them were very colorful parrots, which were a delight to see.

"I'll take the first room we looked at Miguel."

"Very well sir, an excellent choice."

I decided we would give the place a shot. It was like cannery row compared to the hotel in Flores, but that's what made it an adventure. Walking back to the office, I heard my first Howler monkey. Judging by the deep, resonant, guttural sounds he threw at us, he must have been a big boy, with a large chest cavity. I searched the canopy around us but didn't see him.

"At night, between six and nine p.m., we run generators to recharge our batteries. It is a good time to recharge your devices as well, as the battery system here can be unpredictable. During the night, should we lose power, there is a lantern on the table in your room that will help you to see. There are more available at the tienda general if you like. Good for reading."

Back at the office he made a copy of my credit card and gave me the key to the room. He told me that I could drive up to the hotel to unload our bags but would have to return the car to the parking lot. I thanked him and left to fetch Myselda.

She was chatting away with the lady from Vancouver, who had been joined by her husband. He didn't look like the kind of person you would expect to see driving a lemon-lime VW bug. He was a big burly guy with a beard, wearing a Harley Davidson tee shirt. Myselda greeted me.

"Hey! You're back. How did it go?"

"Pretty good. I think you'll like it."

"This is Tamara and her husband Lev."

"Hello again Tamara. I'm Seth Lev, glad to meet you!"

"Nice to meet you Seth," he said as we shook hands.

"Like your car."

"That was all they had left at the rental and being six feet two inches, it's a liddle rough on the knees."

I grinned. "Ah, the things we do for love."

"The salesman said they are very popular with the Americans, so they keep plenty in stock. Go figure!"

They had accents like Boris and Natasha on the old Rocky and Bullwinkle Show.

"They were gonna stay at the Jaguar Inn too," Myselda said, "but they changed their minds."

"It's dee allergies you know," said Tamara.

"Yes, yes, the allergies," agreed Lev. "It is better in town."

Should I tell them about the cases of cholera in Flores? Isn't it obligatory to give them a heads up? Even if it's unpleasant. I took Lev aside and told him about the cholera, the water and the veggies. He said he already knew, and that they were taking precautions. I apologized for bearing bad news.

"Your concern is most appreciated. Of course we take it in the spirit in which it was intended, and we thank you. Tamara it's time we should go. It's getting late."

"Go-shmo. Hold your horses, we have plenty of time." Tamara was so Natasha. "We will talk later Myselda. I will see you here. Maybe when there are no husbands around."

They got into the Volkswagen, talking over each other in Russian. I could still hear them arguing a good way down the road.

"So, the hotel is okay?" asked Myselda as we got into the Jeep.

"Yeah, it's okay. It's *very real*. We can drop the bags off, but then I'm going to have to bring the Jeep back here. There's no place to park up there."

"So, I guess we won't be making any quick getaways in the middle of the night. . . . Don't look at me like that. You never know, anything could happen."

"The pool is kinda' messed up," I said, changing the subject. "It's been emptied so they can work on it. Other than that, the room is bright and airy and almost antiseptically clean."

"That's comforting."

"It will help keep the creepy crawlies away, and all the things that slither in the night."

"Gee. Thanks, Seth. Real comforting."

"It'll be fine Sel. We won't be spending a lot of time there anyway."

We drove past the cantina and around the sign post. *Time*

to have some fun! I passed the entrance and circled around again.

"Is this the scenic route?" Myselda said, laughing. "Or are you trying to make me dizzy to lessen the shock?"

I continued in wide circles around the sign post.

"It's the long way home, through downtown Yax Mutal. I want you to see and savor the ambience of this once thriving metropolis. This is the Times Square of Tikal!"

"Oh boy!"

"Nothing's too good for my girl!" I said, slowing down to pass through the gate of the hotel.

Myselda looked at the sign, and then at me with her 'Are you serious' look. "And why the theatrics?"

"I don't know. I guess I'm a silly man."

I parked in front of the office where Miguel was there to greet us. "Welcome to the Jaguar Inn. Mucho gusto señora!" Miguel took her bags, leading the way.

As we passed the pool Myselda looked straight ahead. I knew I would be hearing about it later.

Miguel placed the bags inside the door and gave us his speal. "I open the oficina at seven o'clock and we will have coffee and pastries ready for you to start the day. The cantina opens at seven as well and dinner is at six. Anything you need, do not hesitate to ask. We will be happy to help you."

Myselda checked everything out with no complaints. She took a seat on the screen porch to take in the view. "So, this is downtown Tikal. . . . Must be hopping on the weekends."

"I'll go and park the Jeep. You settle in. I'll be right back." I gave her a kiss on top of her head. "You're a trooper, luv!"

On the way down to the Jeep the howler began to roar. He was joined by a couple of his friends and they created quite a din. I kept going without looking back. I knew what

Myselda's reaction would be and I was glad that I was not there. I took the Jeep to the lot and parked in the closest available spot. Walking back, I felt very small amongst the towering trees. They were giants in a vast, endless jungle that felt like it stretched forever. The upper canopy was a city in itself, with pathways, grocery trees and meeting places for some serious 'monkey watching'. The birds occupied the lower part of the canopy, darting to and fro, singing as they flew by. I figured the ruckus in the canopy above was too much for these happy spirits.

Other than Miguel and the Russians, I had not seen anyone else since we arrived. *Where is everyone?* No cars, no tourist, no workers, no activity at all. We had the place all to ourselves. Still. *Where the hell is everybody?*

When I got back to the room, Myselda was on the bed reading one of the books we had brought with us about Tikal. She held her finger in the air indicating she wanted to finish what she was reading.

"Hi. I was just reading about the hero twins in the Mayan creation story. They were abducted by the gods of the underworld, right from the road outside our door. The road to Uaxactun."

"Yeah, the Popol Vuh[2] can get pretty strange. Uaxactun was a large city and we should go see it if we get the chance. It was a sister city to Tikal."

"We have the Jeep."

"Let's play it by ear, see how everything goes. You know, with the weather and all. But if all goes well, we should be able to squeeze in a day trip. We just have to keep an eye out for the denizens of XIBALBA!"

---

[2] Mayan equivalent of the Bible.

"Let's get out of here and take a look around!" Myselda said, leaping out of bed.

"Sounds good." I stowed my stuff, put my laptop under the mattress.

"A lot of good that will do"

"You're right, but I don't know how to do anything else."

It was midday. The sun was very bright, and the lazy air was warm and fragrant. When we reached the signpost, Myselda saw the sign to Uaxactun and moved to the safety of Tikal on the other side of the road. I continued on the Uaxactun side pretending to be pulled down the road by an invisible force.

"I can't see. . . . I can't see. . . . Something is pulling me. I'm falling down the road. . . . Help!"

"Seth, stop it!"

"But I think I'll get something to eat first," I said and strode away to the cantina.

The cantina was a large room, with the kitchen and the serving stations in the center. There were clusters of tables in each of the corners and Guatemalan flags were placed around the room. A lady came from the kitchen, wiping her hands with her apron, greeting us with a big smile. I told her we were staying at the hotel and would be stopping by for our meals while we were there. She was a walking, talking, smiley face. She was short and plump, with jet black hair and a classic Mayan nose. Her brown, round, animated face made her look like a Kachina doll.

"Would you like to buy a ticket?"

She said the cost of dinner was a ticket. Drinks were extra. Three drinks for one ticket. A ticket cost fifty pesos, which came to about $2.50 American. *Delightful!* Now I became the smiley face. "Two-thousand pesos, please."

Pulling out my wallet, "That's a very interesting system."

"Very easy, very simple," she said while counting out the tickets.

"And very efficient, I'm sure."

"We begin dinner at six o'clock and finish at seven thirty. The cantina bar will remain open to serve you after that. Tonight, for dinner, we will have pollo asado y frijoles con arroz. (Roast chicken and beans with rice.)"

"Ah, mucho gusto, gracias señora," I said, showing off the Spanish I had learned from my phrase books.

"Hasta luego!" she said, disappearing back into the kitchen.

Outside, out of ear shot, I asked Myselda, "Did you notice?"

"Notice what?"

"She was Mayan!"

"Duh! Considering where we are, I'd say that fits."

"Think back. . . . In Guatemala City, at the restaurants, at the hotel or in the shops, all the service personnel were Mestizo. Not a single Indian to be seen. They're considered unattractive and an embarrassment. Only at the Mercado (market) did we see the native folk."

"Now that you mention it—"

"Yes?"

"You're right, and they all looked very young."

"Colonial hubris. The face of the up and coming Guatemala."

* * * *

The General Store was fully stocked with food, stoves, lanterns, clothes and more. A corner of the store was dedicated to local crafts. There were samples of textiles, wood carvings, jewelry and even a Mayan grandma working a loom while her adorable granddaughter sat beside her. They were both dressed in colorful Mayan outfits, probably made by Grandma herself. Myselda took out her camera to take a picture. Grandma held up her hand for her to stop.

"Camera shy?" quipped Myselda. "Maybe superstition? Do you think she's afraid of losing her soul?"

"She wants five pesos," said the cashier, flipping through her magazine.

"Cinco pesos," grandma said, holding up the five digits of her open hand. Placing the child in her lap, she repeated, "Cinco pesos."

I didn't have anything smaller than a fifty-peso note so I gave her that. She was delighted. She lit up like an electric kachina. Myselda snapped the picture and grandma indicated we could take more. We really made her day and that felt good.

We sat in rocking chairs on the front porch of the store taking in the view. It could have easily been the location for one of the Gabriel Garcia Marquez novels--the makeshift signpost, the fading jaguar gate, the birds in flight circling the pyramids. This definitely could have been the setting in one of his stories.

It was late afternoon, so we decided to go back to the inn to rest, shower and get ready for dinner. We would wait until morning to begin our exploration of the site. I didn't want to be wandering around in the dark, trying to find our way back to the hotel. The place was strange enough as it was.

When we arrived back at our room, we discovered we had neighbors. I was glad to see them, safety in numbers and all that. They were a couple from Oklahoma. He was an archeologist doing his graduate work on the Indigenous People of the Americas. He was full of energy and seemed ready to take on the world. She was a media major who could not resist visiting such an exotic place. They were going to be married in the spring and this was their "trial" honeymoon.

I took off my sneakers and lay down while Myselda showered.

"I didn't get their names, did you?" I said, drifting off.

* * * *

I dreamed the birds outside had become transparent spirits, darting about like hummingbirds. They had a message to deliver. They were beginning to spell out words. The spirts had become butterflies, hovering in place to reveal their message. Myselda came out of the bathroom singing lines from Kurt Weil's *Youkali* and woke me up.

I sat up on the bed, yelling, "Mariposa! La Mariposa!"

"Mariposa to you too stranger! What have you been dreaming about? Whoever Mariposa is, she sure got you going. Will she be in your story? Am I gonna' have to wrestle in the mud with someone named Mariposa?"

"No. No. . . . They're butterflies. It was a wild dream. First they were birds, then spirits who became butterflies. They were trying to send me a message. They were spelling it out in the air for me when you came in. Then they flew away."

"Humm . . . . Members only. . . . messages scrolled upon the air. . . . Literate butterflies! It dosen't get any better than that, Seth."

"It was a far-out dream."

"In a far-out place."

30

"I should take a shower."

"You can't wash it away Seth. You have been chosen!"

* * * *

It was still light outside when we left for dinner. I brought the table lantern with me for the return trip.

"Miguel was right, we should get another lantern."

"He sure was," I said. "I'll pick one up tomorrow. I'm sure it will come in handy."

"Pick up two."

There was Mariachi music playing in the cantina. Lively music, happy music, even when about misfortune and unfaithful lovers. The waitress came out to greet us. She showed us to a table facing the road and brought a basket of tortillas and glasses for the table.

"Agua minerale por favor," Myselda said.

"Tienes tu boleto?"

"Seth?"

"She wants a ticket," I said. "I'll take care of it. Si, tienes boleto . . . cerveza para mi por favor. Señora, permiso, cual es tu nombre?" asking for her name.

"Mi nombre es Isabel," she said, blushing as she left.

"Are you flirting with our waitress?"

"I couldn't help myself. I think I made her blush."

"How can you tell? . . . You have no shame flirting like that, and right in front of me!"

"You're my one and only, Sel."

"until Isabel comes back."

Which she did at that exact moment, bringing our drinks, napkins and silverware.

"Cloth napkins! And the beer is ice cold!"

31

"Ah! Nirvana!" Myselda quipped sarcastically. "Cold beer and oversized napkins."

"Beer is how we know God loves us and wants us to be happy."

"Clever."

"It's a Ben Franklin quote. One of my favorites."

Isabel returned with two plates of roast chicken with red beans and rice.

"Buena cena, señor, señora."

Myselda dug right in. She was ravenous.

"This is really good. So tangy. How did they do that?"

The rice and beans were tangy as well. I started on the roast chicken with a knife and fork, but after the first bite I abandoned that, cut the half chicken in two and picked it up with my hands. It was so good. I felt no shame as the juices ran down my chin.

"Yo soy el barbaro Americano!" I said to Myselda.

She agreed. "Me too!"

I didn't give a damn. I ate like there was no tomorrow.

Our new neighbors came in and joined us at our table. We wiped our hands and faces with the large napkins. I understood now, why they were so large. The folks at the restaurant knew what they were doing. Myselda pointed to her nose to show me there was food left on my face.

"Welcome," I said, "Excuse the table manners, but we're starved. We haven't had anything to eat all day. By the way, this is Myselda and I'm Seth."

"Hi. I'm Adam and this is Christine. Smells wonderful in here!"

"I see we beat the crowd," quipped Christine. I could see she and Myselda were going to get along just fine.

"The food is really good," I said, sopping up the juices on

my plate with a tortilla. "And the beer is ice cold!"

"The chicken is so tangy," Myselda said to Christine. "And the beans and rice are zesty as well. I've got to find out how they do this."

"It's the lime," Adam informed. "They add it to their food. Some believe that maize, or corn, mixed with lime is what fueled all the growth in Mesoamerica."

I was impressed. "Wonder how the Maya figured that out?"

"Trial and error, I guess. They used it early in their history, two— three hundred BC."

Isabel came by and set their places. Adam ordered a beer and Christine ordered two.

"uno boleto por favor."

"Of course. Here you are. Thank you! . . . As I was saying Seth, adding the lime made an otherwise poor food source, the staple of civilizations. There were large populations that had to be fed, and every city-state had to have a stable supply of maize if they wished to survive. Ah! . . . And here's our food now."

Isabel brought out two plates of food that looked exactly like the ones she'd served us.

"Buena Cena señor, señora."

It was getting dark outside and we decided to wait for Adam and Christine to finish their dinner, so that we could all go back to the hotel together. I ordered another beer and Adam and I chatted about the Maya. They ate their dinner with perfect table manners. I could tell they were enjoying the food, but they were able to contain it within the precise movements of their utensils.

Myselda and I are such philistines! But ignorance is bliss and a hell of a lot more fun.

Back at the inn, Myselda decided to turn in early. I took my laptop out to the porch to jot down a few thoughts. Talking with Adam brought to mind questions I had been asking myself for the past year or so.

How did people who lived on opposite sides of the globe, who had no known contact with each other, come up with so many of the same basic paradigms? In language, in architecture, in astronomy and agriculture. In husbandry and religion, as with numbering systems and social constructs, they all seem to be built on the same foundational templates.Although modified, due to location and climate, foundationally they are basically the same. The fruit of the maize plant was little more than two inches long before our clever ancestors genetically modified it to become a foot-long powerhouse. The same work took place in the Steppes of Asia and on the plains of Europe. All humans have areas of the brain, Wernicke and Broca's area, that are used to process sound into language. The people of the world apply meaning to a sound and then categorize and place it in a lexicon. But birds do the same thing? Where and how is the bottomless trunk of songs the mockingbirds sing stored? They must be wired for it, just like I am, and the Bonobo and the wolf. The plot thickens! Perhaps there is a primeval template in all of our DNA. Most critters have a basic nervous system, which is modified as they move up the food chain. A good many have an ocular system, as I do, and use it for the same purpose. Lungs to breathe with, a heart to circulate the blood, filled with nutrients. The Hox gene is common across many species and is responsible for the five digits on my hand and the ability to manipulate them. Even a horse, whose digits have atrophied, has the Hox gene. In the plant world, the number five is ubiquitous. Maybe there is a core template, a fractal of the genome we transport about, that is basic to all life forms. Or at least to the larger ones that require a skill set that can organize billions of cells into a functioning unit. What does it matter that my ears and nose are shaped and placed differently? They both share the same purpose. I have more in common with everything living around me than I have differences with them.

It was getting late, and I wanted to be fresh in the morning, so I decided to pack it in. I heard voices coming up the pathway, first muffled, then becoming more distinct as they got closer. They were speaking in German. The concierge was leading them to their rooms. The man who was complaining, was followed by two women dragging suitcases behind them. I didn't speak German, but I knew this guy was cursing his brains out, to a chorus of "Ja. . . Ja," from the ladies.

It sounded like the first Panzer Division when they went up the old wooden staircase. The man spoke to the concierge in English.

"I called from Chi-Chi[3] and specifically ordered two full size beds for our rooms. Two single beds will not work for three people!"

"I will tell Miguel señor."

"What time does he get here?"

"Actually, he will not be here tomorrow. He has other business, but his cousin will be here with coffee and pastries for you to start your day!"

"Very well. I will see him in the morning. In the meantime, till we straighten this out, we will be using both rooms."

"Si, señor. I will leave a message for Raul to see you in the morning. Buenos notches, señor. . . . señora. . . . señora."

There was chatter in German after the concierge left. Some laughter and bursts of what sounded like bravado. Stepping into our room, the plaster walls muted their voices to a muffled drone. I took a shower, slid in next to Myselda

---

[3] Chichicastenango. Cultural center of K'che Maya

35

and fell asleep immediately.

I awoke early, shaved, brushed my teeth and got dressed. This was going to be a big day. Myselda was still sleeping so I went down to the office to get coffee and cake for us. The young man behind the counter looked agitated. I could feel him watching me as I poured the coffee. When I finished, I introduced myself.

"Hi, I'm Seth Parker. My wife and I are—"

He cut me off with a rant about how rude and arrogant Americans were. How they talked down to people and were offensive. A gratuity did not buy the right to abuse people who wish to make their stay more comfortable.

"I think you've mistaken me for someone else," I said, which didn't work.

"I don't understand you people. You act like you own the world!"

"I think you've mistaken me for someone else. You'll see. Have a good day!"

"Yeah, sure. Buenos Dias."

Myselda was up, dressed and ready to go when I returned with the coffee. We sat on the porch watching the sun climb into the sky. The howlers moving about in the tree tops, became more vocal. The birds did their morning business with the verve of a choreographed opera chorus.

"It's nice you have Adam to talk with about all that heavy Mayan stuff," she said between bites of her pastry. "And it's nice to talk with Christine about things not Mayan. . . .Humm, this turn-over is stuffed with fruit."

"Yeah, Adam's good for somethings, data points, a few cultural quips, but I think he's kinda' old school . . . Eric Thompson's old school."

"Ah yes, the entrenched oligarchs!"

36

"He is very focused though. I think he's working towards a job in academia. You've got to support the team if you want to join the club. Hey, I didn't tell you what happened at the hotel office this morning. You slept through it all, but last night some German people took the rooms upstairs. The man was very loud, rude and obnoxious to the concierge. He had two ladies with him, and there were not enough beds in the room or something, so the guy went off on the kid. I'm surprised it didn't wake you."

"I did hear the thunder, but it didn't last long."

"That wasn't thunder, that was the First Panzer Division going up the stairs! Anyways, the guy at the desk thought I was this rude German guy and started raving about Americans and how rude they are."

"What did you do?"

"I told him he was mistaken and would find out soon enough who the rude one was. They have a meeting later, over the bed situation, and they both may have met their match."

"Tikal, the soap opera!"

"Hey, what do you say we get going, get a good start? Do you want to stop at the cantina before we head out?"

"No, I'm good for a while. I put some water and trail mix in our bags."

"We should pack the flashlights that we brought with us. Ya never know. Remind me on the way back to pick up a lantern at the general store."

"Pick up two."

* * * *

Trees had been cleared forming a gateway to the rear of the

pyramid complex. In the trees on either side of the gate, Howler monkeys spared no effort in letting us know of their displeasure at our presence. I flipped them the bird yelling,

"I'm walking here. I'm walking here!" and they ran higher up the trees.

They must have seen the movie.

"You tell them Seth Parker. Tell 'em good!"

We passed along the backside of Temple I. Attached to it was a wall of scaffolding, with colorful umbrellas on each level to provide shade for the workers. No one was there. We followed the pathway around the backside of the pyramid until it opened onto the Great Plaza. It was like entering the Coliseum in Rome. Like the Coliseum, the plaza pulled you in, holding you in place with holographs of all that might have taken place there. In front of me was Temple I, the burial tomb of the great Ah Cacao. His image, carved into the roof comb, stood like a giant, towering over the plaza.

To the left was the North Acropolis where building began as early as 400 BC. Over the centuries one temple was built upon another. To the right was the Palace Complex with terraced balconies and an ornate façade. Built by the Great Jaguar Paw during his glory days, it was the Versailles of its time. That was until the Great Jaguar Paw was defeated by Teotihuacan and put to death. Behind me was Temple II, the Temple of the Mask, standing sentry at the rear of the plaza. Built by Ah Cacao and dedicated to his wife, its broad shoulders left no doubt as to who ruled the city. Her face was carved into the lintels of the doorway.

We were the only people there. We had the whole place to ourselves. I found the center of the plaza and sat down to take it all in. Myselda continued on to the stelae[4] at the base

---

[4] An upright carved standing stone.

of Temple II. She photographed them and went on to climb the pyramid. The incline was very steep with short steps leading to the summit. She looked like she was climbing a rock wall.

I closed my eyes and took deep breaths. The air was still cool and moist from the night before. My body worked to adjust to the energy patterns in the plaza. This was a powerful place. I was at the vortex of an energy center. The silence thickened with the deep, resonant sound of a flute. Traveling overhead in colored ribbons, the sound undulated on its way through the plaza. I opened my eyes and they found Myselda at the top of the pyramid, playing the bamboo flute we bought at Uxmal. Very soulful. I got up and walked to Temple I.

Climbing the temple stairs like Spiderman, I couldn't help but wonder, *Did they design this stairway so that you would have to walk up it like a monkey? Was this a way to humble the supplicant? Was the incline meaningful or was it just economics?* I had to stop and rest half way up. *What were they thinking?*

I sat on the top step, in front of the doorway of the sanctuary, to catch my breath. Myselda was playing her soprano recorder, sending across to me bird like calls complete with trills and sweeping melodies. I clasped my hands together to form my conch horn.

"OH eeeee oh. OH eeee oh." resonated through out the complex, sounding like a hoot owl. We dominated the airwaves. All we needed were dancers in the plaza below.

There were three chambers in the sanctuary. They were dark and dank and moldy. The light from the entrance diminished as it passed through successive doorways and rested on the back wall. I had to take out my flashlight to see into the last room. It was pitch black in there. There was to be no light escaping from that black hole. It probably looked a lot better in the flickering light of candles with murals of dancers painted on the walls and incense censers to freshen the place up. I felt I should get out of there and did. I stepped outside onto the platform and was frozen in place as I viewed the panorama before me.

How powerful the Lords of Tikal must have felt viewing their minions below.

I saw Adam and Christine examining the stelae in the plaza. Myselda was on her way down the pyramid—butt first. She bounced on every step on the way back to Mother Earth. I couldn't help but laugh. The howlers joined in with a good round of hoots. When I started down the stairway, I soon discovered there was no other way to go down the steep steps. The rise of the step was high, but the landing was short. Standing straight up on the stairway made me feel top heavy. I leaned back so I wouldn't lean forward, which created a swaying motion. The swaying motion made me feel dizzy, and that made me sit down. I had to sit or risk falling into the abyss. Myselda, Adam and Cristine met at the bottom of the pyramid and had a good laugh watching me bounce down the steps. The howlers and spider monkeys joined them with a round of simian jocularity.

Adam told me he was going to explore the excavations underneath the North Acropolis and asked if I wanted to go along. I told him I was definitely onboard. I had read about the excavations below the North Acropolis and the faux pas made in the early excavations. This would be a real treat. The plan worked for the girls as well. They could go off on their own and explore at their own pace. I took the flashlight from Myselda's bag and gave it to Adam, knowing he would not have thought to bring one. The girls took pictures of the stelae, while we set off to our mountain of temples.

On the side wall of one of the larger temples was a makeshift canopy. A doorway had been cut into the wall. Five, steep, wooden steps led down to a narrow passageway that was about four feet wide and seven feet high. It was dark and ten degrees cooler down there. Dark and dank at the top of a pyramid and dark and dank below. Using the flashlights, we could see everything and found ourselves standing in front of a Chaac, the Mayan rain god. We were eyeball to eyeball with the god and had a street level view. All four sides of the temple would have been decorated with similar stucco masks. The lowland Mayans did not have cenotes(cisterns) to store water, so they had to be very attentive to the deity in charge of the rain.

"Look! . . . over here Seth. There is still some of the old red paint left on the wall. And here is some of the black. It's incredible that it has survived after all this time . . . and in these conditions."

"This mask is huge" I said, "Look at the size of the eyes! Viewed from the plaza, it must have made quite an impression in its day."

"The nose is in good shape, laying to the side rather than projecting outward but—"

Adams voice became background noise, drowned out by the questions running through my mind. I was thoroughly absorbed in what I saw and the world view that created it. I had seen Chaac Masks at other Mayan cities and this one looked different. Guessing that the temple was dedicated sometime around 300 A.D, it was an early version of the more elaborate mask found further north in the Yucatan and Puuc regions of Mexico. In the north the nose was more akin to an elephant's trunk. Our mask had a nose like Falstaff. The ornate Chaac Masks of the north decorated the cornices and facades of the buildings. They looked like water spouts. Sometimes several on each corner. The later mask at Uxmal and other places, always reminded me of Ganesha, the scribe from the Mahabharata.

Is this another example of archetypes shared across continents?

It's like there was a common language of archetypes built into us along with our neural networks. Archetypical images carried forth and imprinted on the cultural milieu. In this case the deities were assigned different roles. Ganesha was the patron god of scribes, the deva of wisdom. Chaac was the deity controlling the rains with his thunder bolts. Likely modified along the way, the paradigms adjusted to the local and manifested themselves in situ. In both cases, the image of the deity with the elephant nose was impressed upon the culture as being a member of an all-powerful group of beings, controlling the world and its destiny. The Moai of Easter Island came to mind. The Long Ears had big noses too.

Using that metric, Jimmy Durante should have been canonized.

I heard voices outside the entrance of the pit. People were gathered waiting for us to finish. I looked at my watch and we had been communing with this Chaac for over an hour.

Tapping Adam on the shoulder "Guess we should give someone else a chance."

I started up the ladder and back into the world. It was very bright. There were five people gathered, three of whom were ladies. They bombarded us with questions. The ladies all spoke at the same time.

"Is it dark down there?"

"Did you see any snakes or spiders?"

"What about bats? We were warned about the bats."

I answered that it was dark, that I only saw artifacts, and

no, there were no snakes, spiders or bats. I stepped off to the side to let Adam field their questions. He seemed to enjoy it.

"You will need flashlights to see where you are going. It's quite a bit cooler down there and musky too. The ladder is very steep so be careful." Adam spoke to them like a parent turning his kids loose in the playground.

"I have a flashlight," one of the men said. He was the "take charge" guy of the group.

"Only one?" Adam asked.

I had to cover my smile.

"We'll be fine," the man said. "If you girls want to wait up here for us, that's OK."

"No, we want to go," the girls said together.

"Good, I'll go first and light the way. You girls follow, and Jeff you take up the rear."

They disappeared, one at a time down the ladder. One flashlight, five people and very little room to move.

"Have a good time!" I yelled facetiously into the pit as we started back down into the plaza.

While Adam was holding class, I had watched Myselda and Christine negotiate their descent from Temple II, butt first. Christine seemed to enjoy it, laughing all the way. When they reached the ground, they both looked like kids stepping off a water slide.

"Adam, that was something else!" Christine said, brushing herself off. "Myselda played a big wood flute in one of the rooms inside and it was eerie! Fun eerie though. And you can see forever. There are some more big pyramids over that way, but I'm starved. We were going to go to the cantina to get something to eat, care to join us?"

"Sounds good to me!" Adam said.

"Seth, after lunch I thought I would take a ride with

Christine to Flores, do some shopping. Wanna' come with us?"

"I don't think so Sel. I have lots more to see here. I'll go on the next trip. I have the trail mix, some dried figs, and the water. I'll be fine till dinner."

"Ok," she said giving me a kiss. "I'll see ya when we get back."

As they walked away I noticed brown stains on the rear of Myselda and Christina's pants. A chronical of their journey down the pyramid steps. I called out to Myselda and when she turned around I pointed to my butt. She looked confused at first, then checked her backside.

"Christine, I think we're going to have to change clothes before we do anything" and they disappeared behind the Temple.

I was glad to be alone. Now I could concentrate on what I was doing.

Where to next?

I was facing the Palace Complex, so I decided to start there. It took me a while to find an entrance to the grounds. There were only two; one at each end of the complex. It was obviously their way of controlling traffic into the area. A short stairway with a guard post at either end led to a platform. This was the Palatine Hill of Tikal. I entered the large balcony that faced the plaza. It was not hard to imagine the pageantry that took place below. Musicians and dancers, priests and athletes, captives with the spoils of war all were paraded past the reviewing stand.

Everybody loves a parade!

Further down, at the end of the plaza, was a ball court. Here the young men would practice the ball game so important throughout Mesoamerica; their prowess on display for a giggling, adoring audience. The "Uptown girls" would have watched the young men from their high-rise balconies. So familiar. In my own culture, large men in tights, chase small balls around a field to great acclaim.

Is it in our genes? Maybe a substitute for a rabbit?

For the Maya, it was about life and death.

The Central Acropolis housed the King, his family and all of the dignitaries of Tikal. Groups of buildings were built on platforms at different elevations. The houses, some several stories high, were built along each of the four sides of a courtyard. It gave the impression of a city skyline with skyscrapers at different heights. There had to be forty or fifty structures laid out across the hillside. The main palace had been added to and occupied by the kings of Tikal since its earliest days. A single-story building with many rooms, the palace was the home of the Great Jaguar Paw. He ruled from here before his capture and beheading by invaders from central Mexico. Good-size rooms, nice big courtyard, the king lived well!

The day was shot. I had been there for hours and had only seen about fifty percent of the Acropolis. The sun had fallen behind the big temple and I was feeling pretty hungry. Our German neighbors were in the plaza. The guy was showing his ladies the North Acropolis. With lots of hand waving and big gestures, his voice carried as though in an amphitheater. When I reached the plaza, even at fifty yards away, he sounded as though he were right next to me. I don't understand German, but his cadence was flawless as he went from stelae to stelae, explaining and describing what they were looking at.

Maybe this guy knows what he's talking about?

I started back to the Jaguar Inn. A group of tourists were

climbing down the steps of the Temple of the Mask. Scattered along the wide stairway, they looked like musical notes on a stave. There was an orange glow from the winter sun. The air was beginning to cool. The howlers yelled at me as I passed through the forest gate, and I yelled back at them. The chicken-shits ran up the tree, complaining.

I stopped at the general store and picked up the lanterns we needed, and a six pack of Coronas. Everything was just as we left it, frozen in time. The same girl was at the register reading her magazine, listening to the radio. The grandma was at her loom, with her granddaughter sitting beside her. The little one was munching on a tamale. I waved to them when I left, but they didn't respond.

I don't think they remember me. Business must be good!

The concierge at the inn waved and was very friendly when I walked through the gate.

"Buenos tardes, señor Parker."

"Hello. How are you?" *Humm, I guess he spoke with the German.*

I kept moving. I really didn't want to talk. I had to go to the bathroom, I was hungry and needed to take a long hot shower before dinner. Myselda had not returned from Flores. I didn't see her phone anywhere in the room and thought about calling her but decided to wait. I picked out some clean clothes and jumped in the shower. I dried off, got dressed and still no Myselda. I sat on the bed and called her number. It went to voice mail. Shadows of worry began to creep into my thoughts.

Who do you call when someone goes missing in the jungle?

We had passed a military compound on the way to Tikal and I figured that was the closest we would get to a police department. The compound was fortress like, with solders walking sentry along its high walls. Machine gun towers were on each corner. It looked like something from Beau Geste. They were the enforcers of the rule of law. Not very comforting.

I decided to give her some more time so I took the laptop from under the mattress and set myself up at the desk. Working on my journal would keep the worry at bay. It had been a full day and I had plenty to get down before dinner. Picking up where I'd left off, I detailed the commotion upstairs the night before and the encounter with the concierge that morning.

Myselda finally arrived, bearing gifts. She had something for everyone and even a few gifts for the undecided recipients of her largesse. She said the Mercado and the shops were very crowded and difficult to move around in.

"The cholera warning has passed and there's gonna' be a festival this weekend with music and traditional foods. The local crafts people and reenactments."

"Sounds like fun! . . . I was beginning to get worried, thinking I might have to call out the army."

"Ugh . . . On the way back they were having drills in front of the prison. I mean the fort . . . or compound . . . whatever it is. They looked ridiculous! When there's no one around to see, why do they bother?"

Myselda did not like the military, anywhere, any time. I gave up long ago, trying to explain to her that the military was necessary, and that an animal that couldn't defend itself was doomed.

"Discipline. It's about keeping discipline in the group," I said and changed the subject. "I worked up quite an appetite out there today. I may have to use two tickets for dinner this evening."

"Me too. Shopping with Christine can be exhausting. She has trouble making up her mind. Hope they have something good for dinner. I should get ready. Your present is on the bed."

"Which one is mine?" There were six or seven gifts on the bed.

"The Indiana Jones hat with the big brim," she called out over the shower. "Take a look at the outfit I got for Erin's new baby. It's adorable."

I tried on my new hat in front of the mirror. It was quite fetching really. A well-made leather hat, with good strong stitching. The wide brim would make for excellent protection in the sun.

"Thank you! This is great." I sat down at my computer to finish what I had started.

* * * *

We were the first ones at the cantina and were a little early. Isabel pointed to her watch. It was not dinner time. We ordered a couple of Coronas and talked about our day. Adam and Christine came in and ordered the same. Adam sat across from me, and I told him about my wanderings throughout the Central acropolis. He said that the Central Acropolis was the main focus of his trip, and he would be spending most of his time there. He said it was a mistake going to Flores with Christine and Myselda when he should have started his research.

"I'll just have to play catch-up tomorrow."

The dinner bell rang, and Isabel and her helper came from the kitchen carrying trays of the evenings fare. Tacos with refried beans and roasted peppers.

"Insalata?" Isabel asked. We all declined. I ordered beers all around and asked for some hot sauce.

"You should taste it first, señor."

It was a warning I had learned to heed. Isabel was collecting our tickets when our German neighbors came in. I greeted them and invited them to join us. The gentleman sat down next to Adam, and the ladies sat alongside him. He introduced himself as Franz. He was from Berlin. The lady sitting next to him was his wife, Eva. Next to Eva sat Greta, their girlfriend. Myselda and Christine were a bit taken aback. Adam and I just smiled as Isabel took their order.

"We will have three dinners and six beers, por favor. We will be having the insalata as well."

"Five tickets please."

"Of course. Eva, give the woman five tickets."

"Yes, I have them right here," she said handing Isabel the tickets.

"Gracias señora."

Franz was a Trader in Mayan textiles, crafts and artifacts. He bought low and sold high. From Germany he would bring movies, blue jeans and trinkets he bought on the cheap, and sell or trade them for Mayan crafts. He said the lava lamps were his big movers.

"eBay will ruin everything!" He said, "When the internet becomes more common here, there will be no need for Franz."

Isabel and her helper brought their food and placed the beer in the center of the table. Franz handed each of the ladies a beer and took the remaining four and put them in front of his plate. He said he liked his beer warm.

In between bites of his taco, Franz turned to Adam and asked, "What brought *you* here?"

Adam looked like the kid in class called on first by the teacher.

"I'm here to do research for my paper. I am a graduate student in Cultural Anthropology at the University of Oklahoma."

"Oh, yes . . .. Good school. Norman press and all. . . . Me too!"

"Me too what?" Adam asked, puzzled.

"Masters in Anthropology . . . . University of Berlin."

A surprised Adam put out his hand to shake, but Franz's hands were otherwise occupied. He scooped the refried beans into a fresh tortilla with a roasted pepper and onion from his salad. He ate while he listened to Adams resume.

"Why did you go into trading?" Adam asked, taking his turn to eat.

"I wanted to study the Maya along the lines of Yuri Knorozov and Tatiana Proskouriakoff. My proctor wanted me to work on the Ephesus project in Turkey" he said biting into his burrito, "so I told him Adios."

I was still hungry, and his burrito looked really good. I grabbed a tortilla, filled it with beans, a splash of hot sauce and went to town on it.

We all ate listening to Franz tell his story. His wife and girlfriend, disinterested, ate quietly.

"So, I decided I would go it alone," Franz continued, "but I had no money to finance it. Trading is what I came up with. I can do my work and make some money at the same time. I should have gone to school in Texas." He went on to say he was working on his own reading of the glyphs. It had taken him two years, but he was close to finishing in Tikal. Then it was off to Palenque and Copan to translate the glyphs there.

Isabel brought out a platter of fresh fruit piled high with

slices of mango and avocado, papaya, guava, oranges and bananas. We ordered another round of coronas and feasted on the perfectly ripened fruit. Once again, the large cloth napkins came in handy as our faces and hands were covered with the sugary juices of the fruit. Even Adam and Christine dug in with their hands; it was that good.

It wasn't long before the discussion became heated. Franz and Adam disagreed in many areas regarding the current interpretations of Mayan culture. They argued most about details concerning the translation, the meaning and the purpose of the glyphs. Haggling over small details, sometimes in raised voices, they were losing sight of the big picture.

It was time to call it a night and Myselda signaled me that she wanted to go. I nodded with a smile and let everyone know.

"Myselda and I are going to head back to the hotel guys. We'll see all of you in the morning. Have a good night. Goodnight Isabel!"

"Buenos noches señor!"

"Wait, I'll go with you," Christine said. "Adam, I'll leave the flashlight with you."

"I guess I'll call it a night as well. It was good talking with you Franz, we'll have to pick it up another time. Good night Ladies. Sleep well."

"Gute nach!' Franz said, saluting with his beer. Eva and Greta did the same.

"Gute nach."

"Gute nach."

* * * *

Myselda curled up in bed with a book, and I went back to work on my journal. I sat, staring at the screen, and waited. Nothing was coming. I couldn't recapture my impressions of the day. I was able to recall the different places I had visited, but I had lost the magic and sense of awe. The screensaver started up and with chin in hand, it lulled me to sleep. Later, I awoke to laughing and loud talking. The thunder coming from the wooden steps sounded like kettle drums in some marital processional. Franz and his "Rhine Maidens" had returned. Once they entered their rooms, their voices became a muffled drone. I undressed and crawled into the bed, spooning with Myselda.

* * * *

The dreams that came were very vivid and continued throughout the night. In the first dream I stood in the main plaza, crowded with people milling about in costume and make-up. Some of the painted faces were terrifying. The crowd was oblivious to my presence. They walked right through me, going about their business, preparing for the big celebration that was about to take place. Banners were placed between the steps of the two pyramids creating a roadway between the temples. It was a ceremonial sacbe. Children in monkey costumes, with painted faces, chased each other in and out of the banner poles pulling on each other's tails and laughing with abandon. A high priest, his having the most terrifying face, examined the processional way, making remarks to a cadre of acolytes in tow. This conduit between the two pyramids would carry a lot of juice. I don't know how I knew it; I just did. I could see and hear everything around me, but I wasn't there. I had no physical body to interact with. I was a diaphanous dimensional being, only as thick as consciousness, moving through space and time in a vehicle called a dream. I followed the High Priest to the foot of the Temple of Masks. I stopped and watched him climb the stairway. I realized the incline of the temple was not to make monkeys of men; it was to simulate the climbing of the mountain to receive the wisdom from above. It was so obvious.

Like Moses, Hammurabi, Nari Sim, they all went to the mountain to receive the Laws set forth by their Gods.

Even in a dream it embarrassed me that I had not seen that earlier.

Is this behavior also in our DNA? Is this grouping together to solicit the goodwill of the gods part of a herd instinct? Is religion and politics programed into us? Religion for identity, politics for resources. As with the zeros and ones of computer codes, is the ATCG code in our DNA structuring our behavior? Pointing us to prior successful strategies, driving us to fulfill the prime mandate to replicate. Powered by an influx of mitochondria that acted as an accelerant, the ATCG programming fueled and populated our biosphere.

I heard the laughing and talking of people in an echo chamber from above and behind me.

"Der mann ist ein papagei! (The man is a parrot!)"

I was pulled backwards, sucked through a tunnel. I opened my eyes to the pastel walls and the white stucco ceiling. It took a few seconds for my body and mind to regroup.

"Ist ein arseloch. (He's an asshole.)" I was back to earth.

Don't these people ever sleep?

I rolled over and slipped back into my REM sleep. The next dream came quickly. I found myself on the top of the temple, still invisible. The Lord of Tikal and his queen stood beside an altar. The high priest with his attendants made preparations for the ceremony. Below, the banners waved, and the crowd sang hymns to the Rain God. The howlers and spider monkeys joined in the chanting. The parrots and quetzal birds filled the air with color and song. In the center of the alter was a bowl filled with wood shavings, a sting-ray spine, and short pieces of woven rope. The high priest handed the sting-ray spine to the Queen. The din of the drums and horns from below pulsated through the air. She passed the stingray spine through her tongue while the priest held the ceremonial bowl under her chin to catch the blood. The Queen removed the spine and placed it in the bowl. She passed the rope through her tongue and the blood ran down the rope and into the bowl. She placed the rope in the bowl and the priest set it on the alter. He recited an incantation over the bowl and raised the sacrifice above his head. He looked like a Roman Catholic bishop consecrating the Host. He set fire to the wood shavings, and a thin column of smoked climbed towards the heavens. The Vision Serpent appeared from the rising smoke. The crowd roared, the horns wailed, and the drums sounded like thunder. This went on for several minutes.

"Seth . . . Seth, wake up. You're dreaming again."

I was pulled through the tunnel and found Myselda sitting over me.

"Keepin' busy are yah? Whatcha' dreaming about?"

Without opening my eyes, I told her I had to finish the dream. "I'll tell you about it in the morning" I mumbled and drifted back to sleep.

When I returned to the plaza, I found myself on top of the big pyramid, Temple I. Everything was the same, only this time the priest handed the sting-ray spine to the King. An

54

acolyte raised the King's apron exposing his genitals. The priest held the bowl underneath as the king passed the sting-ray spine through the flesh of his flaccid penis. He passed the rope through and placed it in the bowl along with the spine. After collecting enough blood to saturate the wood shavings, the priest added fire and began the consecration ceremony. The smoke rose and formed the Vision Serpent. The crowd cheered with one voice. The Lord of Tikal had secured their sustenance for another year. The Chaacs would release the rains, the crops would grow, and the maize would create another generation of men. This was an incredible, spectacular, spectacle to behold. The King's family and entourage played flutes and conch shells, cheering wildly from the reviewing stand of the palace. The priest and acolytes on the North Acropolis held streamers that danced in the wind while they chanted and praised the Rain God.

All was well in Yax Mutal, and the people would continue to flourish. A cause for celebration!

I lost my train of thought as I traveled through the tunnel yet again. I was getting to know this tunnel pretty well having established landmarks along the route. My body was exhausted. It needed to rest and recharge. Dreaming could be hard work. I didn't open my eyes when I returned to the bed. I rolled over, spooned with Myselda and fell into a full body sleep.

* * * *

I woke early, refreshed and recharged. The hotel office and the cantina were not open yet, so I went to work on my journal and detailed the events of the prior day: Myselda and her flute, Adam and the subterranean Chaac, my wanderings through the palace and the central acropolis. I relived and wrote of my dreams. They were still very vivid. I captured the trips back and forth through the tunnel, the rituals and ceremonies atop of the pyramids and the ecstatic raptures of the minions below. I captured the whole spectacle, and the musings of the night before.

Myselda woke up and started dressing. She offered to go to the office and get the coffee for us.

"You keep working, I'll go. I hope the coffee's fresh and they have more of those turnovers. Be back in a bit."

I was on a roll. I couldn't type fast enough to keep up with my thoughts and impressions. Myselda returned with a tray full of goodies.

"I ran into Christine on the way down to the office, and we're going to have breakfast in the cantina together. I brought you a cruller and a turnover to have with your coffee. How's it going?"

"Good," I said continuing to work. She placed the coffee and cakes on the desk and kissed the top of my head.

"I'm off. See you later."

"Have fun!"

I dunked my cruller in my coffee and typed with my other hand. Several hours had passed before I finished. It was almost noon and I still had a good bit of the central acropolis to see before I moved on. I jumped in the shower and put on some clean clothes. I needed some more coffee, so the first stop was the cantina. On the way there I saw tour busses lined up in the parking lot, which meant we would be sharing Tikal today.

I opened the door of the cantina and was stopped by a group of Japanese tourists; all of them trying to get through the door at the same time. They moved in a group to the

56

general store led by a tour guide waving a Japanese flag. Another group came through the door and followed the others into the general store. I hurried inside before the next wave arrived. A worker walked by with an overstuffed burrito on his tray, and it looked so good I ordered one and washed it down with my coffee. Sitting down, I checked our itinerary and to-do list. We were on track to get to see all on our list, and maybe some free time to make a day trip.

* * * *

When I entered the plaza, I felt like I was dreaming again. The Japanese tourists were climbing up, and bouncing down the pyramid steps, giggling and squealing. They were all over the place, and there was still more to come in the general store. They looked like the pop-ups in a pin-ball machine. The plaza sounded like a bird cage. They laughed a lot but it was a nervous laughter rather than the funny-bone kind. I sat on a low wall, taking notes, and jotting down impressions in my notebook. This was so surreal.

Maybe my travels last night were real, and this is the dream. Or maybe both are dreams and I'll wake up to a dream within a dream. Maybe they take turns, switching back and forth.

Were it not for the burrito I was digesting, I might not have been able to discern which was which?

There were fewer flags on the North Acropolis, which meant fewer people. That would make a good start. The tourists were gathered at the entrance to the subterranean Chaac, so I walked on to the far end of the hillside. From a courtyard above, I heard chanting. Navigating a make-shift pathway to the top, I found a group of women in grey robes, hands joined in a circle, chanting elusive harmonies in what sounded like Latin. It was very lovely music. Calming and soothing, totally appropriate to the place. I sat in the lotus position, closed my eyes and followed the chant. The music ended abruptly with the women exiting through a doorway at the end of the courtyard. They must have seen me sitting above, deferred and moved on. I guessed they were a very private group.

This must have been a beautiful temple in its day. Standing three stories tall, it was a true mountain. It must have dominated the plaza before the big ones were built. Temples to commemorate the passage of time were built on top of each other over the centuries. Monumental architecture in stone began around 250 BC and continued at Tikal until around 900 AD. While the first temple was being built, well below the upper one, the Chinese Emperor was building his terra cotta army and massive funerary complex. Ashoka in India was consolidating his power. Rome was at war with Carthage, had set its sights on the Mediterranean, and was struggling to hold the Italian peninsula together. From the boot to the Apennines, they fought tooth and nail with local tribes to establish the foundation of what would become an empire.

The nuns returned, followed by a gaggle of tourists. They looked as though they were being chased. Like ducks waddling single file, they crossed the plaza past the big pyramid and disappeared into the wilderness. I sat on the lower steps of the necropolis, behind the stelae, and tried to imagine what the plaza looked like before the two great pyramids were built. A husband and wife team had put it all together. Temple I, built by Ah Cacao, the husband, served as his tomb and a monument to his glorious reign. His image was carved into the roof comb. Temple II, the temple of the masks, was built right after and was dedicated to Ah Cacao's wife. Not to be forgotten, her portrait was carved into the lintels of the building. They were a powerful couple.

Ah Cacao was true to his ancestors. Like the temples of the Sun and Moon in Teotihuacan, he built his pyramids of the Sun and Moon following the astronomical lay-out used at his ancestral home. I sat between the two buildings, looking back and forth between them. Knowing nothing is ever simple, I imagined the conversations at the dinner table of the glorious king and his illustrious wife.

"So, you're going to build a great temple and dedicate it to yourself?" She was an agitated queen. "What about me?"

"It is going to be my tomb. I will be buried there."

"I want a tomb too!"

"Only Kings have tombs."

"Well that's going to change. I was with you from the beginning. If not for me, my uncle would not have appointed you commander of the southern army."

"I will always be grateful for your help. You must admit, you have done well as my queen." The queen was not listening.

"While you're away making war, who is it that takes care of business? Who is it watching your back, uncovering usurpers in the ranks, while you are off being 'The Great Warrior'? I want at least a pyramid, and a big one! And a grand stela to commemorate the dedication to my illustrious person."

However it happened, the end result was that he had a temple tomb with a huge cache, and she had a temple, almost as grand, dedicated to her. It made me think of my own wife.

Where's Myselda? I haven't seen her since she brought me coffee. I better find her.

Approaching the tree gate, I yelled at the monkeys and beat them to it. They ran up the tree cowering, complaining of my rudeness.

I found Myselda and Christine beside the pool. There were several empty bottles and a six pack of Corona on the table. They sat in folding chairs with rain umbrellas attached to shade them from the sun.

"Well, there's my better half now. Seth!" She waved me over. "Come join us at the pool!"

Myselda was best with sarcasm.

"Darling, we are thoroughly enjoying our poolside cocktails. With this beautiful view and marvelous ambience, we couldn't have a better time anywhere . . . not even if we were on the Riviere."

"Like the hat," quipped Christine.

"You've got it dirty!" Myselda moaned.

"That's what happens when—"

"Have a beer cowboy," Christine said handing me a Corona.

"It's for show! You're not supposed to get it dirty."

"Have you seen that wrangler of mine?" Christine asked.

"No, not all day. He must still be working."

"Still out on the prairie, aye."

"Guess so."

"Seth, I have to compliment you on your choice of lodgings and accommodations. The waiter hasn't arrived yet, so you'll have to get your own chair if you want to sit. Aesthetically, it could not be more pleasing. Why just before you arrived, the monkeys serenaded us from the balcony!"

"Too many basses," said Christine joining in. "And the sopranos were a little shrill."

"But what is most touching, Seth, is that you, knowing

60

that this is the one chance during the year when I can forget about the world and relax, have chosen the most beautiful, relaxing and romantic place on earth for me to enjoy."

"Myselda, you wanted to come—"

"Order! Order in the courtroom! The gentlewoman has the floor," Christine said, reaching for another Corona.

"Hors d'oeuvres?" Myselda said, handing me a jar of peanuts.

It was obvious they were both a little bit toasted. They looked silly and it was funny to watch. I grabbed a folding chair from the stack and sat opposite them.

"So, what have you been up to today?" I asked Myselda.

"Well, we had breakfast in the Cantina where we met Tamara and Lev—"

"Interesting couple," Christine said. "They remind me of Boris and Natasha from the old Rocky and Bullwinkle show."

"Me too! I was saying the same thing just—"

"Yeah, yeah," Myseld said. "As it turns out, she's into that Russian woman you always talk about. . . . Tanti Anna Pros . . . Pros—" She was starting to slur her words.

"Tatiana Proskouriakoff."

"Thank you. Turns out she's really into Tatiana's work. That's why they're here. Boris wanted to go to Los Vegas."

The howlers started up again and it looked and sounded like the "Ride of the Valkyries" as they jumped from one group of trees to another, then back again.

"Where else could you find such enthusiastic entertainers?" I said, opening my arms to the canopy.

Myselda laughed. "On a New York subway?"

"Karaoke night in Oklahoma City?" Christine said.

A damp mist was moving in as the sun set behind the pyramids. I needed a shower and to put down a few more thoughts on the day's events.

"I think I'll head up to the room and get cleaned up."

"Clean the hat," Myselda quipped.

"Not a chance. This is authentic! I'm taking this dust back to New York with me. Remember Sel, there's a two-hour window for dinner. Fresh fish tonight with yellow rice. Isabel says it's very good." Putting my chair back into the rack, I grabbed the remaining Coronas, thinking they'd had enough, and took them with me to the room.

After showering, I opened a bag of tortilla chips, grabbed a Pepsi and went out to the porch to put my feet up. I could see Myselda and Christine's head above their chairs. They were still yapping up a storm. Further out I could see the round-about and the road signs catching the last rays of the sun. The cantina and general store lay just beyond. The Russians came along and went into the cantina. They were early and would have to wait. Soon after, Franz and the Rhine Maidens also came along, entering the cantina as well. They too would have to wait. This was going to be interesting.

Myselda and Christine put their chairs away in the rack and started up the hill. The howlers and spider monkeys raised hell as they walked up the pathway, competing with each other for the "most obnoxious" award. Myselda came in the room singing *Youkali*. She grabbed a bottle of water and joined me on the porch.

"We were serenaded all the way home. A very talented group these simians. All they need is a couple of guitars and sombreros and they'd be ready for prime time."

"I know, I heard. You gals bring out the best in them. . . . Ya'll looked pretty toasted down there. You going to be able to make it to dinner?"

"After a shower and change of clothes, I'll be fine. I have

62

to get some food in me. I was getting a little lightheaded. Christine can really put them away. I couldn't keep up with her."

"You don't want to. It's a rabbit hole."

* * * *

We took our lanterns and headed down the hill to the cantina. The horizon was brightly illuminated by the rising moon and the pyramid cast a shadow on the tree tops. We took some pictures and continued on our way. We arrived at the cantina a little after six. Everyone was there, seated, waiting for dinner. Lev and Tamara on one side of the table and Franz, the wife and girlfriend on the other. Adam and Christine were next, and we sat across from them at the far end of the table. Myselda was not feeling her best and wanted to stay out of the action. Her instincts were spot on. Everyone sat silent as Isabel cleared the table of beer bottles with the help of a young girl holding a large tray. The air was tense and I could tell that more than a few harsh words had passed between them all; they were taking a break while waiting for their food.

The food was as good as Isabel said it would be. The fish tasted as if it had jumped straight from the lake into the frying pan. The yellow rice was rich and tangy, the beer was cold and the napkins large. Christine and Myselda quietly nursed iced teas.

"But the roads were passable, yes?" Tamara said, questioning Franz about a trip he had taken earlier that day.

"If you can handle a four-wheel drive," he said.

"Tamara, if there's a question about the roads being passable, why would we risk it?" Lev asked putting his open hands down on the table.

"But Lev, darling, the connection between the two cities is major. Maybe I'll see something new, make a discovery. The mythology suggests the road to Uaxactun is where the entrance to Xibalba is to be found. We can do this!"

"We could go straight to hell."

"Where is the adventurer who wooed me back in Toronto?"

Lev was beginning to cave. "I guess so," he said reluctantly.

Myselda and I knew exactly what she was talking about and wanted to make that trip ourselves, but it wasn't sounding too promising. Tamara turned and handed me a folder.

"Seth, Myselda has told me of your interest here at Tikal. I thought you might be interested in looking at my portfolio. Let me know what you think."

"Oh. Okay. Thank you."

They continued talking about Uaxactun while Myselda and I looked through Tamara's portfolio. Her work was exquisite in detail and in spirit.

"Sel, this woman is a true scholar."

The conversation at the other end of the table became heated. Myselda and Christine having little patience for such decided to go back to the hotel.

"We have our lanterns. We'll be fine," she said. They wished everyone a goodnight and left.

I passed Tamara's portfolio across the table to Adam. "You should look at this, she is doing incredible work."

Adam opened the portfolio and became immediately engrossed, lost to the world.

"Perhaps we should go as well Lev." Tamara explained to

everyone that "this morning the concierge at the hotel told me that there have been reports of soldiers taking off their uniforms at night and becoming highwaymen. The rogue soldiers are stealing from tourist. He said to keep a look out as they have powerful guns and few morals."

"We should leave right now!" Lev said slamming his hands on the table. "Good night everyone. Tamara, say goodnight."

"Goodnight all." She reached over my shoulder to take her portfolio from Adam, "Sleep well," and followed Lev out.

"Goodnight you two, have a safe trip," I said sliding one chair closer to Franz and company. I could hear Lev's voice outside. He was agitated.

"Why did you not tell me this earlier?"

"Lev, calm down. It's a liddle drive. We will be fine. Besides, this was a good trip. I think they very much liked my work."

Franz didn't miss a beat. "The Russians are so cocky. They think they won the war single handed."

"You're talking about World War Two, right? The one that ended fifty years ago."

"The very same," Franz said in his obnoxious manner. "Europeans don't forget as easily as Americans do. It seems your nation has a short attention span."

"I wish they would keep their ballet to themselves" Eva said. It was the first time I'd heard the wife comment about anything.

"Who needs Pushkin anyway?" Greta said. "We already have Goethe?"

The girlfriend also spoke! Adam and I looked at each other in amazement.

* * * *

When I returned to the room Myselda was just crawling into bed.

"That guy was so creepy, I had to take another shower."

"He's not so bad if you don't take him seriously. The sorry bastard is still fighting World War Two. Hey, I found out that it's the spider monkeys that throw their shit at you. Howlers don't do that. And if the monkeys see they are successful, they do it with a passion. Franz suggest throwing it back at them right from the beginning, but I'm not there yet. Not willing to go that far."

"Missed you today," Myselda said, cuddling her pillow.

"Me too, Sel. Tomorrow we should go off by ourselves. Bring a lunch, spend the day together. What do ya say?"

"That sounds sweet, Seth. I—" She was asleep before she finished the sentence.

I sat at my computer to make notes about dinner and our conversations that evening, but my mind went as blank as the page in front of me. Like Myselda, I was tired of Franz and company and didn't want to deal with them anymore, so I decided to turn in. The bed was welcoming, and I drifted off to sleep immediately.

* * * *

The next morning, thoroughly refreshed, we talked enthusiastically about our plans for the day.

"We have to stop at the cantina and get some food for our picnic," Myselda said emptying her knapsack.

"Today we dine at the Mundo Perdido!" I said, clapping my hands over my head, feigning a Flamenco dancer; albeit a challenged one.

"That would be a great name for a restaurant . . . Mundo Perdido. Maybe somewhere in lower Manhattan."

"It would! I'll make a note of it. Don't forget your flashlight Sel."

"Yes dear. Let's gooo! I don't want to run into Christine and Adam on the way out. I would like just one quiet day."

"Ready and able luv. We're off to see the wizard!"

"Shush!" she said sealing her lips with her finger. "We want a clean breakaway."

"Ziti, ziti," I whispered as we went out the door.

We gingerly stepped down the pathway, past the pool and the office, until we reached the gate where we broke into a rousing finale.

"Because, because, because . . . because of the wonderful things he does."

Myselda pulled me to the right to avoid the road to Uaxactun. "I don't want to lose you before lunch."

The cantina was open. Isabel was busy wiping the tables down and preparing for the day.

"Buenos Dias, Isabel. Como esta?"

"Buenos Dias. You're here early, señor. We are just getting started cooking. We have some coffee ready if you like."

"That would be great Isabel. Thank you. We were hoping you could put something together for us to eat."

"We are going to have a picnic at the Mundo Perdido," Myselda said with a big smile.

"Pik-a-nik? No entiendo. (I don't understand.)"

"Almuerzo . . . fuera. (Lunch outside) Picnic."

"Ah! Si! We will make something nice for you," she said, leaving. "Pik-a-nik. Pik-nik. Picnic!"

"Were going get out of your way Isabel. We'll be outside

on the porch."

"Bueno señor Seth," she said disappearing into the kitchen.

We sat outside and waited for our coffee. There wasn't much going on. A few howlers grumbled as the songbirds began their morning oratorio. Isabel brought our coffee.

"Pik-nik. Picnic! Se me le gusta la palabra picnic. (I like the word picnic.)" The three of us had a good laugh and Isabel went back to work.

"I'll bet the hotel office is open," Myselda said, leaping from her chair. "I'm going to get us some pastries. Be right back."

She walked around the signposts avoiding the Uaxactun road. As she passed through the archway of the hotel, the howlers began their protest. *Must be something territorial.* They howled again as she passed through on her way out with her bag of pastries. She looked as though she was carrying contraband, eyes searching, almost jogging. She arrived at the table flushed and breathing heavily.

"Got them!" she said collapsing into the chair. "And they look really good."

"You're the best, Sel," taking a pastry from the bag, "Did I tell you today that I love you?" I asked biting into it, savoring the taste. "Hmm . . . almost as good as you!"

We sat quietly, drinking our coffee, eating and taking in the view. Isabel came by with her coffee pot.

"Mas café?"

"Yes, thank you, Isabel," I said holding out my cup.

"Thank you. It's very good." Myselda said holding out hers.

"Señor Seth, I check with Miguel and he say tonight is your last Cena with us. We cook you something special. A favorite of the royalty of Yax Mutal. It is called subanik. Very good, señor. And I make xocolati for you señora. It is also very good."

"That sounds wonderful, Isabel. You and your cooks have made this trip very special. We will never forget."

"Muy bien. Con gusto! I will bring back your food for the pik-a-nic."

"I know xocolati is their chocolate drink, but I've never heard of subanik," I said after Isabel left.

"I've read about that chocolate drink. They call it the 'Ambrosia of the Gods'. And the *main* dish is fit for kings. We're being treated like royalty and it's all due to my husband's charming self. Who has it better than us?"

"Better than the Riviere?"

"Better than the Riviere, and exotic as well!" she said laughing.

Isabel came back with our lunch and set it on the table.

"Dos boletos por favor. And don't forget to come early esta noche."

We took a look into the shopping bag to see what we would be having for lunch: tamale's and avocado wedges, a stack of tortillas still warm, salsa, two Coronas and a bag of chips. We looked at each other,

"Who has it better than us?"

We shouldered our bags and headed out for the Mundo Perdido. Myselda looked as though she was crossing central park to go shopping. I hadn't noticed the writing on the shopping bag before. Bergdorf-Goodman was written in big gold letters, printed on both sides. It glittered in the morning sun. I had a feeling it was special to Isabel. A souvenir from the Super Mercado del Norte, thrown away by some tourist but treasured like a relic by Isabel. We would have to take special care of it and return it in good condition.

We passed through the forest gate, past the ball court and the pyramids to the road that would take us to Temple III. This east facing temple was the last to be built in Tikal. Finished in 810 AD. It stood over a hundred eighty feet tall. Massive. It is believed to be the funerary tomb of the king called Dark Sun. Restoration work had just begun so it was closed to the public. The stairway would have been a challenge to climb anyway as only half of it was intact. Unbridled vegetation still blanketed its massive base.

Further along the road was the Bat Palace, also called Palace of the Windows. I had read in a guide book that the complex had functioned as the "University of Tikal." The two-storied building had many rooms which very well could have housed the students studying Mayan cosmology, mathematics, religion and art. The vertical openings to the rooms resembled tall French windows, hence its alternate name. Central was a rectangular courtyard with stone bleachers on all sides. Here the knowledge of the ancestors would have been passed on to a new generation of scholars. I imagined sitting in on a lecture on the procession of Venus. The calendar was central to the Maya and was at the heart of all aspects of Mayan life. When to plant, when to celebrate. They even scheduled time for "Tlaloc-Venus Warfare" (A war timed to the rise of Venus), which they practiced after the arrival of the Teotihuacanos. Meandering through the rooms, I came across the fragments of a lintel at the foot of an entry way. I assumed they were broken pieces of the Sapodilla wood from the beams above the door. I was tempted to collect them and bring them home with me to New York. I have always had a soft spot for psychometry and the ability to learn an objects history by touching it. It balanced out my

70

other interests which were more impersonal, data driven, and perhaps even cold. But the "good citizen" tape played in my head, instructing me to leave everything in place when visiting archeological sites so that the people of the future would have it as well. Something I totally agree with. I walked away feeling good about my decision.

Continuing along the sacbe, the roof comb of Temple V towered over the trees. To the right the paved road continued with plazas opening up along the way to the Mundo Perdido.

Temple V, built around 650 A.D., was a pyramid with several anomalies. The road was not paved and the stairway faced north. Usually important buildings had causeways and were aligned along the east-west axis line. There was only a single room at the top of the temple where three rooms were the norm. Its architectural style employed elements of construction used during the early classic period, with wide balustrades along the stairway, rounded corners and an abundance of Chaac masks.

This is old school. Was the king trying to bring back "That Old Time Religion"?

This mortuary temple, built during the reign of Nun Bak Chaac, the twenty-sixth ruler of Tikal, was one of the largest building projects in Tikal's history. Due to a natural depression in the landscape, though now dried up, the area to the north of the stairway was used as a reservoir. It seemed fitting as the building was dedicated to the rain god, but the reservoir had made access to the temple difficult. Enclosed by other structures with no clear egress, the mighty temple had been neglected and fallen into disrepair. The paved causeway bypassed Temple V on its way to the ceremonial center, and the Maya left Temple V on its own. Strange that a people with the energy to build such a monument, couldn't find the energy to maintain it.

There has to be more to the story.

I scaled the stairs like a monkey, using all fours to steady myself on the steep incline. Myselda stayed below taking pictures. The one-room shrine was long and narrow with a high corbeled arch.

What could you do in here other than burn incense?

It was very damp and moldy and smelled unhealthy. The roof comb above was a monster. Even with the lichen and mold covering much of it, you could still make out the carvings of the rain god and his entourage. I started down the stairway backwards, the reverse of my ascent, using hands and feet to steady and balance myself. The steps were green with moss and my hands were getting pretty funky. It seemed like it took a lot longer going down than on the way up. Myselda was there to greet me when I reached the bottom.

"You looked so small standing up there with the roof comb behind you. I took some pictures."

"I felt small too. There's something strange about this place."

"The whole city is strange."

"There's never a reservoir around when you need one. Look at this. My hands are covered in gook."

"I have some water in my bag . . . hold out your hands." Myselda poured the water over them and I rubbed the gook off the best I could. She even had paper towels to dry them with.

"For the pik-a-nik!" she said with a big smile.

We returned to the causeway, passing another pyramid that was yet to be restored. Ahead, the "Lost World Pyramid" grew larger and larger the closer we got to it.

"The restaurant is just ahead My Lady," I said taking her hand and continuing on the road.

Standing before the great stairway of the pyramid, Myselda held onto her hat and looked to the top. "I hope they have a table available."

The Mundo Perdido, or Lost World complex, was ancient. From the earliest times it served as an astronomical observatory, necropolis and major ceremonial center. The site was anchored by the pyramid and its surrounding dance platforms. Around 300 A.D. people from Teotihuacan moved into the area and made it their own. The emblem glyphs representing that great city were carved into all of the dance platforms; and eventually throughout the entire city. It was from here, the plot to overthrow the existing dynasty was hatched. Sadly for Great Jaguar Paw.

"Care for some lunch?" I asked.

"Let's walk a bit. It's still early."

"As you wish. Let's go this way and see what's on the other side."

I felt the size of an ant walking alongside the giant structure. The pathway opened up to a plaza, sparsely planted with trees. The Seven Temples complex was before us. Billowing clouds and the shade from the trees created dappled light patterns on the landscape. Turkeys grazed nonchalantly, foraging in small groups.

"Sel look! Turkeys . . . over by the 'Seven Sisters'."

"Wow! They're beautiful!" she whispered, taking pictures. "Much more colorful than the ones back home."

"I don't think we have to whisper," I said raising my voice. "It's more likely that they would chase us out of here than the other way around."

The sound of my voice bounced off the surrounding

buildings, creating an almost, but not quite, echo effect. We continued thru the plaza obeying the silence of the serenely surreal setting. There were three ball courts on the far side of the plaza.

"Why did they need three Seth?"

"I don't know. Practice courts maybe? Competing games at celebratory ceremonies?"

The west staircase of the pyramid looked ominous with large Chaac reliefs greeting you at various levels of the ascent. This ceremonial center had been in use for eight hundred years when the pyramid was built. It remained an important temple to the very last days of Tikal; the complex was the last part of the city to be abandoned after the collapse.

I was getting hungry and wanted to get to the top of the pyramid while I still had the energy. "What do you say we skip the rest of the buildings for now and have our lunch?"

"My thoughts exactly."

We tied the shopping bag to my backpack and started up the stairway.

"I recommend using the monkey-method for climbing the stairs. It worked really well for me on Temple III."

"I prefer to tackle it as a rock climber if you don't mind. Enough monkey business Parker. Start climbing!"

"Well, well. Looky, looky, looky at you, Myselda Edelman."

Banter was good. It kept our minds busy while slowly moving forward. By the time we reached the top we were both winded; the pyramid was over a hundred feet high. We sat facing the Great Plaza in the distance below. The vanity pyramids loomed large in the magical landscape, as did all the pyramids rising above the canopy; "otherworldly" best describes it. Myselda took her flute from her bag and began playing soft and low. I chose to daydream.

This temple was rebuilt five times. It took this form in 250 A.D. following the old tradition of building one temple on top of another. In the distance, Temples I through VI dominating the canopy now, would have to wait another four hundred fifty years to be built. This was the tallest building in Tikal for most of its history. Below, the great plaza would have been flanked by the temples and the tombs of the North Acropolis on one side, and the palace and administration buildings on the other. This and the North Acropolis were the two major ceremonial centers in the city. At important celebrations, the high priest would have paid homage to the gods and the ancestors at the North Acropolis. Then leading a processional past the palace, joined by royalty and dignitaries, they would proceed along the same causeway we took to get here. The population, after circling the great pyramid, would gather below to celebrate the marking of time. Using the smaller buildings and platforms as markers, the Mayan priests were able to predict the equinox, the solstices and the rising and setting of Venus. For fifteen hundred years this ceremonial plaza would have emoted, at regular intervals, the celebratory cries and jubilation of a grateful populace.

"Seth, I'm getting hungry. Are you ready to eat?"

"Yes, I do believe I am. We have a table waiting in the very center, right this way."

I had put a towel in my bag to use as a tablecloth and brought a lantern along in place of a candle.

"Don't you go attracting no extraterrestrials or spaceships with that thing," Myselda said, passing me a plastic knife and fork wrapped in paper towels.

"Or the Vision Serpent!" I laughed.

"Ahh, even worse!"

We unloaded the shopping bag and feasted on the tamales, salsa and avocado. The beer was a little warm but tasted really good and the location more than made up for it. Fortunately, there was some cloud cover and a nice breeze, so it never really got too hot. With the clouds hovering above the canopy and the mysterious buildings, the place did look like a Lost World.

"You look so content. I never thought I would see the day Seth Parker would be happy with paper napkins and warm beer."

"It's the tamales. They have a calming effect on me."

"Go ahead, blame it on the tamales," Myselda said while biting into hers. "I'm not buying it. You've been a little bit vacant ever since we got here. You've been totally preoccupied with this place . . . and those dreams of yours."

"I love it when you get all ethnic with me. Your hands speak perfect Brooklyn. . . . I thought we were having a nice lunch."

"We were having a—are having a nice lunch. Okay. Never mind. . . . It's the tamales."

We ate everything Isabel had prepared. Myselda wiped her hands and went back to playing her flute. I laid back, watching the sky. The clouds were so close I could almost reach out and touch them. I closed my eyes with a sigh,

"Mi corazón contento, y mi barriga llena." (My heart is happy, and my belly full.)

* * * *

Voices rose from the courtyard below. As in the great plaza, the acoustics produced by the surrounding buildings amplified sound. It was a group I had encountered the day before. The professor was lecturing about the plaza and the temple.

"And right where that man is sitting," he said pointing at me, "the Mayan priest would predict the eclipse of the sun and moon."

"It's him again!" yelled one of the grey-haired ladies.

"The nerve of him, listening to our lecture again, after we—" clamored another.

"That's right ladies, it's me again. And I was here first! Hah!" I said jumping around like a string puppet. Myselda came over to see what was happening,

"Seth, what's going on?"

"They're saying that I am listening in on their lectures again. They've already paid, so what the hell do they care."

"Look, he's got an accomplice!" They began to sound like a mob.

"I can hear every word you're saying ladies" I yelled down at them.

"I'm gonna shut that son of a bitch up" screeched the lead grey-hair, scrambling up the pyramid.

"I want a piece of him too!" followed another.

To my astonishment the professor joined them in what was now a frenzy. "He's been a thorn in my side ever since yesterday."

"Harriet, you said you weren't going to start any fights this trip," an elderly man pleaded.

"Gregory, you're either with us or against us. Make up your mind!"

"Ah shit. I'm coming," he said, scrambling to catch up.

"Seth, what are they doing. . . . People!" she yelled. "You're gonna' have heart attacks!"

"We'll see about that missy," one of them yelled back.

"Myselda, let's get out of here. These old broads are crazy."

We ran across the platform, gathered our stuff and monkeyed our way down the stairs to the bottom.

"Let's go!" Myselda cried impatiently.

"No, let's wait a minute. Oh, there they are. Hello ladies!" I said waving. "I know you can hear me."

"Chicken-shit," Harriet yelled, shaking her fist at us.

"Seth! Seth, wake up." Myselda shook me. "You're dreaming again and you're gonna get sunburned. Put your hat on."

"You're right," I said sitting up sleepily. "Where did the clouds go? Where's my hat? Oh, here it is right behind me. Okay, so yesterday I had a little row in the plaza with a lecture group from Pennsylvania. They were being obnoxious and I was tired and pretty salty," I rubbed the sleep from my eyes. "I just dreamed they were being hostile, making violent threats and chasing us off the pyramid. And to top it off, worst of all, I was provoking them. I egged them on, delighting in their rage. I made them very angry with me . . . which wasn't hard to do."

"Well we should leave your dream on top of this pyramid and head back down. I'm gonna' pack up."

"Works for me."

I carefully folded Isabel's Bergdorf Goodman shopping bag along its well-established creases. "When we get below, lets pick a shady spot and hang out for a bit. I'm not quite through here yet."

"Okay. What's that? . . . I hear voices." She walked to the edge, looked over, and came back. "Just a bunch of tourists with their guide."

"Humm. Were they an elderly group?"

"Yes."

"And the tour guide with them was tall, thin, with horn-rimmed glasses?"

"Yes. How did you know? . . . You mean—"

"The people from my dream! Let's go this way, down the other side."

"Now I'm being chased by a dream. What's next, Seth? Jaguars? Dragons maybe? I don't want anything to do with any of them. Save them for yourself, keep them in your head."

"Yes dear. Shall we monkey our way down this monster?"

"I prefer rock climb—"

"Yes dear. Maybe we can find common ground. Perhaps with something like a spider"

"Spider. . . . I like that. I can work with that."

"Spider it is then! Let's spider down this monster!"

"Not that it matters what we call it, because this time tomorrow, I'll be on my way to Guatemala City and the nomenclature of Tikal will have become moot."

"Time sure has passed quickly," I sighed. "I feel like I'm just getting settled in, and it's time to go."

"Quickly? It seems like we've been here forever!"

When we reached the bottom, Myselda stood up straight and adjusted her backpack. She put her hands on her hips and let me know what had already been decided.

"Next year, I am going to pick our vacation spot. A vacation should be a vacation, not an endurance test. I can guarantee you that there will not be noisy generators or howler monkeys keeping us up at night."

We found a shady tree in the center of the plaza between The Seven Sisters and The Lost World Pyramid. The turkeys grazed and the parrots bounced from tree to tree. We munched on our granola, quietly taking everything in.

"All we need is a jaguar to pass by to complete the picture."

"There's an armadillo over by the ball court," I said pointing.

The dreaded study group turned the corner of the pyramid and entered the plaza. They stopped at the west stairway. The professor described the ceremonies that would have taken place there, and in the plaza and moved on. The armadillo scurried into the ball-courts, the howlers hooted, and the turkeys scattered to the four corners.

"Those people didn't even notice you! They looked right past us as though we weren't here."

"Well, it was just a dream after all."

We took our time walking to Temple IV, savoring our surroundings. The grounds were comparable to any public square, in any capitol of the world. Walking through the residential area, I was reminded of the Luxemburg Gardens with its palatial homes overlooking the park, the Topaki Palace in the shadow of the Aya Sophia, Central Park cradled by mansions and skyscrapers.

Back in the day, this would have been the address to have.

The closer we got to the temple the farther back we would have to bend our heads to find the top; one could have easily gotten neck strain. It was like looking for the top of the Empire State building in New York while standing right next to it. Myselda stayed below, taking pictures. There was a tourist group on the platform above having lunch. I had the wide stairway to myself. The climbing had become much easier. Like a Ninja, I stealthily scaled the ledged wall, silently melding with the temple, moving so evenly my movements were hardly perceptible. The platform at the summit was quite large, offering plenty of room for a full entourage during ceremonies. There was a locked iron gate at the entrance to the shrine. I took out my flashlight and looked through the bars into the first room. The folks on the platform gathered around me to get a look at what was inside. Beyond the first room, the light was useless, as though it was not permitted to shine any further.

"Looks like another smelly, moldy room," Myselda said, standing behind me.

I turned to find her smiling. "Hey. You made it!"

The tourists started down the stairs in two's, bum first, bouncing all the way. We sat on the top step and watched them ride the stairs to terra firma. They were from England and Norway, sharing a bus to Belize for bird watching. A quirky group, but very nice people.

"Look how the pyramids line up . . . like dominos," Myselda said, snapping pictures.

"That's the east-west axis."

"They did a pretty good job."

"I wonder what they used as a sight line through the forest. The temples in the plaza, One and Two, were built in the early seven-hundreds. Then Temple Five, over on the right, was built soon after. This temple was built around 740 A.D., so it would have been aligned with the two in the plaza. The one in front of us, Temple III, was built seventy years later in 810 A.D. I guess they snuck it in along the axis line. It was the last large building project taken on by the great city. A hundred years after that, this magnificent metropolis became a ghost town, reclaimed by its landlord."

"And who might that be?"

"The jungle, Sel, the jungle. It's all a mandala. All that

81

you see . . . Here one day and gone the next. Just a transient mandala."

We sat up there for over an hour, talking and taking pictures. Many great ceremonies would have taken place, right where we sat. Beneath the imposing roof comb rituals petitioning the gods would have been performed. As incense burned, a sacrifice would have been made. The ecstatic minions below would fill the jungle with their collective roar of approval. Temple IV was the apex of their building history. It was the tallest building in Meso-America, in the known world! A declaration made to the universe, it would proudly proclaim, "I AM ANOTHER YOURSELF,"[5].

Only this one, Temple IV, rose above the lost world pyramid.

How powerful the Priest/King must have felt looking out upon his well-ordered world.

His universe was governed calendrically, numerically, and by his divine right to be king, protector and intermediary to the gods. It was the glue that held the cosmos together.

The day was moving along. If we wanted to rest before dinner, we needed to start back to the hotel.

"Shall we spider our way back to earth?" I asked.

Myselda leapt onto the stairway backward, like she was jumping into a swimming pool. "Someone should include this stair climb in a fitness program."

"Maybe that someone is you," I said, trying to keep up with her.

We made it to the bottom in record time and our hands weren't even that dirty.

"We can take this road back to the hotel." I wasn't sure I

---

[5] A Mayan Aphorism.

knew what I was talking about, but it was heading in the right direction, so how wrong could I be? "Hey, there's the service road. I saw it from the top of the temple. I'll bet it's a shortcut to the compound. Wanna give it a try?"

"If guess so," Myselda agreed hesitantly.

A pathway through the trees took us down a hill to the service road. It wasn't very wide, and it would be difficult for passing cars to get through. The canopy above was thick and dense, which made it damp with all the accompanying smells. It was very quiet, and through the forest I could see a cluster of trailers colorfully painted, each with a fenced garden. They appeared the be where the workers lived. We walked silently for a while, but everything looked the same and it seemed we were getting nowhere.

Myselda became anxious. "Is this the road to Uaxactun? . . . Have you put me on the road to hell? This is the road Tamara was talking about, isn't it? . . . Seth, Xibalba is not on my itinerary. I will not be sacrificed!"

"Hey, hey, hold on. Take it easy. The road to Uaxactun is on the other side of the park. The compound has to be just ahead."

"I hope you're right."

"Think about the fine dinner Isabel and company are getting ready for us."

"I hope you're right."

I wasn't right. We walked for another twenty minutes until we reached the entrance to the park. I explained to the gatekeeper that that we were staying at the hotel, and that we took the wrong road on the way back.

"Best to stay on the park roads señor."

It was another ten-minute walk to the hotel. Miguel was standing at the gate and greeted us.

"Buenas tardes, señor . . . señora."

I told him of our adventure on the back roads. He listened, shaking his head.

"It is twice as far señor. That is a service road, not for convenience. Best to stay on the park roads, señor."

We got back to the hotel room overwhelmed, grimy and spent. It had been a long day.

"We made it!" I said flopping onto the bed. "That was a work-out." There was a knock on the door. "Would you get that, Sel?"

"You're not going to fall asleep and start dreaming again, are you?"

"I promise. No dreams. Not until after dinner."

Christine was at the door looking as though she just came from a spa.

"Hello stranger, long time no see. My . . . you look like you've had a full day."

"Just another relaxing day with Seth," Myselda answered sarcastically, turning to glare at me.

"We covered the whole back end of the city. We had lunch on top of the Lost World Pyramid. That is until we got chased off by a dream. . . . Oh, and then we got lost in the jungle."

"We were never lost," I said, disputing Myselda's account.

"Sounds like a full day. Adam wanted me to go with him, but I told him I had a headache."

"Does that still work?"

"Does for me. I get pretty cranky when the headaches come. I think Adam was glad to get away," she said laughing.

The howlers raised a din that flooded the room through the open door.

"That must be him now," I said, fluffing up my pillows.

"You're right." Christine waved. "He's walking up the pathway right now."

"The howlers are like a door bell," I said.

"More like barking dogs," quipped Myselda.

"I meant to ask Miguel if they hoot at him when he walks through the gate. Could be just for strangers."

Adam arrived looking as haggard as I felt. He kissed Christine and came inside.

"I looked for you guys. You just get back?"

"About ten minutes ago," I said.

"Isabel told me they're making something special for dinner in your honor, subanik. I've heard of it. They say that it's pretty good."

"There you go Myselda," I said. "That should make up for us getting lost."

"You got lost?" asked Adam.

"No, not really . . . a detour."

"Well I'm going to get cleaned up. I'll see you at dinner," Adam said leaving.

Christine followed him out. "See you at dinner Myselda. I want to hear all about it."

Myselda picked out her clothes and carried them to the bathroom.

"No dreaming! You should go work on your computer."

"You're probably right. Go take your shower."

I didn't feel much like writing, so I made a list of the day's events: the buildings we visited, the geriatric Pennsylvania mob, getting lost. I changed the getting lost part to taking the long way home. The day had provided a ton of material to write about. The bulleted list took up an entire page, and the day wasn't over yet.

* * * *

My timing was perfect. I was dressed and ready to go to dinner by ten to six. We met Adam and Christine as we were leaving. Myselda gestured for me to take the lead.

"The guest of honor should go first."

"As it should be," said Christine bowing, "Your excellence."

"U dah man!" Proclaimed Adam, stepping aside to allow me to pass.

I played it up as well. I squared my shoulders, held my head high and walked regally to the front of the group. "Follow me, loyal subjects, and we will embark on a journey of epicurean delights."

"Lead on Sire!" my entourage sang in unison.

We arrived at the cantina to a full house. Lev and Tamara, Franz and the Rhine Maidens, were all seated, waiting for the six o'clock hour. Even Miguel, the concierge was there, although not looking too happy about sitting across from Franz. Obliviously the allure of subanik was very powerful. Isabel greeted us at the door.

"Bienvenido señor Seth. Señor, señoras. This way please."

Adam and Christine took their place at the table. Isabel took two rainbow colored place mats from her apron, set a place, and invited us to sit. I gave her the folded Bergdorf Goodman bag and thanked her for the lunch.

"Mucho gusto, señor. Mucho gusto." Isabel flashed her kachina smile, practicing her "pik-a-nik" on the way to the kitchen. She returned with her helper and beers for all; four for Franz, two for Christine and one each for the rest of us.

"How's been everyone's day?" I asked enjoying my new-

86

found celebrity. They all grumbled various complaints, mostly about nothing. I tuned them out, choosing to focus on the uniqueness of the moment. Raul, the other concierge, arrived, greeted everyone and sat next to Miguel. He reached for one of the beers on the table and was quickly stopped. Franz grabbed it from his hand and put it back in its place in front of him.

Miguel, watching the tension build, called for Isabel. "Isabel, por favor, una cerveza fria para mi compatriota. (a beer for my compatriot)"

"Si . . . uno minuto," she called from the kitchen.

Miguel and Raul spoke to each other in Spanish. Franz and the girls spoke in German, and Tamara explained to Lev in Russian, what was happening. Christina talked of making a movie about the cantina. The atmosphere was electric.

Isabel and her helper brought out the food. In colorfully painted bowls lined with mashan leaves, the meats in the red-orange broth welcomed you. With that she served a small bowl of rice, sliced mango and warm tortillas. It took them several trips to fully serve the table. When finished, she wiped her hands on her apron and gave me a big kachina smile.

"Buen provecho, señor." Then she said to the group, "buen provecho a todos! (Have a good meal everyone)," and returned to the kitchen.

Miguel gave us a little background on the dish. "This was the favored ceremonial dinner of our ancestors. They called it 'The Meal of the Gods.' If subanik was being served, you knew it was a very important occasion. My ancestors would be very happy that people from across the globe have come here to Tikal to enjoy this wonderful, traditional food. Enjoy my friends, salud!"

We all raised our glasses. "Salud!"

Eating heartily, no one spoke a word. We were all thoroughly engrossed with our meal. It was a dish that engaged all of the senses. It brought a tear while making you smile. The aroma was commanding, the texture compelling. We all finished about the same time and everyone had a smile on their face. Subanik was made with several different chilis, so the beer was copiously consumed to temper the heat. The chilis, along with tomato, onion and spices, were cooked down to a puree. The beef, chicken and pork were placed in bowls lined with mashan leaves. The puree was poured on top, the bundle tied and placed in a pit of glowing coals for several hours. It was so delectable the gods must have truly had something to do with it.

The conversations at the table picked up with each group conversing in their native language. Myselda was telling Christine about her near escape from the denizens of Xibalba.

Tamara joined the conversation, "The road to Uaxactun is on the other side of the park. I know, I was there today. It's not passable. We couldn't get through."

I gave Myselda one of my "I told you so" smiles.

Lev was not too happy with their road trip to Uaxactun.

"I had to stand in the mud to push the car out," he told us "I was covered with mud. . . . I will have to throw away my shoes."

Franz, with curled a lip, spoke audibly to his companions. "Ha! . . . And he's Russian. You think they would be use to mud by now."

Lev was quick with his comeback. "Fortunately, it was a cheap German car with a sewing machine engine, so I was able to push it out of the mud. If it were a Russian or American car, it would take two or three men to get it out."

"Good one, Russki!" Franz laughed, raised his glass. "Cheers."

"And to you too." Lev said raising his glass. "Herr Sauerkraut!"

There was a good bit of laughter that night, with a strong and infectious comradery. Even Miguel and Raul loosened up and told humorous stories about the "Goings on" at the compound.

Everyone was a story teller. Each of us took a turn spinning tales of our adventures, punctuating them with swigs on our Coronas. Franz was especially funny when talking about monkeys and their behaviors. He spoke freely, rhapsodizing about his encounters with the local primates.

"The ones that yell like banshees? They are the spider monkeys. The others, the ones that sound like eight-foot demons, are the howlers. The howlers, as big and ugly as they are, are really quite docile. Violence within the group is rare and never between the sexes. I think it's because they're physically dimorphic. In cases like that, your girlfriend might kick your ass."

He was passionate when he spoke of his simian friends, which was a side of Franz we had not seen. It was obvious that much of his churlish mannerisms were practiced, and for effect.

"It's that uber hyoid bone that makes them sound so fierce. It's what gives them all that resonance. You can hear them for miles around."

We all listened, amused, and the Rhine Maidens giggled at every pause.

"Now the spider monkey! That's a different story. That's a matriarchal society. The alpha female leads them to the food and holds the troupe together. She is judge and jury. The frau spider monkeys have a penis-sized clitoris that seems to embolden them. That's got to confuse the hell out of the mannlich. . . . Ah, you know, the guy monkeys. Just imagine if you had to deal with that," he said directly to Adam who looked thoroughly confused. "Their brain is twice as big as that of the howler."

Speaking directly to Myselda, who had been contorting her face the whole time, Franz continued. "They are the ones that throw their shit around and urinate on the tourist."

He really did have a gift with words. He would have made a great stand-up comic were it not for his snarly disposition.

"So, what have we got here?" he asked. "A four-foot-tall monkey with a big clit and a big brain. Clever little demons that follow you on the jungle pathways, terrorize and throw their shit at you. . . . I love these guys! If I were not already an archeologist, I would become a primatologist."

"That is so very German!" quipped Lev and we all had a good laugh.

It was getting late and the long day showed on everyone's face. Myselda yawned and the reflex soon passed around the table. It was time to go.

"Seth, we have a lot to do tomorrow, maybe we should call it a night."

We hugged everyone in turn, exchanging emails, vowing we would stay in touch. Franz and company were leaving in the morning. Adam and Christine had another day, and Lev and Tamara were on their own time. We thanked Isabel profusely and said we would stop by to see her before we left for Guatemala City.

* * * *

The next morning, I awoke early. It was still dark outside. The sun would not rise for another half-hour. Rested and full of energy, I grabbed a piece of fruit and turned on the computer. Scrolling aimlessly, not able to focus, I turned it off. I had a compelling urge to return to the Bat Palace and claim a piece of sapodilla wood. Just a small piece that had fallen from the lentil. Evidently the rules and mores were different that morning. *What about leaving everything insitu, so that the people after us can have the same experience?* I fully rationalized it to myself. *It will just lie there and rot or be trampled underfoot by endless tourist; unless of course another myself comes along and picks it up.* Based on that premise, I was saving it. I made up my mind. I would go to the Bat Palace and be back before Myselda woke up.

I grabbed the backpack with the lantern in it and quietly opened the door. The crickets roared, deepening the darkness. In the distance, "Rosy Fingered Dawn"[6] illuminated the roof combs of the pyramids. I stealthily walked down the pathway not wanting to wake anyone.

When I reached the gate, I heard Franz's voice. "I heard something! . . . Someone is out there."

The hike to the Bat Palace was incredible. The Great Plaza glowed orange as I passed through it. The radiant blush was the color of the subanik we'd had for dinner the night before. The breeze was cool on my face. My nostrils flared, greedily taking in the negatively charged air. It was like fuel, thrusting me forward. The daylight creeped in steadily. I could feel the solar winds.

The Bat Palace was just ahead. I quickened my step, almost to a jog. I slid into the building and went directly to

---

[6] From Homer: Iliad.

the room where my sapodilla trophy was lying. I put it in my bag and left the same way I'd come. My body language declared that I was a thief. And so I was. But my criminality was soon forgotten, enchanted once again with my efflorescent surroundings. I slowed down. This would be my last pass through the plaza this trip.

Maybe forever. I should have had brought the camera.

But the camera would never have captured the subtle hues of light. My memory would have to record it all. I made sure I noticed everything.

Myselda was awake and packing when I got back to the room. I felt guilty about what I had done and lied.

"Well that was a great walk! I needed to take one last look around. Thought I would be back before you got up."

"Franz woke me up. He was yelling, 'Something is out there! I know what I heard.' He must have had a bad dream."

"I'll go and get some coffee," I said. "Be right back."

The office was empty so the goodbyes would have to wait. The pastries were arranged attractively, displaying all their goodies. I was the first one down that morning so I had my pick. I glanced over my shoulder, looked about the room, then took the two best cakes. I poured two large coffees, put it all in a box and hustled off to the room like the thief I was.

"I know your gonna miss these pastries," I said setting up the table on the screened porch. "A table with a view for madam."

"Ah yes, a view of the business district."

We enjoyed our coffee, talking, revisiting all of our adventures. Myselda admitted that it had been different kind of vacation, and maybe even interesting. I was a little sad about leaving. I was going to miss the old signpost, Isabel and company and even the howler monkeys. I was satisfied though; I'd gotten what I came for. I now had a physical, visceral, cerebral understanding of the ancient Maya. Plenty to ruminate and speculate over when I returned to the canyons of Manhattan. But now I too looked forward to going home, sleeping late and not having to follow an itinerary. No complaints, all in all it was a pretty good trip and it wasn't over yet. We still had to schlep back to New York; that should be the easy part.

"Let's make a list of what we have to do before leaving." I pulled the notepad from my shirt pocket. "Let's see . . . finish packing—"

"Done."

"Okay. Get the Jeep."

"Up to you."

"Check out . . . say goodbye to Miguel---"

"Right there with ya."

"And of course, Isabel."

"God bless her soul."

"Alright. We don't need a list. I've just a few things to pack."

"I'll finish packing, you take care of the Jeep."

Myselda was getting anxious. She wanted to set the "going home" in motion. She was adept at playing the passive aggressive, and if she didn't get her way, only my meanness and insensitivity would be to blame.

I went straight to the parking lot. I would make the stops for the goodbyes later. The Jeep was just as I'd left it. I had felt uncomfortable leaving it in the parking lot at night and checked on it every day. The worry was for naught. I drove through the Jaguar Gate and parked in front of the office. Myselda, along with the bags, was standing there waiting for me. She had already said her goodbyes to Miguel and was ready to go. I shook Miguel's hand, thanking him.

"You've made our stay very pleasant. Thank you, Miguel."

"Mucho gusto, señor. Raul has asked me to convey his apologies, once again, for the mix up earlier in the week."

"Not a problem Miguel. Please thank Raul for us."

"Well, we ready to go?" asked Myselda.

"No, not yet, I have to check the room."

"I packed all your stuff and checked the room before I left."

"I still have to check for myself. I don't want to be two-hundred miles away and realize I'd forgotten something."

"But why? I've already checked it!"

"Because I have to." I turned away and walked back to the room. It checked out, Myselda had packed everything. But now I had removed all doubt and could put it aside. I washed my face and hands and walked back to the office.

"Thank you, Myselda, You got it all." pointing to the bags in the Jeep.

"You're welcome. Can we go now?"

"You bet," I said, jumping in the Jeep and turning the key, "but first we say goodbye to Isabel."

"Oh, I'm sorry. I completely forgot. Of course."

I parked in front of the cantina where we could see the Jeep from inside.

"Where's my computer bag? I should take that with me. You know Sel our flight is not until three o'clock. We have plenty of time. There's no need to rush."

"I will feel better when we're waiting safely at the airport. Suppose the Jeep breaks down? There's no AAA down here. Or suppose the army decides to close the road. We would be in the hands of a renegade military junta. Held for ransom in

94

some rat-infested dungeon. And my parents are mad at me for coming down—"

"Here we go . . . Myselda that's enough! Tamara and Lev made the very same trip every day. Hell, twice a day! You weren't worried when you went shopping with Christine."

"That's true."

"So, calm down. We will say our goodbyes, drive to Flores and catch our flight. End of story."

The cantina was empty when we arrived. Isabel was cleaning up after the last busload of tourists.

"Señor Seth . . . señora, so good to see you. Please sit, I will bring some coffee."

Isabel brought three cups of coffee and this time sat down with us.

"Isabel, you and your people have made this visit very special. You have made us feel right at home. We will always remember your kindness."

"Mucho gusto señor. Mucho gusto. We are happy that you came. Señor Seth, part of your heart beats alongside ours. You will always be welcome here."

"Isabel, permiso por favor. We have a handful of tickets left and we would like to give them to you and your crew as a thank you for everything you have done for us."

"Muchas gracias señor, but we are not permitted to take gratuities. But that's okay. Everyone says that watching your faces while you were eating was the best. Better than a gratuity. But señor Seth, if you would like, we can take these tickets and buy meals for some of the old and the poor people of the village. That would be best, señor."

"I believe it would, Isabel. It certainly would. I thank you even more."

We finished our coffee, talking quietly until it was time to

95

go. I stood up and held out my arms.

"Un abrazo por favor? (A hug please?)"

She stood, took off her apron and wiped her hands. With open arms she gave me a big hug. "Que tenges un buen viaja, señor. (Have a nice trip.)"

She gave Myselda a hug and then ran into the kitchen.

Myselda teared up. "That was beautiful," she said wiping her eyes. She took my hand, and we left.

We climbed into the Jeep, backed up and entered the circle. Both of us were sad that we were leaving our new friends. I hit the gas and we drove around the plaza at what seemed top speed: fifteen miles an hour. Myselda looked surprised and a little frightened. But then she smiled, waved her hat above her head and let out a big *Yahoo!*. We passed the Jaguar Inn, the cantina and general store. Dust clouds trailed behind us like a streamer. I laughed raucously, took one more spin around the plaza, then headed down the road to the federal highway.

Conditions were excellent. We had the whole road, in both directions, to ourselves. I had checked the oil and the tires. We had most of a tank of gas and everything was present and accounted for. All was good. Time to sit back and enjoy the ride down the modern sacbe to Flores.

It was a very scenic drive. Smoke rose from the chimneys of the homes as children played in the front yard. It all looked the same as when we passed on the way to Tikal.

"Nothing's changed," I shouted to Myselda.

"It hasn't even been a week since we passed . . .so? . . . What did you expect?"

She was right and I laughed along with her. With no traffic we could drive along leisurely, at our own pace. We had lots of time to look around. It was like we were driving through a theme park. Flores was only forty-five minutes away and it went by quickly. We drove over a hill and Flores and Lake Petén appeared below. The landscape was more beautiful than a theme park. I smiled at Myselda and even though she was looking straight ahead, I knew she could see me.

"We're not there yet," She grimaced.

The paperwork for the rental was ready and waiting when we arrived. We even got a discount for the half-tank of gas that was left. The terminal was very busy. The kiosks overflowed with shoppers looking for last minute souvenirs. We checked our bags and got our boarding pass.

"Well, now we have to find a home for the next two and a half hours," I said looking for available seats in the terminal. I spotted a couple close to the main entrance, and we hustled over there and grabbed them. This would be perfect for watching the goings on at the baggage drop off outside, as well as the entire terminal. A two and a half hour wait at an airport can drag on, but there was plenty of visual here to keep us busy. After we settled in, I sauntered off to a large gift shop in the center of the terminal. I was hoping to find a notebook as I had checked my laptop with the luggage. I found a yellow legal pad and I picked up a couple of postcards with excellent views of Flores, Tikal and Lake Petén. On the way to the register something caught my eye: a rack with leather gloves. Why winter gloves would be needed in Guatemala confused me, but I knew right away that I should get a pair to protect myself from Myselda. It would make a good joke as well.

When I returned, I handed Myselda the picture cards and sat down.

"Did you bring anything to eat or drink?"

"No, I didn't think to. They have sodas and snack stuff at the gift shop, and there are food vendors over there too."

"You'll like my pictures of Lake Petén," she said, shuffling through the cards. "I'm gonna get something to eat. Hungry?"

"Yes," I said, a little embarrassed. "Maybe some peanuts and an iced tea."

I made notes on the morning's journey. From 'Rosy Fingered Dawn' through the goodbyes, the highways and our arrival at the airport. I jotted down profiles, mannerisms and descriptions of the people; fawning over the colorful handmade clothes the Mayan ladies wore. Myselda returned with our snacks.

"You look like an artist sketching the people around you."

"I am sketching the people. Words are my colors; sentences my brush strokes and paragraphs my setting," taking my iced tea and peanuts from her. "This here yellow pad is a canvas of words."

She sat munching on chips, flipping through a magazine,

"I like this airport. They should build a new one like this in Guatemala City. Replace that 'Candy Land' shack they have now, with a real airport."

"Tikal is Guatemala's jewel. When the tourist industry is successful here, rebuilding the capitol will follow."

The rest of the wait passed by quickly. Our flight was called over the loudspeakers and we packed our stuff and headed for the gate. There were six people in front of us and two behind. This was a packed flight. We walked the bouncing ramp to the cabin, stowed away our gear and took our seats.

"You take the window seat Seth."

The stewardess was the same gal we had on the flight to Tikal. She recognized us and greeted us warmly. "Welcome, so good to see you again."

The pilot came aboard, put his bag in the cabin, and introduced himself. "Good afternoon everyone. My name is Juan Felipe de la Cruz, and I will be your pilot."

"He has the same last name as the other pilot," Myselda whispered behind the cover of her magazine. "You know, the kid. Maybe he did take his father's uniform."

"Ah bull," dismissing Myselda's theory. "The kid was great. His landing was perfection. I hope his father is as good. How do you know this guy didn't steal his son's uniform and is pretending to be a pilot?"

The pilot grimaced at us for not listening to his speech and continued. "Please, enjoy your flight, and I will see you in Guatemala City."

The engine whined as we taxied to the runway. I put on the gloves I had bought earlier. Myselda leaned back into her chair and grabbed my hand.

Feeling the glove, she turned to me. "You're so mean."

"I know, but I need that hand."

The flight was pretty calm, no turbulence or drama. We signaled to the stewardess that we wouldn't be needing anything and settled in. I daydreamed, looking out of the window, watching the landscape change below. Myselda dozed off holding my gloved hand. She slept the entire flight. When the pilot announced our descent, I had to wake her.

After another excellent landing, we were soon bouncing down the gang plank on our way to the luggage carousel. A driver, holding a sign with our names on it, was there waiting. We let him know we had arrived and would be right with him. Without saying a word he changed signs, which now read, "Robert and Mary Kelly."

"Over here driver," someone called out. He acknowledged them and changed signs again.

Our bags came, and we all loaded into his shuttle bus. The ride to the hotel was a tour of the real Guatemala City. In the place of grand monuments and plazas, there were furniture stores and street vendors. Smoke billowed from portable kiosks where food was being prepared; a fractal of the monster volcano looming in the distance. That giant covered half the sky.

Everyone on the street looked busy and focused on their business. The traffic patterns were crazy and erratic, bordering on chaos. Our driver drove calmly, as though he didn't have a care in the world. Incense burned in the ashtray, as he weaved through traffic. Driving for him was like breathing in and breathing out, as though it were meditation. We arrived safely at the hotel and I gave him a good tip for his tai chi dance through the city.

The hotel was a modern twelve-story building with a spacious lobby, elevators and even a restaurant on the top floor. All of which we welcomed after our stay at the Jaguar Inn. I could see Myselda was reveling in anticipation of the amenities; much deserved and understandable. Bathtubs, television, and room service were all part of the natural order of things; as the world should be. We took the elevator to the seventh floor, found our room and flopped onto the twin beds. Munching on the complementary chocolates, we decided we would have dinner at the restaurant in the hotel.

"We've been authentic enough," Myselda said, making her case.

It was fine with me. I certainly didn't want to go schlepping through the city at night looking for a restaurant.

100

We had the whole next day to explore Guatemala City.

Tonight, we chill. After a shower and a nap, dinner upstairs will be perfect. I'll bet they don't have subanik!

The restaurant was nice. The elevator opened to a waiting area with plush furniture and an imposing station for the maître d'. European landscapes, tastefully framed and lighted were displayed on the wall. Two steps below was a large dining room with bright white tablecloths, sparkling crystal and highly polished silverware. Rather elegant, but the place was practically empty. There was another couple dinning, a dinner group of five, and us. The waiters stood on either side of the steps, anxious and eager to serve. They were very Latin looking. Tall, thin, with high cheek bones, tight fitting clothes and jet-black hair. The maître d' brought us to our table handing us a rather large menu and introduced us to our waiter. His name was Jorge and he looked thrilled to have his job. Myselda was having white wine and I ordered a cerveza fria, something the waiter found amusing. It was a pretty extensive menu. Just about any kind of meat, fish or fowl you might want was there for the asking—but no subanik. Myselda ordered the salmon with rice pilaf. There were too many choices on the menu for me to make a decision, so I ordered the steak and fries.

"Un bistec cocido raro, por favor. No insalata, y otro cerveza. (A steak cooked rare please. No salad and another beer.)" Once again the waiter found my Spanish pronunciation amusing. For some reason everything I said brought a quick laugh and a smile to his face. I could see the maître d' nodding in approval at the waiter's mirth.

Maybe I sound like a New Yor'Rican speaking Spanglish?

On the balcony to the left were two musicians with different sized guitars, waiting to be called into service. Their outfits looked more Mexican than Guatemalan, but who's to say where the boundaries lie when it comes to haute couture. I waved them over to our table.

"Señor, señora. What would you like to hear?" said the tall one carrying a small guitar.

"We know many songs," said his partner. He was a short man with a big guitar.

Both were very pleasant fellows, but their outfits needed a dry cleaning. There was an atmosphere that accompanied them and their music. Myselda and I consulted and decided on *De Colores*, which was a rallying song south of the border. I thought our choice would be appreciated; the "Norte Americano" was "simpatico" with their hope for a just government, governance and all that.

The musicians fidgeted nervously. They looked to the maître d', but he was busy on the phone. I guessed they didn't know how to say "no" because they hesitantly began the intro. They sang the first verse in close harmony. Myselda and I had sung this song at many a party, so she was right there with a piercing soprano. Delighted, I jumped in with a continuo in the bass. By the third verse everyone knew where everyone else was going with the harmony and we gave the song a full blend of voicings. When we finished, we received a round of applause and nods of approval from the other diners.

Our food arrived and we dug right in, talking away. When we finished the maître d' approached our table. I could see he had something he wanted to say.

"Señor . . . I should like you to know that this is not a cantina, and that your behavior does not, shall we say, suit the decor. Please refrain from any other similar behaviors, and please pass it on to your equals."

"Well, I think I understand," I said leaning back in my chair. His name tag read Pedro. "Peedrooo, worry not," affecting a southern accent, "I cannot foresee any circumstances where such events would come about. We hope you will pardon our manners. We usually travel on the continent where a rousing aria at dinner is well appreciated and applauded. We understand you have your quaint rules of decorum and of course we will respect them."

"Another capitalist trained in rhetoric, Hah! Thank you señor," he said with a smirky smile and marched off.

"I know you enjoyed that," Myselda said raising her glass. "I especially liked it when you rubbed your stomach while talking. That was perfect."

"I was just giving him what he wanted to see. He's never going to change his view, no matter how hard you try. It's okay with me. Good for the journal too." I passed her the credit card and wispered "you pay the bill."

I signaled the waiter for the check. When he came, I pointed to Myselda and watched the head waiter grin. Myselda gave Jorge the card and he took it to the maître d' to be processed. Jorge came back looking worried. This was obviously an embarrassing part of his job.

"Señora, lo siento (I'm sorry), your card has been rejected. Have you another card you would like to present?"

"That won't be necessary Jorge. It is my name on the card. I'll handle this." I signaled to the maître d' to join us. I switched to my New York accent which took him by surprise.

"Señor, we seem to have a data entry problem here. I use this card whenever I travel. It has taken me to a great many places. As a matter of fact, my accommodations at this hotel have been paid for with this card. I am in room seven twenty-three. Please run the information again and let me know when the billing goes through. I will sign for the charges and let Visa know you are having problems with their service. Thank you señor. I will be in my room." He turned on his heel and walked away somewhat perturbed. I called after him.

"And I like your shoes señor . . . very shiny."

We returned to our room to settle in for the night. I made notes on the dinner and the confrontation with the head waiter. Myselda didn't care for the guy at all.

"What a pompous ass that guy was. If he were any more full of himself, he would explode!"

"He's just an uppity mestizo. They're all wannabe Che Guevaras."

There was a knock on the door. It was our waiter. Dinner had been placed on our hotel bill directly. Jorge looked embarrassed.

"Señor, I am very sorry. I have nothing to do with this. I only work here."

"I understand, Jorge. Good service," I said handing him twenty pesos, "Buenas noches."

Myselda didn't care for the whole situation. "I wouldn't have given him anything. It makes no sense to reward bad manners. I'd be more inclined towards revenge. Like inviting Franz and the Rhine Maidens to dinner and watching *Peedro* deal with them."

"That's brilliant! You're a genius . . . devious perhaps, but still a genius. Let's put that on the back burner." I continued making notes while Myselda got ready for bed. She came out of the bathroom wearing only her panties, looking for her night gown. I dropped everything, wrestled her to the bed, and we made love.

"You have two days to make up for cowboy."

"Yes ma'am."

We drifted off to sleep. It had been a full day, and the pillow was welcome. Tomorrow we would explore Guatemala City before heading home.

* * * *

Mayan warriors, some with wings, were spewing out of the doorways of all the temples of Tikal. They were like bees leaving the hive to fight an invader. They were on a search and destroy mission and I was the enemy. The high priest, face painted, ready for war, stood on the platform of Temple I. His army surrounded him, so numerous they blocked out the sun. He spoke angrily, directly to me. Even though at a distance, his voice sounded like he was standing right in front of me. I could feel his fiery breath on my face.

"You will be bound and made to watch your family being sacrificed. Even this is not enough to atone for the insult you have made towards us. You will be taken to Xibalba to walk the gauntlet of angry gods. Then you will be placed on the altar stone where your heart will be ripped out, and fed to the vultures."

Isabel appeared. She had come to help me.

"Señor Seth, por favor, listen closely. In Antigua, near the Mercado, there is an old church which is crumbling and falling down. Underneath this crippled monster is a great Mayan temple. In former times it was a great power center, and a sister to the volcano there. If you return the wood to this sacred site, it will absolve you of your trespasses. With the permission of the high priest, we can make amends." She bowed at the waist and signaled to me that I should do the same.

"I will accept that, but it must be done immediately! . . . Make it so foreigner!" bellowed the high priest. He then passed through me filling me with terror. His minions followed him in waves, passing through me like a tropical storm. After what felt like an eternity they disappeared. So did Isabel.

I awoke, drenched in sweat, shaking uncontrollably. Terrified, I ran to the desk and wrote down everything so as not to forget any detail. Our lives depended on it. It was five a.m. Sunrise was at least an hour away; it would take another hour after that for the city to wake up. I put on my clothes and packed a travel bag.

How am I going to get to Antigua?

It wasn't far away, but we certainly couldn't walk there. I went down to the front desk and asked about transportation to Antigua.

"There is a tour guide company that has a shuttle bus twice a day to Antigua. They leave at eleven a.m. and one p.m. from the front of the hotel. There is a local bus that runs all day, but it is crowded with locals and makes many stops. It takes over an hour to reach Antigua."

"How far is the bus stop?"

"Not far. When you leave the hotel, turn right señor. Then, when you reach the corner you will turn right again. Walk straight for two blocks and you will come to the bus stop. It is the first and last stop for the bus to Antigua."

I thanked him and returned to the room. It was time to get Myselda moving. I would have to explain why we were changing our plans, and why we were in emergency mode. I went over the story in my head, and it didn't look too good. I was going to have to wing it. Back in the room, Myselda was already dressed, looking worried.

"Seth, are you all right? Your pillow is soaking wet! You look pale. . . . Where have you been?" Myselda searched my face for what was happening. "It was another dream wasn't it? Seth Parker, you tell me right now! What's going on?"

"It was a dream."

I told her about the high priest and how he was going to sacrifice my family and his plans to feed my heart to the vultures. I told her of his minions darkening the sky and creating tremendous winds that terrorized every cell in my body.

"I'm going to have to walk a gauntlet of angry gods!"

"What about me? Am I going to be sacrificed? After all, we don't have any kids, and we're not related by blood or anything."

"I didn't see you there, just my kids. He was pointing to my kids. They would be sacrificed . . . along with me of course."

"Oh, that's good. There's no reason I should be involved in—"

"Anyway, Isabel showed up and saved the day. She came up with a way I could atone for my trespasses."

"Trespasses? What trespasses? Seth what have you done now?"

"I took a piece of sapodilla wood from the Bat Palace."

"Is that what this is about? A piece of wood? That's where you were yesterday morni—"

"Isabel said that if I returned the piece of sapodilla wood to an old Mayan temple in Antigua, I would be able to absolve myself. The high priest agreed, so we are going to Antigua today."

"Antigua? How are we going to get there? And we have our flight home tomorrow."

"It's not that far. There's a local bus that runs all day, a couple of blocks from here. A little change in our plans is all."

We stopped at the lobby café and I ordered a large coffee and buttered roll for each of us. Fortified, we passed through the lobby and entered the roar of the city. The morning rush was in full swing. A steady flow of traffic and pedestrians passed the hotel. It was very loud, between the car horns and the stop and go of the traffic; many of the cars were without mufflers. Turning the corner brought us face to face with the volcano. So very there, so still, so peaceful — for the time being anyway. As simple as the directions were, I carried them, and read and re-read them many times, making sure we stayed on track. They were spot on. We came to a parking lot where several buses, colorfully painted in a rainbow motif were parked. Strung together, they did look like a rainbow. There were two doors, front and rear, and a luggage rack on the roof. A group of locals waited for the next bus to leave. All Indio's in colorful outfits. Women with suitcases and tied bundles of their crafts, waited patiently with their children. An old man carried chickens in a wooden crate. Two young men who looked very hung-over, slept back to back, waiting for the bus to leave. They reeked of alcohol. The volcano dwarfed us all.

A man with a Mets baseball cap jumped out of the bus yelling, "Antigua . . . Antigua!" He collected the fare, which was one peso, and threw the bundles onto the roof. For a small guy, he was pretty strong and tossed the bundles around like beach balls. All the while yelling, "Antigua . . . Antigua!" He was very theatrical and appeared to enjoy his work. The bus back-fired, sputtered, and we were on our way. We traveled down a narrow, cobblestone side street with sidewalks wide enough for only one person. Iron bars covered all the windows at street level. A few of the apartments had window boxes on the second floor. Some with jeans drying in the wind, but most of the street was stark and bare. When we reached the main thoroughfare of the city things picked up. Stores selling kitchen wares, appliances, electrical supplies had their hawkers out front pulling in customers to see their goods. A military convoy passed in the opposite direction. Shopkeepers sweeping their sidewalks, the people on the street, stopped and silently watched the convoy pass by. The bus made stops every few blocks. The ticket man would call out, "Antigua . . . Antigua!" all the while flirting with the young girls on the street and throwing bags onto the luggage rack. People were getting on, and no one was getting off. The bus was getting crowded. By the time we reached the highway, there was not an empty seat.

Leaving the city, we followed a road that closely hugged the hillside. In the distance below, at the base of the volcano, was Antigua. The town, with its sprawling suburbs, looked as though it was supplicating itself before the great mountain. The chickens clucked, the children cried, and the young drunks snored. The bus sputtered along, laboring with each shift of its gears during its decent. The folks on the bus eyed us with great curiosity. The women were especially interested in Myselda; but she didn't notice. Her eyes were glued to the window, transported, enamored by the Disney like setting. It was slow going for which I was glad because it was a long way down to the bottom, and the breaks squealed as we crept along at ten miles an hour. The volcano loomed larger and larger the deeper we drove into the valley. When we reached level ground, we both breathed a sigh of relief.

Myselda had taken my hand on the way down and had inscribed her fear on the back of it. She never said a word. I hadn't noticed or felt a thing, being absorbed myself, with the steep drop-off on my right. The town was only a couple of miles ahead. On either side of the highway were milpas (farms) well-manicured and cared for. Cattle and sheep grazed bucolically on the hillsides. Corn fields separated by rows of beans and squash and tomatoes brought us to the edge of town. We rolled into antigua like a ship returning to port after a battle at sea. On the outskirts of town was the barrio.

It seems there is always a barrio, even in Shangri-La.

The barrio turned into the suburbs. Row houses, neatly kept, lined the wide streets. The closer we got to the center of town the larger the homes became; Antigua certainly had a healthy middle-class. I saw the ruins of an old church through the openings between the buildings we passed. It looked to be a couple of blocks away. I knew instinctually that it was where I had to go. I turned and smiled at Myselda. She didn't look too happy. She was brewing something; more so then the volcano. We drove a little further and pulled into the terminal area. It was a busy place. Shuttles, cabs, tour busses were all either picking up or discharging passengers. The open-air Mercado was across the street. The good folks gathered their belongings, calmly left the bus in single file, and formed a line outside. We watched the parade of chickens and children go by before making our move. The driver walked to the back to wake the young party-goers.

"Despierta (wake up, let's go) . . . vamanos . . . despierta!"

The young men grumbled, arranged their clothes and left. We followed with the driver behind us. The ticket man had climbed onto the roof of the bus and handed the bundles and suitcases to the driver below. The passengers took their precious cargo and left for the Mercado.

When the last bag was retrieved the driver jumped back behind the wheel and the ticket man waved his cap in the air yelling, "Guatemala . . . Guatemala!"

The bus backfired and leapt forward leaving us in a cloud of grey and black smoke.

I shrugged, my shoulders giving Myselda my helpless-hapless look.

"Now you have a farting bus to add to your story, Seth. I'm outta here. I have to use the bathroom." She darted off to the terminal building. I followed along.

As long as the volcano doesn't fart, we'll be all right.

It was more of a gift shop than a bus station. Textiles, pottery, statues, all beautifully crafted lined the shelves; ad nauseam. So many they began to look like tchotchkes. Other than an interesting array of post cards showing the volcano in various stages of activity, everything looked like trinkets.

Myselda returned shaking her head. "I won't be using that facility again. I had to wash my hands three times."

I could see one of the crumbling towers of the church above the rooftops of the buildings.

"We have to go this way. I saw an old church when we were passing through town and I think that's where we have to go."

"As long as it's not the road to Xibalba."

"If I don't find this temple, life will become the road to Xibalba!"

"That's the part where I go shopping."

"Thank you love, it's so heartening to know you're with me every step of the way."

"I'm not walking a gauntlet of angry gods. I have nothing to wear."

We followed the broom swept streets to the tower in the

distance. The buildings were freshly painted and had large impressive doorways. I couldn't tell if it was one building with multiple doorways, or independent units with separate thresholds.

A group of school children passed on the other side of the street. They were obviously Catholic school children. Dressed in uniforms of pressed white shirts, ties, knickers and skirts, they were well groomed and cared for. Exuberant and enthused, they were eager to get to school, carrying slide rules and squares with bookbags strapped to their backs. This was a strange blast from the past. It was everything I had rebelled against in parochial school; yet now so refreshing to see.

Myselda was wide-eyed. "In my school, we are teaching kids how to put condoms on bananas . . . and little else."

"Why don't you say something?"

"The union says we can't insult the cliental."

"Oops. . . . There ya go." *So much for progressive education.*

The next street opened to a plaza, with the old church at the far end. It was empty and the sound of our boots echoed throughout, bouncing off the buildings. Only one of the large wooden doors remained at the entrance. The threshold was intact, but the supporting walls to the left side of the building lay in a pile of rubble at its base. Climbing three wide steps, I entered the church. It was an ambitious endeavor with which the Spanish had hoped to make a big impression on the natives. The center nave was a very large, open space. The supporting walls for the roof were further apart than usual. The builder's ambition was the buildings demise and the evidence of that lay at my feet. In the rear of the nave was a mural of Jesus with his flock. That was where the alter would have been. I searched the side alcoves, climbing over broken pews and debris from the roof. I really didn't know what I was looking for, but I would know it as soon as I saw it. Over by the mural was an area where the floor had collapsed and I worked my way over there.

This is it!

I found what I was looking for. Four or five feet below was one of the stone talud-tablero platforms of an old temple. Part of its stairway remained intact. I worked my way around to the mural wall where a section of the floor, about a foot wide, was still attached. I hugged the wall and inched my way along, as though I were on the ledge of an apartment building, until I reached the stairway. Climbing down I saw the remains of Chaacs. They looked like they had been intentionally defaced; parts of their nose and eyes were still lying on the platform. The stairs continued further down until it reached the fill that had been used in the construction of the church. I couldn't return the sapodilla wood there; the fill was put there by the Spanish and that would only make the gods angry.

That won't work.

I monkeyed my way up the steps to the platform where I found a crevice between two large blocks of stone, beside the Chaac.

This will work! One hundred percent Mayan.

Taking the wood from my backpack, I placed it in the deep crevice. Picking up a branch, I pushed it further into the niche. I felt a thousand pounds lighter. Total relief.

"Oh yeah! Thank you Isabel!"

I considered carving my name into the stone, but thinking it might add insult to injury, I finished with a celebratory dance. I could feel someone watching me from above. It was Myselda.

"How ya doin' buddy?"

"Great! Couldn't be better. I was just thanking Isabel."

"I know, I could hear you all the way back in the plaza. Does this mean that you've done what you had to do?"

"Yes ma'am, I am now a free man."

Climbing the stairs back to the ledge, I eased myself along the wall.

"Take it easy Seth. Go slow, that looks dangerous."

"I'm okay," jumping onto the floor, I gave her a big kiss. "Let's get something to eat. I'm famished."

We worked our way out of the old church and into the plaza. Walking down the now familiar streets, everything looked brighter and more inviting.

"Slow down Seth, what's your hurry?"

"Sorry luv, but I feel so light . . . like a bird in flight. Take my hand, I'll take you with me."

"No thanks, I'll save my flying for tomorrow."

We passed the bus terminal and entered the labyrinth that was the Mercado. Myselda always felt better after shopping and there was plenty there for her to quell her anxieties. I told her to pick out something nice, that I wanted to buy her a gift for being such a patient trooper.

"Myselda, you should take advantage when I'm in such a generous and gregarious mood."

Going shopping is just a replacement for the five hundred thousand years we spent searching the forest floor for mushrooms, tubers and roots. The plants, the fruit, the nuts and berries were so necessary for life that it was programmed into our DNA to forage for them. Shopping is the modern way we fulfill that genetic mandate.

Myselda went from rack to rack, totally focused on what she was doing.

114

"I know I want a dress," she said examining the various materials, the stitching, even smelling them. "I just can't make up my mind."

"Why do you smell them?"

"I don't know. . . . They're all so beautiful. I just can't make up my mind."

"The skimpier the better."

"That'll narrow it down. Let's go to lunch and come back after. Seth . . . look. It's Franz and the Rhine Maidens."

"Damen schauen, es ist Seth und Myselda! (Ladies look, it is Seth and Myselda.)"

"Hello!" We called, greeting them.

"Schönen tag (Nice day)," the ladies said, giggling.

"Schönen tag," Franz said. "I'm glad I ran into you. We are having dinner tonight at the hotel where you are staying. One of my clients has an account there and has made it available to us. We would like for you to join us."

"That's sounds great Franz. What do you say Myselda?"

"Sure."

"What time, Franz?"

"Around seven o'clock would be good for us."

"Then seven it is. We'll be there. We're on our way to lunch right now, care to join us?"

"No, we have more business here. The bargaining is rough today and we have to stay at it. But I do know of a good restaurant close to here. The best in Antigua. Follow the old cobblestone road for a block or so. After you pass through the arch, the restaurant will be a few doors down, on your left."

"Good then, we'll see you at seven. Schönen tag, ladies."

"Schönen tag."

"Schönen tag."

Antigua is a story book little town with winding streets, murals depicting the daily life of the native people and of course the ubiquitous volcano. We came to the arch and Myselda became very excited, jumping up and down.

"Ooh, ooh. Take my picture under the arch, with the volcano in the background. I've seen it in the brochures and on the post cards!"

Myselda was becoming manic. I took the pictures wondering which was going to blow first, Myselda or the volcano."

Franz knew his restaurants. It was a great place and would surely cheer Myselda up. The dining area was a courtyard, partitioned with bougainvillea vining on lattice and along the beams of the pergola above. In the center was a large Chaac fountain with water flowing from its nose. The sound of the flowing water was calming and soothing. On the plaster walls were murals of Antigua. Its volcano, churches, the mercado and the arch we just passed through.

The waiter showed us to a booth. Myselda ordered white wine and I ordered a beer. The next moment she was whimpering with deep sighs, drying her eyes with her napkin.

"Myselda . . . are you okay? What's up?"

"I'm just tired I guess," She blew her nose, heaving and sobbing.

The waiter came with our drinks looking confused and concerned.

"Is everything all right, señor?"

Myselda answered for me. "Yes, I'm fine. I'm tired and hungry, and I want to go home."

"Lo siento (I'm sorry), señora. When you are ready, I will come back and take your order."

"No, no . . .I know what I want," she said blowing her nose again. "I'll have the salmon with the basmati rice and string beans."

"Very good señora. The salmon is perfectly fresh."

"I think I'll try your Tikal burger with the fries."

"Very good. Will there be anything else?"

"I'll have another beer."

"I'm good, thank you."

After the waiter left, I handed her my napkin and tried to find out what was going on. "So what's happening Myselda? Why are you so upset?"

"I'm tired of it all, Seth. I'm tired of the jungle. I'm tired of smelly, old, cold, moldy buildings. Tired of the monkeys and the conquistadors. I'm tired of nothing being normal. I'm tired of it all. I want to go home!"

Taking her hand, I tried to comfort her,

"Tomorrow morning, we'll be on our way. By tomorrow night, you'll be in your own bed surrounded by all your comforts. After a good night's sleep, you'll have all of New York at your disposal. Who has it better than us?"

The waiter came with our food and we ate in silence. The food was very good but Myselda hadn't perked up any. When we finished, I paid the check and we left.

"Let's go get that dress Sel. It's out there on a rack waiting for you."

On the way to the mercado, Myselda didn't even notice the arch when we passed through it. She was walking with her head down and shoulders hunched. I was hoping the foraging would bring her back.

Franz was swimming in his emporium, going from booth to booth, haggling with the locals for their goods. It sounded as though he could bargain in Spanish like a native. We

117

stopped to talk with him. I told him we were going to find a dress for Myselda and then catch the next bus back to Guatemala City."

"Why are you taking the bus?"

I told him the tour bus didn't leave until eleven o'clock and I didn't want to wait.

"The concierge said the local busses run all day long."

"For twenty dollars American you can take a cab, and it only takes thirty minutes. Expensive I know, but much easier."

Myselda looked at me wide eyed and walked away.

"I didn't know!" I said calling after her.

"Whatever price they ask for the dress, pay half!" Franz yelled as I took off after Myselda.

I caught up with her in the heart of the mercado. She had already bought a poncho and handed it to me. "This will come in handy back home. What do you think of this dress?"

"It's beautiful and you'll make it even more beautiful when you wear it."

"Quanto (How much?), señora?" Myselda asked the saleswomen.

"Cincuenta dolares. (Fifty dollars.)"

"I will pay . . . treinta y cinco, no mas. (Thirty-five, no more.)"

"Very good, señora."

"Franz said to pay half," I whispered to her.

"I'll leave it for Franz to cheat the little people. A lot of work went into this dress and I'll not take advantage of them."

"I agree, good for you Myselda."

We crossed the street to the bus terminal. It was very busy, being late in the day. People were coming and going with a slow kind of urgency. The local bus was being loaded with cries of "Guatemala . . . Guatemala!" Four or five taxis waited in the queue. We went to the first taxi in the line. The driver tipped his hat and held the door for Myselda. It may have been a Toyota hatchback, but he treated it like it was a grand limousine. I got in behind him on the driver's side.

"Quetzal Hotel por favor, Guatemala ciudad."

"Very good, señor." He had a clear speaking voice with almost no accent. "You know folks . . . Yo hablo ingles. (I speak english.)"

He was funny. Even Myselda laughed. He said he was a night club comic working part time as a taxi driver. He entertained us all the way to the hotel. When we arrived, his voice and his demeanor completely and abruptly changed.

"Twenty dollars American, señor."

I had forgotten about the exchange rate,

"Por tu . . . cuarenta pesos amigo. Gracias. (For you, forty pesos friend. Thank you.)"

"Dollars, señor. No pesos."

Back in the room, Myselda went immediately to the shower. She was in there a long time, and I drifted off to sleep. I slept until six o'clock. Realizing we were running late, I called out to Myselda to remind her we were having dinner with Franz and the Rhine Maidens. The covers were pulled up over her head and she spoke through the blankets.

"I don't feel up to it this evening Seth. I think I'll stay in the room and catch up on my sleep. Make my apologies for me, will ya? Tell them I have allergies."

"Okay." I laid out my clothes and jumped in the shower. When I came out Myselda was still buried beneath her pillows and blankets. I called down to the front desk.

"Hola! . . . this is room number seven twenty-three. We'll

be checking out in the morning and would like to have our bill ready. . . . Yes, early. . . . A wake-up call would be nice. Make it six o'clock. Thank you. Buenas noches."

"That sounded soooo good," Myselda said, her voice muffled by the pillow. "Don't worry, I'll get you up in time."

"I know, you get your rest, I'll be back in a couple of hours."

"Have fun."

When I stepped out of the elevator, the maître d' looked surprised.

"Señor, I didn't expect to see you again."

I really didn't want to joust with this guy; he was annoying and not worth the trouble. Franz and the Rhine Maidens, already seated, waved me over to join them.

"What- a- surprise. Will the wife be joining you, señor?" the maître d' asked.

"No, not tonight." He handed a menu to Jorge and the waiter walked me to the table.

"Good evening, señor," he said quietly with a big smile.

"Good evening Jorge. How are you?"

I made my apologies for Myselda to Franz and company, explaining that she'd had a rough day and wasn't feeling well.

"She did look stressed," he said sympathetically.

The waiter came with six bottles of beer and set them in front of Franz; he knew the routine.

He has been here before.

"Señor, for you?" he asked, turning to me.

"Cerveza, por favor."

"Very good." I almost expected Jorge to click his heels.

"So, you guys are regulars here? Looks like everyone knows you."

120

Franz, speaking to the ladies, "I love the way the Americans call everybody *guys*. It's so egalitarian. Yes, we come here whenever we are in town. The food is good, reasonably priced, and my ladies like to get away from the monkeys. Just one of the vergünstigungen . . . ah . . . perks of my business."

"The head waiter is a bit of a jerk. He gave me a hard time last night. Wouldn't accept my credit card. I don't think he likes Americans."

"I'd say you are right. He went to university in Havana and believes he knows how the world should be ordered. I tell the politicos I'm from East Berlin and they call me comrade."

The Rhine Maidens were in good spirts, laughing and giggling along with everything Franz said.

The waiter came back with my beer and took our order. The ladies ordered the salmon and Franz ordered the pork chops.

"They are delicious," he said, "and very thick."

"I'll have the pork chops as well then. And Jorge, I'm from the east Bronx."

Franz was in good form that night and kept us laughing throughout dinner. I signaled Jorge for another beer and Franz held up three fingers indicating he wanted a refill as well. The maître d' returned with the waiter and asked Franz if everything was satisfactory.

"Yes, very good Pedro, thank you. You can put the entire table on señor Vasquez's bill."

I smiled at Pedro thinking his name should be Simon, Fidel or Che. The pompous poppycock scowled at me, reciting a prepared statement that he'd obviously rehearsed.

"Tell me, señor . . . how many people have to work to

121

support your meaningless and frivolous lifestyle?"

"Not too many Peedro, only a few. Mostly me, myself and I. We're a motley crew, but we get the job done. It is our good fortune that we were born in a place where a schoolteacher and a construction worker can afford to travel the world and see its wonders. Travel to your beautiful country and study it's wonderful heritage. At least those things that the conquerors missed in their holocaust."

His face dropped. He looked unsure of himself as he searched his mind to find the official party comeback.

"Yes, but at the expense of how many señor?" He turned on his heels and sauntered back to his station, visibly upset. The waiter smiled at me and followed Pedro.

"Sorry for not backing you up, mein freund. Business and all, you understand. Don't want to upset the locals. Besides, there was no need; you handled yourself pretty good."

"Understood. It doesn't matter what he thinks, or what I think, or even what you think. That was a great dinner with good company and lots of laughs. Who could ask for more?"

It was time to go. I told them I should check in on Myselda and pack my bags for the morning. We promised to stay in touch, and Franz gave me a big hug. The Rhine Maidens also gave me a big hug, pressing themselves onto me in a rather intimate way. Both of them.

"Auf wiedersehen, Seth."

"Auf wiedersehen," the ladies said, holding hands and giggling.

"Are you sure you want to go?" Franz asked with a Cheshire grin.

"I think I'd better. Thanks for everything!"

I walked to the elevator, passing the maître d'. We ignored each other.

When I got back to the room, Myselda was sleeping. I undressed, brushed my teeth, and slipped into bed. I thought about what it would be like to roll under the covers with the Rhine Maidens. With that thought, and its accompanying smile, I drifted off to sleep.

* * * *

"Rise and shine!" Myselda said, clapping her hands. "Let's go, we have a busy day in front of us. Rise and shine."

"Whooh . . . What time is it?" I said trying to wake up.

"It's getting late, that's what time it is. Come on, let's go! I'm already packed."

"Hold on sarge. It's two hours before the shuttle leaves. Take it easy. You have ruined my dream of searching for the Rheingold."

"You and your dreams. Haven't you had enough of them?"

"This dream was different."

"Well save it for later. We have a lot to do. Let's get cracking."

Myselda's suitcase was open on the bed, waiting for the last few items before lockdown.

She was a little manic, but cheerful and energetic. I was anxious to get home myself. I was looking forward to the time when I could flop down into my Lazy Boy, flicker in hand, and watch the most insultingly stupid television shows I could find. I breathed a sigh of relief just thinking about it.

I was ready to go within an hour. Our checkout went smoothly, and the woman even apologized for the maître d'. She said an employee had told her of his tantrum.

"His behavior was unacceptable and should not be seen as a reflection of the hotel and its staff." With hushed tones she added, "You see señor, his mother is on the Board of Directors." She nodded her head as she spoke.

I told her that we had a very pleasant stay and that the food at the restaurant was excellent, in spite of the maître d'. We stopped at the café for a coffee and buttered roll.

"I know we're a little bit early Seth, but it's better than rushing around trying to get everything together at the last minute."

"Sure . . . makes no difference to me weather we wait here or in the room. It's fine."

Afterward we sat in the lobby by the picture window, and watched the city come to life. Myselda had different colored socks on. She didn't notice the clash of color on her feet, so preoccupied was she with getting out of town. The shuttle bus came, and we got on board. We had the whole bus to ourselves at first and leisurely spread ourselves out. But soon the driver stopped at another hotel and a large group of people came on board with their suitcases. Sitting uncomfortably close, shoulder to shoulder the entire way, there was no sense of loss when we arrived at the airport and went our separate ways. We checked our bags and breathed a sigh of relief.

We had thirty-minutes to kill until boarding. We wandered around looking at the magazines, surfing the gift shops. Myselda checked her purse every ten minutes or so to make sure our tickets and passports were still there. The time passed quickly and soon we were waiting in line at the gate. The large 747 American Airlines jet brought a smile to Myselda's face. We found our seats and stowed our carry-on bags. Myselda sat by the window. We both buckled up and settled in with a sigh and a smile.

"We're on our way!" I said, reaching for her hand. We

were both wearing gloves and had a good laugh.

"Very good Myselda, that's funny." Leaning back in my seat, I closed my eyes. "Think of the Hudson River and the George Washington bridge lit up at night. Think of the Palisades, Fort Tryon Park and the Cloisters. Think of Times Square and the Staten Island Ferry."

The jet took off whistling and humming. I could feel the giant bird turning north. It was a direct flight to New York, and we would be home for dinner.

"Who   has   it   better   than   us!"

THE QUEEN OF THE EVERGLADES

"Jedidiah Bozeman, you is the craziest man that has evva' walked the face of dis earth," Eunice said holding the screen door open, pontificating while clutching the railing. The aroma of her cooking escaped through the kitchen door and joined the lazy summer air. The falling sun seemed to set the landscape in the distance on fire. As Jedidiah worked, a flock of pelicans swept in on a breeze from the canal. He counted thirteen birds flying in formation with a choreographed Tetradactyl grace. Stationary in flight, riding the wind as though they were resting in lounge chairs, the pelicans hovered, observed Jedidiah for what seemed to be a long time and flew on. From the corner of his eye Jedidiah saw one from the flock sweeping around, flying back. Like a parachutist, the pelican landed on the roof of the shed, tucked its chin into its chest, and there sat motionless.

"You stop dat craziness right now for yo dinner gits cold."

The cigarette dangling from Eunice's mouth issued smoke signals at regular intervals as she spoke. "You listenin' to me! . . . Damm skeeters," she said cursing to herself under her breath. "Ya' know I hate ter eat alone!"

She waved her hands about her head fighting off a cloud of mosquitoes. With the waving of her hands the seagulls leapt into the air with hysterical calls of surprise and the ground critters scurried about with much anxiety.

"Come on now, enuf' is enuf'," she said, punctuating her soliloquy with the slamming of the screen door.

"Yeah, yeah, be right ther." Feeling unappreciated Jedidiah consoled himself. "Women never know when a man is upta big things."

He grumbled in a low thunder as he limped across the yard balancing a large box that seemed to pull him forward with its own momentum. His short arms barely reached a third of the way around the box.

Pointing his nose in the direction of the brown shingled house, he yelled at the vacant screen door. "It's all fer you Eunice that I'm doin' this ya' know."

He knew Eunice could hear him, and he also knew she wasn't listening. Dropping his burden, he opened the door of the shed. Without lifting the box, he tried to negotiate it through the door, twisting it and rolling it as though he was trying to put a square peg into a round hole. He worked it through the doorway and disappeared along with the box into the shed.

Jedidiah Bozeman was a troll of a man with a head the size of a basketball. Clumps of hair protruded from his ears like some primeval flora, which he would twist unconsciously at times with an apprehensive intensity. The wart at the end of his bulb-like nose exaggerated the features of his shiny round face. The red and grey patches on his face marked the places he would inevitably miss while shaving in the morning. His eyes were set deep behind big, bushy eyebrows, which cantilevered over the dark pools that searched nervously like a squirrel in an open field. He walked with an undulating limp, which raised his head a full six inches into the air, rising and falling like a buoy bobbing on the ocean. Some people in town complained of seasickness while watching him walk down the road. Others complained that poor people shouldn't own such valuable property as theirs; and some folks complained because they were just plain mean. But anyone who bothered to look closely could see that Jedidiah Bozeman had a beautiful soul.

He emerged from the shed, as would a thief checking to see if the coast was clear. Satisfied, he closed the door, put three heavy locks into their hasps, nodded to the pelican and hobbled off to the house to have his meal.

"Ain't gonna' get no more in the shed, that's for sure," Jedidiah said as the screen door slammed, ushering him into the kitchen. "Just as well, done spent all my money anyways."

Eunice had been waiting to tell him what she'd heard at the market that morning.

"Emma Crowley said she saw the manager of the Lucky Market chasin' ya outta' the store da otha day, yellin' like hell, tellin' ya not to come back no mo'. Sit down and eat somethin' Jedidiah." She set a bowl of cabbage and sausage in front of his place at the table while he washed his hands. "She said he was yellin' somthin' 'bout ya buyin' all he had, and wasn't gonna' sell ya no more, dis and dat. . . . Uppity fella that store manager. I never liked him anyways." She sat down at the table, lit a cigarette and finished her dinner in a cloud of smoke.

The kitchen was farm-size and in former times had been the hub of a growing family. Now it needed painting and was occupied only by Jedidiah and Eunice and the spirits that filled their memories.

"Yup. . . .He said I was nuts, but we'll see who's nuts once dem 'puters don't work no more. Good cabbage, Eunice. Some people are so smart they don't know what's right in front of them. Pass the biscuits, please. I figure were gonna' take advantage of what folks don't see."

Jedidiah explained to Eunice that on one of his trips to the public library in town, he'd read about a change in the future. All about the coming event called "Y2K." He told her that the letters meant "Year Two thousand" and that the "Experts" were saying that the world, as people had come to know it, would grind to a halt. He told her that computers couldn't tell time too good and come New Year's Day computers weren't going to be so smart anymore. The experts—he liked the word expert and pronounced it slowly while emphasizing the X—were telling folks to save up their money and put away food for the coming hard times. He told her that was how he came to have the idea of selling toilet paper to people figuring everyone would overlook the simple things that they would be needing every day.

"What you goin' on about Jedidiah Bozeman? You're talkin' 'bout turlit paper not somthin' nobody ever heard of before."

"That's the beauty of it, Eunice. While folks are puttin' away their money and gettin' their gasoline stored-up, they're gonna' be too busy to think about the little details, the things that might be hard to come by. Paper money won't be worth nothin' no more, but turlet paper will become precious, you'll see."

"You're a crazy man!"

"Crazy I may be, darlin', but I'm gonna' make ya the "Queen of the Everglades," he said, talking with his mouth full, wiping his plate clean with his biscuit.

"Jedidiah, the Everglades be a hundred miles from here!"

"I know that. We're gonna' move there when we buy 'em. Didn't I tell ya Eunice?" He washed his biscuit down with iced tea. "I picked out a big house just outside the town of Chosen, where your Granddaddy is from. That's where we're gonna' live in sublime splendor Eunice, like I always told ya we would."

"If ya did tell me I wasn't listenin'. Jus' like the time ya was gonna' put saddles on Alligators so the tourist could ride 'em, I wasn't listenin'. Or the nature walks thru the swamp you was gonna' take folks on with dem wearin' 3-D sunglasses, I surely wasn't listenin'.'"

"Folks get bored, they're always lookin' for somethin' new to do." Jedidiah smiled acknowledging his stroke of brilliance.

"Or the miracle tonic you were gonna' sell what cured ingrown toenails."

"It worked for you didn't it?" Leaning back in his chair, he grinned like the Cheshire cat.

"I was just tellin' ya that Jedidiah! I didn't wanna' hurt your feelin's."

"You was glad when ya got my tonic, and ya could walk regular again."

"You're a crazy man!"

"Well this time you're gonna' see. Like Shakespeare

William said, 'There is a method in his madness' and my two-ply in assorted colors are gonna' make me the Kingfisher 'round these parts."

"Well I ain't listenin' to any more of dis craziness. Next thing ya know I'll be standin' 'beside ya sellin' rolls of turlet paper, talkin' 'bout peoples privies."

"That's my dream Eunice, you and me. That was a 'specially good dinner darlin'."

"Now wake up and smell the coffee, will ya Jedidiah!"

Eunice Bozeman cleared the plates from the table and began to clean the dishes. Her appearance was close to that of her husband. What they say about people and pets beginning to look like each other over time was true in their case; though by now it was long forgotten who had absorbed the features of whom. Eunice stood about five foot two, a robust woman with a low center of gravity. Her hair was as wild as the surrounding landscape. Her ears reached her shoulders and she had a large gap between her teeth. The housecoat she wore kept a record of the meals they'd had for the past week. Her face was a happy one, and when Eunice laughed everyone laughed whether they wanted to or not; Eunice had that effect on people. Like Jedidiah you really couldn't say how old she was exactly, just that she was somewhere around "getting old." She had lived in the same house for most of her life, except the one summer she spent in Biloxi Mississippi with her Aunt Flora. Her father was on trial for robbing a Federal train, and Eunice filled her summer by playing in the waters of the Gulf of Mexico. She never saw her daddy again and her father's brother moved in to comfort her mother. He would take Eunice fishing and tell her all about how the critters in the swamp lived and how the plants grew. He knew all about the medicine of plants and was respected throughout the county as a healer. A couple of years later, Eunice's mother died and her uncle moved away. Folks said he couldn't live with the fact he failed to heal her, and one day jumped on a freight train to parts unknown. Sometimes, people still talked about him and his knowledge of healing plants.

Eunice's grandfather, on her mother's side, moved in and things were pretty stable for Eunice for several years. Her grandfather was a tall, thin, weathered gentleman who read aloud to her, books by authors with foreign names. Eunice, to that very day, would tell you she learned more from her grandfather's books on those quiet evenings—about life, the world and its people—than she ever did in school. Sometimes her grandfather would work at the local truck farms; mostly cause he liked to work. Sometimes he fished. They enjoyed each other's company and talked a lot about anything that came to mind. When her grandfather passed away, he left a small fortune in local real estate. During the time she lived with him, Eunice became a young woman, and soon after his death she met Jedidiah.

Jedidiah was passing through town on his way to Miami, collecting seashells and trying hard not to have to work. They met at the Harvest Festival. Jedidiah was standing on a milk crate, pointing to the sky and telling the crowd of people before him about Thuban, "the star between the dippers" and how it used to be the North Star at the time of the building of the pyramids. Something about him reminded her of her grandfather. They fell in love, married themselves to each other, and had never been separated a single day since that time.

The summer months turned to fall. Jedidiah made plans for the coming of winter and the approaching millennium. He went to work cleaning and polishing the old trailer beside the banana tree. Each morning the pelican would return to its place on the roof of the shed, tuck its chin on its chest and follow the progress of the work with its eyes. Jedidiah cut a big opening on the trailers best side and attached the French window shutters he had found alongside the road. He put air in the tires and gave the body a new coat of paint. Jedidiah, as he worked, would step back, wink at the pelican and admire the old trailer as though it were a fine painting in a museum.

Sometimes Eunice would stand on the deck and call to him, "You're a crazy man, Jedidiah Bozeman, and ya made that bird crazy as well."

Jedidiah just went about his work humming to himself, delighting in each improvement he made to the trailer. Occasionally he would take a rest from his work, hobble over to the willow tree where he had a chair set under its canopy, and smoke his pipe. He would sit, admire the trailer, and concoct elaborate daydreams.

"Gonna' be the prettiest damn trailer in all of Okeechobee, Florida. Folks gonna' pass by just to look at it."

In his reverie Jedidiah saw himself, Eunice by his side, standing proudly at the window of their wondrous trailer being interviewed by newspaper reporters.

~ ~ ~

"My name is Jedidiah Davidson Bozeman. I'll try to recollect the best I can 'bout my personal history. I ain't sure about the year of my birth exactly, but I can tell ya I was born sometime before the World War of the Forties, 'cause I remember my Pa wearin' his army uniform around town and tellin' folks 'bout the war and the foreign' lands he been to. We was livin' in

133

Hehaw Louisiana at that time. Not much of a town, Hehaw. Mostly a couple muddy roads with some houses strung along them haphazard like. That's where I got my first schoolin'. Went to the fourth grade there. Missus Vance, that was my teacher's name, she said I was purty smart and would do real well in the world, if I stayed in school and learned somethin'. She was real nice Missus Vance was. She was the person who taught me how to read and write, cipher and study maps. After fourth grade, we moved around a lot, and I never went to school regular no mor'. My Ma would save the books that the rich folks throw'd out when she was cleanin' house for them, and I kept up my readin' that way. I guess readin' from the books my Ma give me, helped me to calculate what folks 'round here consider to be my peculiar ideas on things. Peculiar or not, that's how I come to be the man I am today. Now, if you'll be so kind as to step aside Mister Reporter, my customers are lined up to make their purchases."

The next person in line stepped up the window of the trailer.

"I got a chicken Jeb. How much paper can I git' for it?" Ed Tyler said, searching Jedidiah's face for conformation of the new respect he has found for him.

"Been gettin' lots of chickens Ed. I had to build a whole nuther chicken coop jus' to keep em' in. What else ya' got?"

"I've got a baseball card with a picture of Babe Ruth on it. How much for that, Jed?"

"Humm. Let me see that." Jedidiah examined the card closely. "One hundred fifty sheets Ed. That's all I kin' give ya'. Take it or leave it."

"I'll take it," Ed said, hands in his pockets, kicking the dirt. "You sure become the businessman, Jeb. I always know'd there was more to ya' than folks said."

"Folks is always gonna' be sayin' somethin' 'bout somethin', Ed. Ya' can only pay so much mind to it." Jedidiah smiled, carefully unraveling the toilet paper. "I'm gonna' give ya' the aqua marine green." He slowly counted out the sheets. "Pretty in the privy and has a nice smell to it. Here's some xtra, Ed. Give our best to the family and to Grandma Taylor."

In his mind he could see the rich and famous folks from nearby Palm Beach parking their cars alongside the roadway, causing traffic jams in both directions. They were coming to negotiate with Mister Bozeman.

Jedidiah decided he would talk respectfully to everyone that came to the trailer.

"Mornin' Governor, back so soon?"

"Good morning Mr. Bozeman. How are you, sir?" the gentleman in the white suit said, wiping his forehead with his handkerchief.

"Just fine Governor. Ain't ya got air conditioning in that fancy car of yours?"

"No, I'm trying to save on gas. I had a mechanic in town disconnect the air conditioning hose. He charged me three hundred dollars to do it, can you believe it?"

"Sounds like a bargin' Gov'. That money you got ain't worth hardly nothin' now a days. What can we do for ya' today?"

"I would like to purchase eight rolls Mister Bozeman. My wife asked if we might have the pastel blue rolls . . . if you have any left."

"I think we can oblige ya', Governor. What ya' wanna' trade em' for?"

"I've brought this fine fur coat that your wife admired so much the last time we stopped by."

Jedidiah smiled to himself thinking about Eunice in her

new fur coat. He knew Eunice didn't really think he was crazy, but when he gave her a new fur coat, she would see that all he had been telling her was true. Soon, she would see that she was the "Queen of the Everglades."

"Jed . . . I mean Mister Bozeman . . . I happened to see the mayor's car in the wait line and would appreciate you not mentioning my stopping by"

"Not a problem Governor . . . happy to oblige. Have a good day and our best to the misses."

~ ~ ~

Jedidiah reveled in his dreamtime. Sometimes leaping from his chair, laughing wildly, he would begin clogging and dancing around the old willow tree, hooping and a hollering. The screen door of the kitchen slammed, and Jedidiah awoke from his dance.

"Now what's all this ruckus about?" shouted Eunice, hands on her hips, trying to figure out what was going on. "You're a crazy man, Jedidiah Bozeman, and ya' got da' chickin's all upset. Dey ain't gonna' lay no more eggs with you carryin' on like dat'." She turned to the pelican. "And you ain't makin' things any better goin' along with him."

The pelican just smiled stoically, motionless. An armadillo scurried into the brush, a doe jumped into the canal with a big swoosh and the squirrels ran to the top the tree. Eunice disappeared behind the loud clap of the screen door.

Jedidiah returned to his chair and sat back down to resume his daydreaming. The pictures that drifted from his pipe floated under the canopy of the willow tree, circling around and around like a carousel.

~ ~ ~

Jim Lubberly, the manager of the lucky market came to the trailer's window.

"Mornin' Mister Bozeman."

"Mister Lubberly. How's things at the market?"

"We had to close for a few days. Can't get no deliveries due to the Y2K, and we run out of almost everythin'."

"Well . . . things will be back to the ways they were 'fore too long. What kin' I git' ya' Mister Lubberly?"

"Jed, I'd like five rolls of your paper for this case of Van Camps Pork-n-Beans," he said, holding up the case for Jedidiah to see. "I know how much ya' like 'em by how much y'all buy."

"I can give ya' (hand to his chin) three rolls of the white single ply."

"How's about four?"

"I don't haggle Mister Lubberly. Take it or leave it. Three rolls of white single ply. What'll it be?"

"I'll take it."

"Pleasure doin' business with ya." He handed him the paper and took the case of beans. "Now if you'll kindly stand aside, the Mayor has been waitin' patiently. Mornin' Mister Mayor. How are ya?"

"Not so loud Jedidiah." His hands pushed down on the air as though he were lowering the volume of their conversation. "I'll take three rolls of your basic white." He nervously looked over his shoulder, shifting his hat into different positions to cover his face.

Jedidiah always liked the mayor. A quirky little man who squealed a lot when he got excited, which was often as he was always in a state of confusion, always overwhelmed by the details of any given situation. But he had a good heart and things eventually got done. He was too scatter brained to be dishonest, and Jedidiah figured folks voted for him so they could just do what they wanted.

"Good to see ya' Mayor. You have a good day now."

"Shuuush! Not so loud." He placed a finger to his lips, nervously looking in all directions. "If anyone asks— If anyone asks, you've not seen me. Goodbye."

~ ~ ~

Jedidiah's preparations were nearly complete. It was time to move the trailer from underneath the banana tree to the center of the backyard for its finishing touches. Though a small man, he never doubted for a moment that he would be able to accomplish the task. He cut down a young pine tree and removed all of its branches. He would use the pine as a lever to move his palace.

Eunice would open the screen door several times a day, puffing on her cigarette, scaring the critters in the brush, calling him a crazy man. Only now it was more from curiosity than ridicule that Eunice watched Jedidiah's progress. Little by little the trailer rolled from underneath the banana tree toward the center of the yard. Jedidiah would work long into the night until he could do no more. He would hobble into the house, dirty and exhausted, collapsing onto the bed with his clothes on. Sleep would overtake him before his head reached the pillow. Echoing through the caverns of his dreamtime he could hear Eunice whispering in the distance, "You're a crazy man Jedidiah Bozeman."

Eunice awoke the next morning to find the trailer on display in the center of the yard. The pelican stood motionless like a sentinel, casting a shadow as would a sundial. Jedidiah was on the roof of the trailer, sun rising behind him, nailing shingles down and sealing them with tar.

"Wouldn't want rainwater to ruin the merchandise," he murmured to himself as he hammered away.

Slowly and methodically he carried buckets of water to the roof of the trailer and poured them over its surface to test its inviolability. Eunice watched him struggle up the ladder, one exaggerated step at a time. He held a pail of water in one hand, the other grasping the rungs of the ladder to pull himself up. Once on top of the roof, he would raise another pail of water with a rope that was tied around his waist. This went on until Jedidiah was satisfied the roof would not leak. He saw Eunice watching from behind the screen door and called out to her.

"I know what yer thinkin' and ya' don't have ta say it."

But it was no longer true, for Eunice had begun to admire Jedidiah's determination, and his crazy scheme began to look as wondrous as he said it was.

Jedidiah spent the rest of the day unpacking boxes of toilet paper and arranging them in the trailer. Each roll was neatly stacked in rows according to color and type; two-ply tissue went to the left, single ply on the right. Eunice stood on a crate beside the trailer, looked through the window and watched as Jedidiah meticulously placed the rolls of paper one on top of another. The layered bands of color formed a rainbow stretching end to end. She gasped when she saw the beauty of it and had to run away. Scurrying back to the house she heard a crash and Jedidiah cussing loudly. She ran back to the trailer, climbed onto the box and looked in the window. Jedidiah was on his back and she could hardly see him except for his feet kicking wildly. He waved his hairy hands in the air in an attempt to clear the rolls of paper that blanketed him. She covered her mouth so he wouldn't hear her laughing and hurried back to the house.

"I can hear ya' out there woman."

Opening the screen door, she turned to look back and found the pelican smiling at her.

One evening after dinner, Jedidiah sat outside enjoying the night air, smoking his pipe and calculating the arc the moon would travel that night. The trailer was but a shadow against the turbulent orange horizon. Eunice arrived with her beach chair and a tray with mint tea. She quietly opened her chair, poured the tea and sat down to join Jedidiah.

"How many boxes are lef' in the shed Jed?"

He gave her an exact account of what was in the shed and what was stacked in the trailer. He told her how he had found that some of the boxes were labeled incorrectly. Inside two of the boxes marked blue, the contents were all white. He had thought about returning them to the Lucky Market store manager, but he didn't think it really mattered.

"Ya' know, Jedidiah," she began, "afta' ya' told me how dem 'puters are gonna get stupid afta' New Years, forgetting how ta count an all, I got ta thinkin' maybe I should put aside some things so as we ain't spendin' all that money we gonna' be makin'." She lit a cigarette and continued. "So I went and got some big trash barrels, brand new, and filled 'em with beans and rice and lentils and stuff."

"That's good thinkin', Eunice," he said, nodding his approval, puffing on his pipe, "real good . . . not that were gonna' be needin' them."

"Well, I was jus' thinkin', it might take a couple of weeks or so for people to run out of der own paper. You know, 'till they start comin' to the trailer an all, and I don't want us

140

needin' too much whilst we is waitin'."

"I like what you're sayin' Eunice." He took her hand and gently pressed it to his face. "It's no wonder I loves ya'."

The cars on the Canal Bridge behind them beat out a syncopated rhythm as the dogs in the distance called out to each other. They sat, quietly holding hands until the moon disappeared behind the pine trees. Jedidiah smoked his pipe and Eunice watched the stars through the smoke-rings she created with her cigarette. They were content knowing that as long as they were together, there could not be a more perfect world.

The next morning Jedidiah awoke to the smell of coffee and biscuits. He could hear the bacon sizzling and Eunice stirring the gravy. A little startled, he threw his stiff leg out of the bed, reached over and pulled aside the window curtain. It was still dark, and he didn't remember hearing the cock crow. Jedidiah was always the first to rise in the morning. He would make the coffee and listen to the weather report on the radio before starting his day. He put on his robe and went into the kitchen.

Eunice greeted him without turning around. "'Bout time you got up." The cigarette in the ashtray on the table burned unattended, its long ash sending a column of smoke straight to the ceiling. "Sit down and have some breakfess' The gravy 'ill be ready in a minute."

He sat in his chair and watched her, amazed, rubbing the sleep from his eyes as she served him his breakfast.

"I was a thinkin'," she said, moving nervously about the kitchen as she spoke, "that it would be real nice if we mixed up the colors, one after anodder to make 'em look like beads 'stead of a rainbow." She sat down in the chair across from him, "You know like dem Mardi Gras beads from Nawlins."

141

"Beads? Rainbows? Nawlins? Eunice, what are ya' sayin'? Have ya been ta sleep yet?"

"I'm sayin', suppose, 'stead of stackin' 'em on atop each odder, we string 'em togedder on some clothesline or somethin'. Make 'em look like dem throws the kids bring back from carnival; not that your rainbows ain't real pretty, Jedidiah."

Having had his first cup of coffee, her idea began to make sense to him. Eunice said if the rolls were strung like beads, they wouldn't fall so easily. They could stretch ropes from end to end in the trailer and slide the rolls on, alternating the colors, so that they looked like beads. They would be easy to get off and easy to put back when they needed to. She put her elbow on the table, rested her head in her open hand, leaned forward while staring intently at Jedidiah.

"Wha'd ya' think?"

He liked the idea Eunice had come up with, and he was glad she was beginning to take an interest in his preparations for the millennium.

"That's good thinkin', Eunice, powerful good. Two heads is always better'n one and yours is so pretty."

"Hurry up den. Finish yer breakfess. We gots work to do!"

"Why Eunice, I do believe you is blushing!"

After finishing the breakfast dishes, Eunice started immediately to work on the trailer. She greeted the pelican and went about her work singing and humming gleeful tunes from long ago. She took down the clothesline that ran from the kitchen door to the shed, promising herself she would get a more modern one at a later time. She put the lace curtains she had been saving for a special occasion in the window while Jedidiah placed rows of nails on either side of the trailer for her to hang her colored beads. He hummed along with her as they worked. Eunice went about adding her feminine touches to the trailer while Jedidiah made signs to advertise their new business.

~ ~ ~

The trailer was ready and it was time to move it to its new location alongside the roadway. The millennium would arrive in a week and Jedidiah wanted everything in place so they could open for business the first day after the New Year. He never doubted that most people would be absorbed in the revelry and would neglect to provide for their privy. He chose a spot a short way from the canal bridge, giving people plenty of room to park their cars. He walked the route they would push the trailer along, clearing rocks and tree limbs and other obstacles that might be in their way. He knew it would be difficult, but now he had Eunice to help him.

Jedidiah approached the problem of moving the trailer to the roadway as he had any other task. The only way to get it done was to get started. He recalled finding a dusty book in the attic of the house and from that book the myth of Sisyphus came to mind. He could see old Sisyphus laboring to push the huge boulder up the mountain, but he quickly dispelled any similarity between Sisyphus and himself. Hills were hard to find in South Florida and for the first time Jedidiah was glad of it.

Everything was ready and both he and Eunice rubbed their hands together as though cleansing themselves of any other chores they might have. They set about the work of moving the trailer to its new home. Jedidiah would place his pine tree lever under the axle, move the trailer six inches or so and Eunice would place large rocks behind the wheels so it would not roll backwards. Each move of the trailer was an event and they treated it as such, as though no other existed. They studied and discussed each move and patiently repeated the process day after day for the next six days. When the trailer reached its designated location and the wheels were locked in place, Eunice pulled beach chairs and a jug of apple cider from inside. Jedidiah set up an umbrella to provide them with shade and together they sat and toasted a job well done. Jedidiah stood and raised his glass in a toast, "To the 'Queen of the Everglades', long may she reign!" Pressing a clenched fist to his breast, he bowed and blew her a kiss.

"Jedidiah Bozeman, you make me wanna' cry! You stop that right now 'cause people can see when they drive by." She wiped the corners of her eyes delicately with her apron, as delicately as any lady that ever lived.

They sat beside the road until the sun fell behind the thin line that marked the end of the earth, and watched as a red moon rose in the east. The highway, now deserted, was quiet and peaceful. They talked and made plans for the future. It had been a full, satisfying day. It was time to return to the house, to sleep and then greet the millennium the next morning.

Jedidiah folded the umbrella and put it in the trailer along with the cider. Eunice closed the French shutters over the window and locked the door. Together they hobbled back to the house holding hands, carrying their beach chairs. They stopped before the shed. The pelican stood tall on its legs, spread its wings and rose into the air. They waved goodbye as it flew away. The soft glow from the kitchen diffused through the screen door shinning a spotlight on the couple, casting giant sized shadows over the lawn.

Eunice threw her arms around Jedidiah and whispered, "Jedidiah Bozeman, you is the most wonderful man that has evva' lived!

The Beginning.

LUCHIA AND THE DIVA

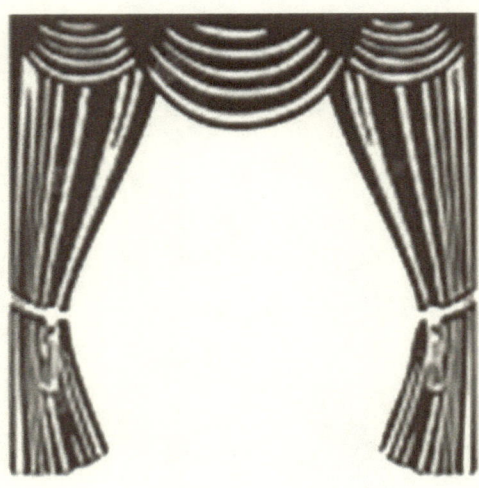

It was snowing pretty hard after the show. On the escalator ride down to the lobby, people were visibly nervous and worried about getting home safely. The wind and the snow pressed against the plate glass windows of the Metropolitan Opera House.

"I told you we should let this show pass. . . . I hope the busses are running."

"It wasn't supposed to start snowing until after midnight," said the man she was with.

When the escalator reached the lobby, I turned to take a look at the people behind the voices. They were preppy, in their mid-thirties and looked more worried than the older folks around them. Opera audiences were mostly composed of grey hairs, some students, a few middle-aged 'use to be' music majors, but mostly grey hairs. Inclement weather does not deter these intrepid aficionados; nothing would keep them from their musical fix.

The wind was blowing hard and it took a good bit of effort to open the door. I held it open, so the people behind me could pass through until someone yelled from inside, "Close the door," which I was glad to do. The plaza fountain was lit so, I could make that out up ahead. It looked like a gurgling cauldron, casting off an eerie amber light. Part of me wanted to warm my hands in its glow. The other part said, "Get the hell home."

The Lincoln Center maintenance crew were working hard to keep up with the snow accumulation. Their snowblowers were throwing the heavy wet mess into piles along Avery Fisher Hall on one side and The City Opera on the other. I turned to look back at the Met and could barely make out the Chagall tapestries. Only the chandeliers revealed the identity of the great opera house. The path to the taxi stand was clear and there was already a waiting line.

"I'll be here all-night."

Amsterdam Avenue looked like a ghost town. The few cars that passed drifted sideways as they moved forward, their headlights struggling to lead the way. The soft red glow of their taillights left nothing but the silence.

"I'd better get home."

I lived in a flat on 82nd and Broadway, which was a good sixteen blocks from the Met. The station below the plaza, which serviced the Number One Train, was closed for renovation. Not a bus in sight. And forget about finding a cab. There was no alternative but to start walking. Fortunately, the wind was at my back and helped push me through the slush. I was glad I had worn my chukka boots. L. L. Bean made a pretty good boot; you could be sure your feet would stay dry for a reasonable amount of time, yet still look kind of dressy. The pristine snow on the sidewalks was packing tight. The quiet, as it always is when it snows, was almost complete. The only sound to be heard was the groan of the snow compacting beneath my feet as I walked. I turned around to look back. I couldn't see the tops of the buildings and my footprints made a jagged line, which led to where I was standing.

Walking up the Avenue only an occasional car crawled by; doing less than five miles an hour, creating a slow-motion timeless effect. Its headlights revealed just how hard it was snowing. I walked along, humming the tunes from Carmen, when I heard the rattling of chains and the murmurs of a bus engine. It made a stop on the block I had just passed and moved on. I stood between the parked cars, waving for the driver to stop and pick me up. I know he saw me, but he went right by, clanking along, only to stop on the next block to drop someone off. I knew I'd never catch him. My voice was muted by the silent snow as I yelled, "Have a good night asshole!"

Seventy-Second Street was just ahead. There I would jump over to Broadway, which would complete the first leg of my journey. This was familiar territory. I often walked that stretch of Broadway as I did my errands, shopped and patronized the sidewalk eateries along the avenue. From there, the rest of the trip would go quickly. Wrong again!

The wind, blowing in off the river, created cyclones of snow. It felt much colder than before. My feet were getting numb, as well as my hands and face. The ice patches on the sidewalk sent me slipping and sliding, fighting to keep my balance and stay on my feet. My coat acted like a sail in the wind, which didn't help matters. There was a tavern up ahead on the next block that I had passed many times. It was one of the last surviving local bars in the neighborhood; the rest having been converted into yuppie dens. I decided to make a pit stop, get a drink, warm-up and start out again. A gust of wind blew hard as I opened the door, almost knocking me on my ass. I struggled to close it quickly, to keep the snow from blowing inside.

"Greetings," someone said from inside the pitch-black tavern. It took a while for my eyes to adjust to the dimly lit bar room having seen only bright white snow on my trek.

"I should put some salt down by that doorway. Have a seat, I'll be right with ya."

I brushed myself off, hung my coat on the rack to dry, and took the barstool closest to me. After my eyes adjusted, I could see the place was just about empty. A couple at the far end of the bar were chatting it up and a wiry, weathered gentleman, sat by the window nursing a beer. He wore an old fishing hat with what looked like lures pinned about it. He sat, still wearing his Carhart coat, staring out of the picture window at the snow. The sign above his head read, 'Mc Gowan's Tavern' The letters were outlined by green neon lights and punctuated with shamrocks at either end. The wind howled like a banshee as it pressed against the window. All of my extremities were numb from the cold. I warmed my hands with my breath and covered my ears and nose to bring them to room temperature.

"What can I get ya buddy?" the barkeep asked, returning to the bar.

"I'll have a shot of Dewar's and a beer please."

"There was a time when that was called a boilermaker,"

the old guy at the window said, raising his glass in a welcoming gesture. "Looks like it might snow!"

"It's not supposed to start 'till after midnight," I said, "but the *'supposed too's* are never what their *supposed to be'*" raising my shot glass I added, "To your health!" He responded in kind and put out his hand.

"Terrence Mc Gowan," he said pointing to the sign, "No relation to the owner."

"My name is Eugene. Glad to meet ya Terrence. Been here long?"

"Only about twenty years. If I'm not here, you can bet I'm in church. I go to work in between."

"You always sit there by the window?"

"Every night . . . the bartenders" he spoke loudly to be heard by the barkeep, "usually keep my stool in the closet by the door, so I always have my spot."

"It won't happen again Terrence" the barkeep said from the far side of the bar.

The Dewar's was doing its magic and I was warming up. I signaled for another which I downed in short order.

"So, what brings you out on this lovely evening?" Terrence asked, finishing his beer.

"The opera."

"I should have known. . . . Devon, I'll have another, and set up my friend here."

"I'm good . . . still have to get home. It's hard enough walking with the wind and the ice, let alone being half in the bag."

"Bullshit! Haven't ya ever noticed a drunk walking through a subway car? He walks in a straight line while everyone else is holding on for dear life. He only gets in trouble when the train stops, and he has to stagger his way to the platform. The wind and the snow and the Dewar's will help you keep you on your feet."

"No, I'm good. I still have my beer. Thanks."

"Have it your way. That must be some opera to drag you out on a night like this. I hate opera. They sound like a bunch of cats in an alley if you ask me."

"Gee . . . someone who hates opera. . . . I've never heard that before! . . . But I think you might like this one," I said trying to remember my Cagney and Bogart movies. "It's about a sexy gypsy broad who is so hot she makes everyone crazy. She twists them around her finger like a string. She takes up with some country boy, corrupts him, uses him up, then leaves him for a bullfighter."

"Lucky for the bullfighter.... hope the kid had a good time."

"Not so good. He winds up killing her and gets arrested by the police."

"Poor kid. That's one expensive dame. That could be worth goin' to see. It don't sound so bad."

"One of my favorites. And it has good songs too. You probably know half of them already from the movies and all. It's special for me, because my daughter and I sang in a production together when she was young. Great memories. We still talk about it sometimes."

"Let's hear about it!" he said pointing to the snow, "I've got time."

The Dewar's had loosened my tongue, so I jumped into my story with both feet.

"I had been singing with the chorus for over a year. Clay, my neighbor, was the assistant conductor of the New Orleans Opera, and Virginia, his roommate, was a soprano singing with the company. That's how I became involved in the

151

chorus, knowing them. They both had just graduated from LSU Baton Rouge. They took their music degrees and headed for the Big Easy. Clay found his way to the assistant conductor's job and Virginia was waiting for her first break so she could begin her singing career. Jenell, my wife at the time, played piano and had a strong grasp of music. It was she that gave our Luchia Della Luna her foundation in music. She worked with Luchia three, four times a week, going over her Suzuki violin lessons with her. The kid could find her way around the piano pretty good too. Our house was always full, and everyone was a something or other. Stage managers, actors, directors, make up people and a lot of singers. Those who were not singers, played cello or viola, harpsichord .... whatever. We were a tight group and had a lot of fun.

So, with all that going on, Luchia was not intimidated by music at all. And man, did she love the theater! The costumes, the sets, the music and the make-believe all thrilled her. When allowed, I would bring her to our musical and staging rehearsals. Sitting in the crow's nest, at the top of the theater, we took everything in. The music and blocking, sometimes repeated over and over again, didn't bother her; she was mesmerized. On the way home, we would discuss the plot, the characters, and sing their songs. So when Carmen came up on the roster that season, it was only logical that Luchia would sing in the children's chorus. Everyone said so.

Clay was her diction coach, and Jenell pounded out the notes for her on the piano. When it came time for our first rehearsal of Carmen, Luchia was ready.

Clay held several rehearsals with the kids to iron out any kinks and to put everyone on the same page with pronunciation and entrances. Like Luchia, the kids in the children's chorus were all related to someone involved with

152

the opera. Sons, daughters, nieces and nephews were all pretty well schooled before rehearsals began. There were even a couple of little ones. Too small to really grasp what was going on, and who would contribute little musically, but were so cute they would bring the house down during the tableau. Audiences love to see children on stage and this group was delightful. Clay had pulled a couple of ladies from the soprano section and mixed them in with the kids to help beef up the sound. The small voices of the children would evaporate on the big stage without a little help. They were lined up according to height, which put Luchia on the far end; she had stretched three or four inches over the winter.

The conductor came to the last chorus rehearsal to be sure everyone was ready for the 'sitzsprobe.' He walked on stage clapping, praising everyone, and thanking them for their hard work. His granddaughter Senta was in the children's chorus, and he took her by the hand and placed her in the center.

"Luchia please come," he said standing Luchia next to her. "Senta, you stay with Luchia at all times, and when she sings . . . you sing." He was one proud grandpa and Jenell was beaming; both of them grinning ear to ear.

"Our conductor was Herr Doctor Knud Andersonn. A tall gentleman with thinning white hair and a thick German accent. A very nice man who was perceived as curt and abrupt due to the standard of excellence he had set with his orchestra and singers. When Doctor Andersonn conducted German opera he shined, especially with Wagner. But he was a master with the French and Italian operas as well. He seemed to have an innate insight and deep understanding of the marriage between music and theater. Our performances were praised and celebrated. He was a very solid, pedantic conductor with no ambiguity in his beat pattern. Some conductors were so flamboyant, jumping up and down and carrying on, that you stressed over finding your entrance. Doctor Andersonn was old school. He said that theatrics belonged on the stage, not in the pit. Before World War Two he was an assistant conductor to Richard Strauss and had worked with him on several performances of the composer's operas. But all that ended when Knud joined the Luftwaffe.

"Dr. Andersonn was my mentor. To this day I don't know what he saw in me, but he gave me a shot. Usually someone auditioning would have a couple of arias prepared. I had nothing prepared and it came down to matching notes and scales. I went there on a fluke thinking, 'What the hell. The worse that can happen is he'll say, No.'

"To my surprise I made it! I wasn't the only one surprised. The members of the chorus, waiting outside to begin their rehearsal, listened to my crude and awkward audition, and they were pissed that I was accepted.

"This company is going down-hill!" was being whispered amongst the various cliques in the hallway. After all, they had worked hard, had their various music degrees from somewhere or other and had to wait for their chance. I waltzed in and got a spot, despite my lack of training. But I proved Doctor Andersonn's instinct had been right. By the end of the season I had a B contract which meant I was being paid. By the fifth year I had an A contract with the company. Some, after a decade, still sang with no contract at all."

Terrance raised his glass saying "You know you're talkin' over my head. . . . are you doin' that on purpose lad?.... Devon, when ya get a chance, I'll have another."

I raised my glass asking for another as well.

"Tableau?" Terrance said. "What's that? And what the

hell is a shits-probe? Sounds like something my proctologist would say."

"The sitzsprobe is a rehearsal with the whole company and orchestra. No costumes or staging, just singing. And you get to sit while you sing. It gives the conductor a chance to hear how the show is going. And the tableau is just when everyone freezes, like in a picture, and the audience applauds the sets and costumes."

The barkeep came with our drinks. "On the house gents," knocking the bar three times with his knuckles.

My mouth was dry from all the talking. *Why am I telling this guy all this?* I couldn't even explain to myself, my compulsion to tell this story.

"Continue mice-trooh! You're learnin' me something here." Terrence took off his hat, scratched a full head of red hair and checked to make sure all of the lures were in their proper place. "This conductor business, what do those guys do anyway? Looks like everybody knows the music, they got it right in front of them. What do they need him waving his arms around for?"

"Well . . . he's kinda' like a guy playing a song on a guitar. The orchestra is his guitar and he gets to play the song anyway he wants. Fast-slow, loud or low; it's his call and everybody either likes it or they don't. Yes, the band knows the music, but he tells them how to play it."

"Gotcha."

"The sitzprobe went well and everyone was in good spirits. Doctor Andersonn came on stage with last-minute comments for each of the principals. We hadn't been dismissed yet, so we were still on stage waiting for our bit from Doctor Andersonn. He brought Shirley Verrett, the lady singing Carmen, over to meet his granddaughter.

"You look so beautiful Senta," Ms. Verrett said, "and I love your name. I want to be a Senta someday and spin wool on a loom."

"Like in the Flying Dutchman …. that's who I'm named after," little Senta said delighting everyone.

Doctor Andersonn and the Diva smiled and laughed, nodding to each other; obviously there had been discussions about future productions, and we could expect a 'Ghost Ship' to be sailing our way.

"And this is Luchia," Doctor Andersonn said, introducing our Luchia. "She is our anchor in the children's chorus."

"Oh, I know. I heard you singing!" she said, shaking Luchia's hand. "I had to turn around in my chair to see where that perfect little voice was coming from. Where did you learn to sing your part so well Luchia?"

"My mom taught me, and Clay helped me with the French. That was the hardest part 'cause I don't speak French."

"Wonderful job mom . . . super!" She spoke to us all like we were old friends. "I am so happy to be singing with you guys and we are going to have a wonderful time. This is gonna' be the best Carmen ever." The great Diva was as generous as she was talented, and we were all star struck."

"Who is this Shirley Verrett broad?" Terrance asked, sipping his beer.

"Shirley Verrett was the most personable and ingenuous person that ever graced a stage. She was one of only a few black opera singers working at the time. She was loved all over the world. And even though she was an international star she made herself at home and worked with everyone to make the magic that is theater. Most divas, both sopranos and tenors, are so full of themselves it's a wonder they can

156

breathe; but not Miss Verrett. Along with her gracious demeaner was a voice that commanded your complete attention. To this day, I measure every performance of Carmen I see or hear to her sultry presentation and luscious voice. She was perfect for the role. It was as though Bizet had composed the music with her in mind. This Carmen could have seduced anyone with a pulse. Don Jose never had a chance. That's the soldier I told you about, you know, the kid."

"How come I never heard of her, this Shirley Verrett?"

"Don't know. I guess she's more popular overseas. They love Shirley Verrett over there and make a big fuss over her. She's famous here too, just not the TV kind of famous."

The couple at the other end of the bar put on their coats and started for the door. They said good night with the thickest brogues I'd heard in a long time. They opened the door and threw themselves into the snow and wind--only to return moments later.

"I think we'll wait a bit. Not the right time yet," the young gent said smiling, brushing the snow from his coat. His lady agreed. "No . . . certainly not the right time."

"Devon!" Terrance cried, "Our friends will be with us a bit longer. They'll be needing something to warm themselves with . . . put it on my tab."

"Comin' up, straight away . . . two rum and cokes."

The couple thanked him and took a table close to the window to watch the weather outside. Devon brought their drinks and a fresh basket of pretzels.

"Continue mice-trooh!" he said, so I did.

"What came next were the staging rehearsals. That's where a director, the stage director, tells everybody where to stand and—"

"I know what a stage director is . . . Jesus man."

"Oh, okay. . . . Sorry. So the blocking part is pretty cut and dried. The kids run out, sing their song and leave. In this case, there's a changing of the guard and the children, carrying little rifles, mimic the soldiers as they drill. They always bring the house down in their uniforms. A bright moment in an otherwise dark drama.

The dress rehearsal came next. Clay played the piano score in the pit, and Doctor Andersonn conducted from a chair at the foot of the stage. The stage director ran around, arranging the children, stopping and starting. The kids were excited, proud of how they looked in their costumes and were a bit more difficult to handle. He looked as though he were trying to herd cats. He made them repeat their entrances and marching drills over and over again. Doctor Andersonn was becoming annoyed as it was taking so much time, and this was just the first act. They almost had words. The diva was in the wings watching, waiting for her entrance. She came on stage and offered to help the frazzled director."

"Ethan, allow me please. I am used to working with children back home and think I might be able to help this along." Turning to the children, she took complete control. "First of all, ya'll look wonderful! No one's gonna notice me once they get a look at you. This will be fun, so come on, buddy up, two by two. . . . That's right. . . . There you go. Wonderful!' She made short work of rehearsing the children and it all came together. Luchia was the tallest in the group and marching next to Senta they made a comical pair, heads held high, believing they were soldiers. Satisfied, the director moved on, and the older kids went to the dressing room to change into their peasant costumes for the diva's big aria."

"That's a song, right?" Asked Terrance.

"Exactly! And I know you've heard this one, from the movies and commercials and stuff. Carmen, that sexy gypsy comes down the stairs of the cigarette factory singing her song and hypnotizes everyone."

The Irish couple had been listening to the conversation and the young man jumped in.

"We couldn't help overhearing your story, and if you wouldn't mind, we'd would like to listen in on your tale. I'm Malachy Creen and this is Coleen Mc Carthy. We're both here from Dublin. I remember ma Da, when I was a lad, brought me to the theater where there was a big stage and huge chandeliers. Everyone was dressed fine and so were we. One of my fondest memories is me and ma Da going to the opera."

"And we love stories about children too, don't we Malachy" Coleen said taking Malachy's hands and warming them with her breath.

"That we do luv."

"Well then, Failte!" (Welcome) I told them, raising my glass. The barkeep brought his stool to our end of the bar and joined us.

"You have a full house mice-trooh!" Terrance laughed.

"Tell us some more about how wonderful the children were," Coleen said.

"Ahem!" Terrence interrupted, tapping his glass with his pinky ring. "If you please. . . . Continue, mice-strooh."

"The staging rehearsals went well, and we were now at a full-dress rehearsal with orchestra. The night before the first performance, we came in the stage door to find David, the stage manager, instructing the parents and children how to behave during a performance.

"People, people, like I told you before, we must have total

silence back-stage during a performance." David was a rather flamboyant character, prancing around with his score, waving his arms, giving orders. He was well over six feet tall and could cross the stage in five giant steps. "If the kids are feeling antsy, you MUST take them to the dressing room, and I will call you on the intercom for your next entrance.... Luchia! Luchia De Lammermoor, the diva wants to see you. Dad, can you bring Luchia to Miss Verrett's dressing room? I have a ton of details to take care of here and ... Thank you! Now people, lets line up and see what we look like.

"We found Miss Verrett's dressing room and Luchia knocked softly on the door. The Diva greeted us in her robe, costume in hand, inviting us inside.

"Luchia! Just the person I wanted to see." The lights from the make-up mirrors were bright and she had her costumes spread out in the room in the order they would be used. She was animated and the air was drenched in the scent of flowers.

"What beautiful roses!" Luchia cried, running to smell them.

"They have just arrived. My husband sent them." She thanked me for bringing Luchia to see her and told me, "Children and their honesty have a calming effect on me. Especially before a performance. Luchia reminds me of myself at her age, wide eyed and filled with wonder. We're kind of kindred spirits." She smiled at Lu, "but you should take care of your own costumes and get ready, then maybe you can come back and help me with my make-up?" Luchia was thrilled, and we left to get ready for the show.

"I dropped Lu off with the costume mistress and went to put my costume on. When I returned, both of us dressed in our soldier's uniforms took our rifles and went to get pancake

160

makeup on our faces, to take away the sheen from the stage lights. We were all set.'

"Can I go to see Ms. Verrett now?" Lu asked. "I have to help her with her makeup you know."

"Yes, I know. Let's go soldier!"

On the way, Lu told me she was getting nervous about the performance.

"Suppose I mess up? Then what? I will be so embarrassed."

"Everyone gets nervous before a performance. I'll bet ya even Miss Verrett gets nervous before a performance sometimes."

Luchia knocked on the door, and from inside with her singing voice, she told us to come in.

"I'll be right with you," she sang in full voice, at the top of her range. She stepped out from behind a screen wearing her first-act gypsy costume. "Ta da! What do you think Luchia? Do I look like a gypsy? I like your costume, fits you well and I see you already have your pancake on . . . Did I tell you that I'm from New Orleans too? Born right here in the Crescent City, but then we moved to Atlanta."

"I was born in New York . . . but my brother and sister were born here."

The diva sat in front of her mirror, tucked her hair into her skull cap and started her makeup. There was a knock on the door and a voice informing her that, "Your makeup crew is here Miss Verrett and the wig mistress is on her way."

"I do my own make-up so I'm good there.... send the wig girl though." Talking to Luchia through the mirror she said, "Wait 'till you see how long my hair is. It's perfect with this dress." Searching Luchia's face in the mirror she asked " you look a little sad, are you okay sweetheart?"

"I think she's a little nervous about the performance. Getting the jitters," I told her.

"That ain't nothin'. Everybody gets nervous before a show. Keeps ya on your toes. Happens to me all the time."

"'Really?' Lu said. 'Even you?'"

"Oh yeah! And that's why I need you for back up. When I start down those steps from that cigarette factory, I'm gonna' need to know you're down there rooting for me."

"Really?"

"Oh yeah,… not to worry…. you're gonna' be great. Wait and see."

The stage manager called for the supernumeraries, the children and the choristers to come to the stage, so we had to leave. "Thanks for everything Miss Verrett. It has been a pleasure meeting you. Luchia, we have to go darlin.""

"Please, call me Shirley."

"I wouldn't even know how to do that ma'am. I'm a big fan."

"Well, Luchia's dad, that was a helluva nice thing to say. I thank you for that; it means a lot to me. See you both on stage."

"There you go again!" Terrance said. "Can't you use regular words? What the hell are super nu mer arees?" he asked adjusting his hat. "That's why most people don't like opera. You never know what they're talkin' about."

"They're like extra's in the movies," Malachy said.

"Where'd you learn that?" Coleen asked, surprised.

"In school."

"I never learned that in school."

"We went to different schools luv. . . . I went to parochial school. They actually taught theater at Saint—"

162

"Ahem!" Terrence said, interrupting them to finish his point. "These operas aren't even in English, so how you gonna know what all the hemmin' and hawin' and fussing is about? How are you supposed to figure out what's goin' on if ya can't understand what they're sayin!"

Malachy laughed. "I guess the French speak French."

"And the Italians understand Italian," said Devon joining in.

"Ditto for the Germans! but let me go on, there's more to the story."

The performance was excellent! Everything fell into place as it always does before opening night. Luchia was thrilled and absorbed everything happening around her. If she wasn't in the wings watching Carmen's every move, or on stage, she was hanging out in Miss Verrett's dressing room, talkin' up a storm. They really did hit it off. The Diva helped Luchia plan her show and tell for school, gave her tips on making an entrance and how to project the voice to the back of the theater. They stopped only to answer the call to the stage for the final act to begin.

The fourth act is pretty loud and violent so only the older kids were allowed to be in the crowd scene; nightmares of the opera were not an option for the little cherubs.

The curtain dropped and the chorus, the super . . . ah, the extra's . . . filled the stage in costume. The curtain rose and we all clasped hands and took our bows. Luchia and I, along with Senta, were in the center per Doctor Andersson's request. The principal singers chose alternate sides of the stage from which they made their entrances, each taking a turn to take their bows to bravos and applause. Don Jose came out . . . the soldier kid who killed Carmen . . . and the crowd went wild with a long, standing ovation. When Miss

Verrett took the stage, the audience roared. Wave after wave of bravos and applause rippled through the theater. She smiled, bowing, blowing kisses and thanked the house for the applause. She came to the chorus line and took Luchia and Senta by their hands and returned to the center of the stage. Flowers were brought from both sides, bouquets for each of them. Smiling radiantly, they held hands, curtsied, and left the stage. Evidently Miss Verrett had worked this all out with Senta and Luchia in the dressing room—and to great effect. There were three performances, each one to standing ovations and thunderous applause. The best Carmen I ever saw!"

"Look! Malachy, the snow has almost stopped," Coleen said, putting on her coat, handing Malachy his. "We should try to make it back to the hotel." Coleen was obviously excited by the opportunity to consummate the evening.

"That was a good story. Perfect for a snowy, winter's night," Malachy said. "I thank ya for helping us pass the time so pleasantly."

"You're very welcome" I said, shaking his hand, "I hope the rest of your trip goes well, and you both enjoy your stay in New York."

"There's no place like Central Park after a fresh coat of snow," Terrence said, raising his hat.

"Thank you both, and safe home yourselves!"

"Good night," could be heard from Coleen, waiting outside.

It was getting close to one a.m. and I started thinking about getting home.

"I should be going myself," I said getting up to put on my coat. "I have work in the morning. Terrence, it has been a pleasure meeting you, and if I see you by the window when I pass by, I'll stop in to say hello."

"Like I said, if I'm not here, I'm in church. Out of curiosity, what is it you do?"

"I'm a wire lather, Local #46."

"For Christ sake! A lather who sings in the opera. What the hell is this world comin' too? I 'm a steamfitter myself, Local #683. Maybe I'll see ya on the job sometime. Don't worry; I won't tell anybody you put on make-up and sing like a songbird."

Laughing, I shook his hand, zipped my coat to my chin and wrapped my scarf three times around my neck. I put on my gloves and thanked the bar key.

"Good night Devon. Thanks for everything."

"Good night, come again, and safe home!"

The streets were still deserted except for Malachy and Coleen, up ahead on the next street. I had four blocks to go but was well fortified by the Dewar's and like Terrence said, my equilibrium was perfectly in sync with the snow and the wind. Nice and toasty, the snow melted as it landed on me. My breath, white and vaporous, scented the air in front of me with beer and pretzels. As I always do when it's snowing, I stuck out my tongue to catch the snowflakes. I was over forty, but like a kid, I still got a charge from catching snowflakes on my tongue. A bus rattled on its way up Broadway, muffled in the quiet. I made a snowball and threw it, hitting the back door. "I didn't want you to stop anyways!" I yelled, throwing another. "I'm almost home so screw you!"

Opening the door of my building I felt sad the night was over.

UNDER THE APPLE TREE

It is forty-thousand years before the present time. One of the last of the dwindling Neanderthal clans are following the reindeer down from the mountains to the valley. Trees with graduating shades of red, green, yellow and gold carpet the rising cliffs. There is a plateau on top of a hill from which you can see the meandering river and the lush valley below. In the center of the plateau lives an ancient apple tree, heavy with the last fruit of the year. The tree has nurtured this passing clan, season upon season since before memory. It is here that Norwac has chosen to end his days. His stalwart companion, First Wife, will accompany him on this, his last journey. The clan, after much discussion, has agreed to Norwac's wish. All is well with the clan, they are a healthy and vibrant group, but must continue to move forward, following the herd, or they will die.

Two men are dragging a litter along a road beside the plateau. Animal skins are tightly fitted to their short muscular frames, with thick protruding hair protecting their extremities. On the litter is an old man, covered with blankets of animal skins and furs. He is mentally vibrant, though physically weak. He is Norwac the hunter, the provider, the leader of his clan for generations. The history of his harsh existence is told by his deep-set eyes and the symmetry of his facial scars. Stories of his prowess, even as a young man, will live on for generations. Norwac has lived his life as the best hunter of all the clans. Now he is lame, and his legs will no longer carry him. No longer can he follow the herd, and so has become a burden to his family.

Walking beside the litter is First Wife; Norwac's mate for most of his life. She is a weathered robust woman, with a full head of hair, prominent teeth, and alert intelligent eyes that reveal her confidence. Draped over her shoulders is an antelope shawl. She wears it proudly. On the other side of the litter walks Spear. He is tall for a Neanderthal and has a commanding stature. Having a deep respect for Norwac, he is reluctant to replace him. He is also wearing the antelope shawl. Norwac smiles at the sight of the ancient apple tree. First Wife takes his hand as the porters, Stalker and Grunt, bring him to the tree.

"Place the litter so Norwac can see the bottom of the sky" bellows Spear while checking the frame and the ties of the litter.

"Make the bedding for First wife beside me," groans Norwac.

The remaining members of the clan arrive and gather under the apple tree. They number twenty, five of which are children; the others at different stages of their life. Spear's booming voice fills the air under the tree,

"Children, gather firewood for Norwac...Grunt, Stalker make a fire-pit for First Wife."

Norwac waves, calling for Spear to join him.

"Norwac, this is hard for us," said Spear imploring Norwac to reconsider

"Not as difficult as carrying me to the winter grazing lands."

"It is more difficult! All of us are willing to share the burden if it will keep Norwac and First Wife with the clan."

"The young men have been carrying me since the new moon. They have used their strength and their time dragging my litter, when they should be with you, hunting to feed the clan."

"This clan has never wanted for food."

"I can see that you are pained to leave us here, but it is part of our ways from long ago. In former times, leaving the old ones to rest at the apple tree was more common. When I put on the Tiger Pelt it was not as it is with you. Man-Bear died in the glory of the hunt while he was still strong and never made it to the ancient tree. Now it is your time to wear the Tiger Pelt. The Antelope clan will grow and do well with you as leader. My son would be proud of you, as am I."

First Wife has brought the Tiger Pelt to Spear and places it on his shoulders. He crouches beside Norwac to receive his blessing and advice.

"Spear, be wary of the new peoples that have come, the ones without hair. They follow different ways but have much understanding of the world. It would be best to learn from them. They are small and look weak but are good hunters and as their numbers grow, the herds will become smaller. It is said they store food in many ways that allow them to winter in one place, in warm caves, away from the wind and snow and the hyena."

"I will crush them with my ax and leave them for the beast to feast upon."

"I said to be wary of them, not to kill them. Better to learn what they know but keep them at a distance. Watch that they don't breed with our women. We don't want weak offspring in the clan. Protect our campsites along the trail from the hairless one and the beast of the forest. If you trade honestly with brother clans, they will be with you in times of troub--" Norwac coughs and the pain that accompanies the flexing of his muscles shows in his face. Looking into the group he continues, "Shiwind has mated with many. It is uncertain who is the father of any of her offspring. It is her flat nose that makes the young hunters crazy for her. That nose will make for trouble someday, and it is best to stay away and let them work it out.... Shisnow over there, will make a good wife to Wulf of the Ibex clan. It will strengthen our bonds again. It is the Ibex clan that gave me First Wife."

Pointing to the children playing, Norwac smiles and continues,

"So many little ones. There will be many able hands in the future and that will be good for trade. You have seven strong hunters ... brave enough to bring down the largest mammoth. All is good with the Antelope Clan as I give them to you Spear. Make them flourish!"

The children have gathered a mound of firewood, each competing to see who could collect the most wood for Norwac. They stand in a line, awaiting Norwac's approval. Stalker and Grunt have made a fire pit of large stones. A small fire burns in its center with a column of smoke rising, dancing in the wind. The old man thanks each of them by

169

name. He is the same gentle giant they have always known.

"Look Norwac, look! The Sun and the Moon are at opposite sides of the sky. Lightning is flashing between the two. This is a sign."

"What does this sign mean First Wife?"

"It means that all is well Norwac" said First Wife reassuringly. Norwac smiles happily about the message written across the heavens. He addresses the clan.

"My people!.... Please... gather and listen." All the members of the clan close in around Norwac, children in front, then the women with the men behind.

"Spear has put on the Tiger Pelt and is now your leader. We are blessed. If you love him as I do, all will be good for the many years to come."

The clan shouts its approval, creating an echo in the canyon below. Spear steps forward, raises his hand and addresses the group.

"Make your fire pits around the tree. Prepare your food for the end of the day. Tonight we will camp with Norwac and First Wife."

Everyone goes to work preparing the encampment for the coming night. Soon, plumes of smoke rise from the campfires surrounding the tree. The moon overhead cast an ethereal light over the plateau. The higher the moon rose in the sky, the further the sun sinks, as though it were being pushed into the darkness. The Children play happily, running and chasing each other, sometimes the hunter, sometimes the prey. The aroma of burnt flesh cast a reassuring calm over the camp. Animal calls echo from the valley below. The cries and shrieks of fallen prey are drowned out by the yipping of the jackal and the howls of the wolf. A lonely mammoth bellows sweetly, seeking its mate in the twilight. The clan, bellies full, gather about the apple tree and its roaring fire to hear and tell stories.

"Norwac, tell us how you hunted the reindeer" asked one of the young men.

"Ah…there were so many. There is part of each of them in every one of you. I never wanted to kill the beautiful reindeer. I cried as I launched my spears. I looked into their eyes as they were dying and told them I was sorry to have taken their life. The brave ones, the ones that fought the hardest, I would take out their heart and bring it to First Wife so she could eat their strength. Especially when she was with child. We must thank the reindeer every day." Norwac sighs and wipes his eyes. Everyone is surprised by his show of emotion.

"First Wife, what will you do if the wolf comes to eat you?" asked Shiflower, daughter of Grunt.

"If a wolf tries to try to eat me, I will cut his eyes out with my scraper. I will cut his face till he runs away crying and is eaten by the jackals."

The group laughed, pounding the earth with their feet, shouting their approval for First Wife's defiant declaration. Shirain, wife to Stalker, steps forward with an antelope skin she has prepared as a present for Norwac and First wife.

"This pelt is very soft First Wife and will fit closely to your body."

First Wife examines the pelt, smelling it, tasting it, studying both sides. Smiling her gratitude to Shirain, she hands it over to Norwac.

"She has been chewing on it for two moons!" shouts Stalker from within the group.

Norwac studies the hide intently, "This is very good work Shirain. Thank you," he said with a groan. Turning to

Spear, "This is what I meant about able hands for trade."

"Now you can have your wife back Stalker," First Wife says with a laugh, much to the amusement of everyone. Shirain, embarrassed, runs into the group to hide.

The crowd pushes a young man out into the light of the fire. From inside the crowd, someone yells,

"Stoneface, tell Norwac what scared you on the hunt today... he ran like a baby! Ha-Ha."

"From a baby glutton[7]" yells another, laughing with the group.

Turning to speak to Norwac, Stoneface anxiously defends himself.

"It was a big baby glutton! He fell from a tree and landed on my shoulder. He tore my covering! .... It surprised me!"

Norwac holds his side to contain the pain accompanying his laughter.

"He wasn't no Stoneface then! He was whiter than a deer tail and his hair stood straight up." This and other mocking words rained upon him from his faceless tormenters. Deciding It was time , Spear steps forward to speak.

"You are the better for it Stoneface. Now you will be aware of what's above, as well as what's in front of you. A good hunter knows his surroundings," reassuring the young man, "that could have happened to anyone, learn from it."

Spear's absolution puts an end to his torment and Stoneface disappears back into the crowd. Young girls drag a satchel in front of the tribunal and wait for permission to speak. Spear gives them the nod and they all talk excitedly over each other, holding in their hands some of the bounty they had harvested.

---

[7] Wolverene (Gulo Gulo)

"First Wife, we bring you roots and tubers" says the tallest of the girls.

"And nuts and berries," sings another.

"With mushrooms and apples" adds the youngest.

The First Wife is delighted, "Children! it all looks so good! You know the forest floor as well as I do. Norwac look, the children have made for us a feast!"

It was just what they wanted to hear. The girls grinning ear to ear, return to the group.

Grunt and his wife Shimoon step into the light carrying tortoise shells of cured meats.

"This meat is well preserved and will last a good long time" Grunt says, bowing, handing his tortoise shell to Norwac.

"And will taste good with berries and apples!" Shirain says, handing her tortoise shell to First Wife.

Spear, seeing Norwac and First Wife tiring, steps forward and addresses the group.

"It is time for us to leave Norwac and First Wife. We have an early start in the morning so return to your fires to rest and sleep." He nods and the women begin to secure the food for the coming night.

"Leave the berries!" calls Norwac.

The plateau grows quiet as everyone settles in for the night. Soon, only silhouettes move about in the evening twilight. Norwac and First Wife lean against the apple tree, eating their berries and watching the stars.

"First Wife, before I sleep, I wanted to speak with you about tomorrow. You are still strong and should follow the clan when they leave in the morning. I will be fine. I have my spear and my axe and plenty of food. I have spent many a night alone in the forest, it is nothing new for me. Dream on it tonight and decide the right thing to do."

"I already know the right thing to do Norwac. You have kept me safe, warm and fed for all these years. You have given me fine children and a place of honor in our clan. I have spent the better part of my life at your side and I don't see how that can change. Besides, in a season or two I will be like you are now and face the same as you do. This way, when I die, I will die with a warrior."

Eating the last of the berries, they hold hands. First Wife rests her head on Norwac's shoulder as they watch the rising moon illuminate the valley below. While star dust lights the heavens above, the sounds of the earth lull them to sleep.

First Wife is awakened during the night. Not by a loud noise or an animal in the brush. She is awakened by an absence of sound--Norwac is silent. She could not hear him breathing. Putting her head to his chest, she could not hear or feel the beating of his heart. His face is serene and his body limp. Still holding his hand, she pats it a couple of times and rest her head on his shoulder. Staring off into the valley, she see's pictures of their life together. From youth to old age and everything in between. She drifts off to sleep again with beautiful memories of all they had shared together.

In the morning, First Wife awoke to Spear, Grunt and Stalker standing over her, checking to see that she was still alive. Having already checked Norwac, they attend to her.

"First Wife...Norwac is gone" Spear tells her, speaking softly, holding her hand.

"I know," she says with a deep sigh. "His spirit left in the night while we slept.... Look at that face" smiling "the last thing he said to me was ....'The stars shine forever.' I awoke in the moonlight and found that he was gone."

Gathering herself together, she stands, wraps her

174

antelope shawl about her shoulders and walks to the edge of the plateau. Staring into the valley she instructs Spear

"He loved this place, and it is here we will bury Norwac. Here by the old tree that watches over the valley." Turning to face Spear, "You must make it so, son of my son."

"As you say First Wife."

"I am no longer First Wife. I am once again Shibear. Your chosen woman, Shismile is now First wife. I will follow her and care for the children… as it should be."

"Grunt, Stalker, gather the clan," commanded Spear, "have the hunters bring their spears to dig a pit. Tell the others to gather stones. Gather enough to cover Norwac's body with a mound. Go!"

Spear approaches Shibear and puts his arm around her shoulder.

"Now that Norwac is gone we hope that you will be staying with the clan. The children will be happy to have Shibear with us, sitting by the fire at night, telling stories of old. It is what Norwac wanted for you."

"I know, he told me. And now it is so," she said wiping her eyes. "But I tell you! had Norwac lived through the night, I would have stayed with him until the end. That I know!"

"Yes, if Norwac had lived I would not question your decision to stay" Spear said stepping back from the tree to survey the area, "Where do you want us to make Norwac's grave?"

Wrapping her antelope shawl tightly around her, she walks the area around the tree. Searching, kneeling, feeling the earth with her hands, she is waiting for the right spot to speak to her. Twice she circles the tree, humming as she goes. Stopping, closing her eyes, raising her arms to the sky, she chooses an area midway between the tree and the edge of the cliff.

"It is here that Norwac will rest." She says, firming up the ground with her feet. "He will like it here."

"Stalker!" yells Spear in full voice surprising Shibear, awaking her from her dream. "Bring your brother. Dig here where Shibear is standing. Dig to the middle of your body.... I will mark out how big to make the grave. Tell Grunt and the others to carry the stones and rocks here. There is much to do. We must bury Norwac properly and have enough daylight to make it to our next camp before nightfall. If we stay here another night, we will be two days further behind the herd, and it will be difficult to catch up."

Stalker tells everyone the day's plan and all busy themselves making it so. The entire clan works together, and everything is ready in a short time. Shibear has been sitting with Norwac at the tree, holding his hand, savoring their life together. Her visions bring both smiles and tears. Spear is busy organizing the preparations.

"I want the young ones to line the bottom of the grave with the pebbles and stones they have brought. Place deer skins on top of them to make a bed for Norwac. Let the women ready everything that will accompany Norwac in the grave." Spear approaches the tree, "Shibear it is time."

"I see," she said holding out her hand. "Help me up Spear, my legs don't want to leave this place." Spear helps her up, puts his arm around her as they walk together. The clan is gathered around the grave. Spear speaks to the men,

"It is time. Bring Norwac here. Two of you step into the grave to receive the body, the rest of you carry him to his resting place."

Four of the men carry Norwac to the grave in a solemn procession. The women hum a soulful dirge as they pass the body down to the men waiting in the pit. Shismile, now as First

Wife, hands them a deer skin.

"Put this underneath his head."

"Place his axe and spear upon his chest and fold his arms across them," orders Spear, circling the grave to be sure everything is right. The food given the night before is placed into the grave along with his favorite scrapers, stone tools and the curiosities he had collected over the years. They cover the body with his antelope shawl. The litter is passed below but Shibear stops them.

"Bring the litter back to the old tree. He may want to look upon the valley later on." Speaking to Spear she adds "Norwac loved the apples."

"As you say Shibear."

The clan stands around the grave, each remembering the life of the great hunter. They moan and sigh as they place the stones around Norwac's body, piling them one on top of another until a mound sits upon the earth.

Spear raises his axe over his head and calls out the great hunter's name. "Norwac!"

The clan answers with the same, in a mighty roar. Three times he calls out the name, and three times the clan responds, creating thunder in the canyon below. After a moment of silence, Spear addresses the group.

"Antelope clan break camp and pack your belongings, it is time to move on. Stalker take your brother and go ahead of us to secure the campsite for tonight. Start the fires and wait for us there. Grunt, you and Stoneface will hunt for the evening's meal. A young deer should serve us all."

"We will bring apples and berries!" cried the children.

"Gather together at the road when ready, and we will start our journey" said Spear leaving to help the new First Wife prepare for the move. When all the clan is ready and waiting at

177

the road, Spear addresses them.

"We can start now. Be aware of your surroundings, and don't rush going down the mountain. Stay together and look out for each other."

Shibear is still standing at the grave site and Spear calls out to her.

"Shibear, it is time for us to go."

"I will be right along."

Speaking to Norwac she says her goodbyes.

"I have agreed to stay with the clan for this season, as was your wish. I will push my body forward and by the time we return to this place next year, I will have reached my time as you have today. I will be buried next to you. Once again we will lie side by side. Goodbye until then." She picks up a stone and places it on top of the grave.

A young girl has stayed behind to wait for Shibear. She takes the child's hand and together they start down the road. Before entering the path to the valley, she stops to take one last look at the grave and the ancient apple tree.

"Goodbye old friends" and continues her way.

THE LAST TIME I SAW KRISHNAMURTI

The last time I saw Jiddu Krishnamurti was at Carnage Hall. Not in the main hall; this stage was on the sixth avenue side, above the theater where the art films were shown. It was a small intimate venue, perfect for lectures and recitals. On the apron of the stage was a simple bentwood chair, a table with a pitcher of water and a glass. A vase with a single rose tied it all together. The quiet little man came from the side of the stage, his white hair shining, his face as youthful as when I had first seen him fifteen years earlier albeit now, he had an assistant to accompany him to his chair. He carried a cane and was a bit more hunched in the shoulders.

He sat, thanked his assistant and leaned his cane against the table. Eyes closed, sitting straight as the chair, he brought his knees together, folded his hands in his lap and took a few deep breaths. He raised his to head to face the crowd, smiled and welcomed us.

"Thank you so much for coming to our little talk. Today, I would like to talk about fear."

It was my third time attending a Krishnamurti talk. The first time was at the University of California at Santa Cruz in 1967. The second was a couple of years later at Ojai, California where he had his home. His New York talk began the same way as the others I had seen. For Krishnamurti, it was in the examination of life's conflicts and struggles that we could glean the most insight. For him, watching the process of fear and its machinations, seeing how it developed and became a default response, gave us the ability to render it powerless. That's where our freedom lies; in the ability to resist deferring to our default wiring. He had no use for psychology or organized religions, political ideologies and especially "Gurus." In the land of cults and crazy ideas, I thought the man made a lot of sense.

In the group I belonged to, Krishnamurti was required reading. As was Dostoyevsky, Freud and Jung, Hesse and Henry Miller. Ginsberg was considered a prophet, Ferlinghetti a personal friend. We lived and worked on a sheep ranch in the hills above Placerville California. We had a large garden, chickens, horses, ducks and a milk cow. We worked hard on the ranch during the day, but come evening the coffee pot was percolating, friends and guests brought bread, wine and cheese, and the country table was strewn with books to be discussed that night. From the poetry of Kenneth Patchen to Solzhenitsyn's 'Gulag' all of the topics of the day were covered. The music ran from Bach to Coltrane. It was my job to feed the record player when the 33 rpm's came to an end.

These bohemians were mostly refugees from the San

Francisco "Beat" scene. They claimed that the media created "Hippies" had invaded their city and the burgeoning Renaissance they had created and ruining what was a really good thing. The hippies were the mirror image of these folks. My Beat friends viewed hippies an anti-intellectual hoard, who's only concern was to intoxicate, copulate, and escape all responsibility. The Beats I knew, contrary to popular belief, were very industrious people. Each of them had found a niche with which to make a living and worked very hard at it. They were unapologetic and sometimes downright snobbish.

I was sitting on the steps of the student union on the Berkeley campus when my friend Ray Holder passed by. He wanted to show me a flier posted on the bulletin board inside. Krishnamurti would speak at the Santa Cruz campus on Monday. We were both a little surprised as Krishnamurti was not that well known, and a bit heady for most. We decided we would go. Ray claimed he "loved Krishnamurti" and would hitch-hike to New York City to hear him if he had to. Ray was an ex-marine, gay, unashamed and not someone you would want to "rumble" with. Two other friends came by and asked to come along with us; they weren't interested in hearing Krishnamurti speak, just wanted the adventure of a road trip. We agreed we would pick up our sleeping bags and a few other things and meet back at the student union. We met up and began our trek to the interstate to hitch-hike to Highway One. We lucked out and all of us caught a ride with a VW bus headed to Ocean Beach, which was right on the coast highway. There we split into two groups agreeing to meet up at the student union in Santa Cruz.

Santa Cruz is not that far from San Francisco, about seventy-five miles. We all made it there by evening and met at the student union as planned. Ray knew of a beach in

Capitola, about ten minutes away, where we could camp and build a fire. Capitola was a sleepy little town on the ocean with grocery stores and all the facilities we would be needing. Best of all, Ray said, was the bakery which sold starter bread (used to warm up the ovens) for a dime a loaf. We all caught a ride together in the back of a pickup. The kid driving said he knew exactly where we were going and that he had camped there himself. He let us off at the Safeway Market so we could buy some supplies for dinner. I left to pick up a bucket of Colonel Sanders chicken. Ray and the guys bought some beer, wine and munchies; macaroni salad, coleslaw and fruit for Ray as he was a very picky vegetarian. We picked up our gear which we'd stashed behind the Safeway and headed down to the beach.

We walked the winding road, following a path that ran through the brush, until we came to a cove hidden from the main beaches. Ray was right. It was a great camping spot. There was even a fire pit set up, waiting for some firewood. Ray said that he had stashed some firewood in the brush the last time he camped on that beach and went to see if it was still there. We set our sleeping bags around the fire pit to settle in for the night. Ray came back, arms filled with firewood, saying there was more should we need it. The sun was setting on the horizon and dusk was rolling in with a bit of fog. We devoured the chicken and drank the beer watching the night sky grow darker and the stars getting closer. The ocean slapping the shore lulled us to sleep. As the tide came in, the waves grew louder waking me; reminding me of where I was. The moon hovered just above the water, soon to be devoured by the horizon. Drifting off, I reminded myself that tomorrow we would go to hear Krishnamurti speak.

When I woke up Ray was just returning from the bakery.

He had also picked up a bag of oranges, a tub of butter and a gallon of water. He had several loaves in a paper bag and the loaves were still warm. *Man that was good!* The butter melted into the warm bread and the oranges were bursting with juice. The sun was rising over the hill and warming things up, reminding us that we had to get a move on.

The talk was held in a pavilion on campus. An octagon shaped building with windows all around. The stage was just a step higher. On it was a straight back chair, a table with a large floral arrangement, a bottle of water and a glass. Krishnamurti stepped onto the platform, hands clasped and greeted the audience. He took his seat, sat straight as the chair, put his knees together grasping each one in his palms. He took a few deep breaths and began.

"The drive here was so beautiful this morning. Everything was sparkling in the dew. The earth welcomed the warmth of the sun. It is so important to be able to appreciate what's before us. But I digress. . . . We came here today to talk about pride and envy. Our journey is not to entertain, but rather to inform."

So began Krishnamurti. He talked for well over an hour until he claimed the "process" had tired him and he would have to rest. Krishnamurti received a standing ovation and the audience left the pavilion silent and introspective. My mind was still processing all that I had heard. Compared to all of the "swami snatch your undies" type gurus running around California at that time, this guy was great!

The second time I saw Krishnamurti was in Ojai California. It had been a couple of years and I was due for a talk by my favorite non-guru. Ojai was a quiet little shire, nestled below the Ojai Mountains in a valley of rolling vineyards. It was not hard to understand why he chose that quiet little valley town for his home and foundation.

I hitched down by myself that time; I didn't want to be distracted. I was in my Siddhartha phase. For months, I called a lean-two home. Alone beside the Cosumnes River, I lived on brown rice, river water, and mountain air. It was time to break out!

It was a long trip from Placerville to Ojai. I said goodbye to everyone at the ranch and caught a ride to the interstate. First leg of the trip was to San Francisco where I stayed overnight with my friend Jen. She had a huge apartment near Coit Tower. The view of the tower was really beautiful when lite up at night. I got up early the next day to get a good start. It was a long stretch to Ojai and I wanted to get there by nightfall. Jen gave me a ride to the coast highway. I gave her a long hug, promising to come by on my return trip.

The hitch-hiking wasn't going so well. An hour between rides was the norm, with most of them being local. I considered jumping over to Highway 101 where I would make better time but decided to stay on the scenic route, which was the aesthetic choice. It was a bright crisp day. The vast Pacific Ocean was on my right. The mountains on my left looked as though they were trying to push the highway into the ocean. It was slow going, but that gave me the time to digest the changing vistas where each turn in the road was more beautiful than the last. I met some interesting people who told me their life stories. Some telling their tale in colorful language, in an attempt to purge themselves of their "lives of quiet desperation." Others, excited by the future, happily described how well things were working out for them. I listened, nodding my head like a therapist. All of them told me how lucky I was to be able to live such a free and unencumbered life. *The grass is always greener . . .*

I finally made it to State Road 33 which would take me inland to Ojai. It was getting dark and I figured it would be tough to get a ride come nightfall on a country road. I walked about a mile, where I found a meadow and settled in for the night. Jen had packed some granola and oblong tea and I feasted on my humble fare while trying to identify the constellations over my head. I crawled into my sleeping bag and drifted off to sleep. I awoke up in the middle of the night to a torrential rain. My sleeping bag was canvas backed so I was able to stay dry, though I worried about mudslides, so common in that part of California. By morning the rain stopped with the clouds being pushed out to sea by the winds coming down the Ojai valley. I washed my face and hands with water from my jug, put on a clean shirt, combed my hair and tried my best not to look like a guy who spent the night in the woods in the pouring rain.

The first ride I caught took me straight to Ojai. I thanked the driver and got out at the edge of town. There was an old motel on the other side of the road and I crossed over to see if I could get a room and a shower. The old fellow behind the desk looked like a miner from the 1849 gold rush. He talked like Gabby Hayes and chuckled at the end of every sentence. I explained I was in town for the Krishnamurti talks and needed a room to shower and rest up. He said check in was not until two o'clock, but he didn't see any harm in my taking the room a few hours early. He gave me the key for room seven and pointed to the sign behind him which stated the rules of the motel.

No alcohol or loud music.
No pets.
Only two people to a room.
Check-out is at noon.

Any time later and you will be charged for another full day.

Then with a complete change in demeanor he smiled, gave me a big welcome and told me that just up the road was a diner with the best home cooked food in town. I thanked him and left to go to my room. There was not a single car in the parking lot and the only soul to be found was the cleaning lady changing the linens. I took a shower and a short nap.

Ojai was a small town, so it wasn't hard to find the pavilion where the talks were being held. This was Krishnamurti's home turf and most of the folks there had followed him for years. The round tent pavilion was open on all sides except behind the stage. On the platform was a straight back chair, a table with a water pitcher and a glass. Behind his chair and on the sides of the platform were a dozen or so large vases with flower arrangements overflowing with incredible energy. He came on stage in a white suit, almost as white as his hair. He sat straight as the chair, folded his hands in his lap, took a few deep breaths and began. That time Krishnamurti spoke of the ego and the ability to be happy. His words flowed easily and were almost musical. He spoke very clearly and succinctly, staring off as he tried to elucidate all that he was seeing. The following day he spoke of compassion and caring.

The frail sage on the stage of Carnegie Hall still had a boyish aura about him. There was only one spotlight to illuminate the dark stage and it was focused on the single rose beside him. Krishnamurti shed his own light, which drifted out and onto the audience.

A couple of years later a friend called to tell me that Krishnamurti had passed away. I felt I had lost a good friend. Even now, years later, I can still hear his voice in my head describing how we all live. The pictures in my mind always bring a smile, and I murmur to myself using the words of the Bard,

"Hail,   good   fellow,   well   met!"

VILLON

From a gopher hole in the heart of Pangaea came Chat Villon. She jumped upon my porch, leapt into my lap and she has been with me ever since. Feral from birth, known in the area as Mamma Cat, she lived in a gopher hole behind Miss Bracken's machine shed. Stories tell that she had two litters while living there. It was agreed upon by all the folks on our road that she was an excellent mamma cat and made and raised fine kittens. What happened after they left Villon was often sad and helped form a characteristic behavior in her. Some of her young would be captured by bobcats or coyotes, some by predatory birds and some were run over by trucks. Lord only knows how many times Villon may have come across one of her lifeless kittens lying in the road, barely recognizable, flattened by an unknowing vehicle. I saw for myself once, down by the bridge, such an event. Villon stood over her little one confused and frightened. She caught sight of me, eyes bulging with fear, and ran off into the woods. I didn't see her for weeks after that.

At the sound of a truck approaching, Villon would run for the hills. Especially if it were a large truck and along with its roar, you could feel it's size by the ground vibrating. Something like a concrete truck would strike terror in her and send her running to the darkest corner of the house, not to reappear until the coast was clear. To this day, when the UPS truck pulls up to the house, she is gone in a flash. Occasionally I would come across one of her offspring on my walks. The ones that survived grew to be large, healthy and confident feral cats; a testament to her acumen.

Villon was a very responsible parent. Many mornings, while sitting on the porch, I would see her trotting alongside the road, calling out to her young, letting them know that dinner was on the way. The side to side swinging motion of the rabbit locked in her jaws, countered her forward motion. Her cries would create a doppler affect as she passed by on her way down the road. That must have been a very happy gopher hole.

Some time had passed and along with spring came the kittens venturing out into the world. I would see Villon running through the field with her kittens in tow, jousting, jumping and playing. They practiced climbing up and down the trees. Climbing down proved not to be so easy, but they kept at it until they became quite good. They looked like a happy bunch. As they became too big to feed from the teat, she spent more time running from, rather than playing with them. Looking back, I think that's why she wound up in my lap.

We crossed paths occasionally, on the road or in the fields. We'd stop, look each other in the eye, indicate that there was no challenge to be made and go about our business.

No problem, there was plenty of room and we had a "live and let live" type of agreement. I have profound respect for critters living in the wild and the genius they employ to do so; I think Villon knew that.

She startled me one morning while drinking my coffee, reading my email and the day's news on my phone. This was a regular routine of mine that had a sleepy cadence of its own. From out of nowhere Villon flew into my lap, spilling the hot coffee on us. I jumped up with a yell, Wolfie barked and Villon ran off. She was a whirlwind, shattering the calm of the morning, turning it into chaos. I cleaned up, got another cup of coffee and resumed our morning routine. She appeared again, walking the railing to where I was sitting and curled up in my lap, purring.

There she was, scenting my chest as though she had known me all her life and was just saying hello. Wolfie got up clumsily and sniffed the stranger in my lap. He had seen her around and smelled her scent all about, but never at his home. The familiarity confused him. He saw my response to Villon and knew, that by petting and scratching her head, I had given my permission for her to be there. He just watched, befuddled, anxious and confused.

All that day Villon followed us around while we went about our business, in and out of the house. I began to realize that I was creating a dependent. She had made herself right at home. She ate kibble from Wolfie's bowl, something no one imagined could ever happen. Not even I ate from Wolfie's bowl! Wolfie just watched, dumbfounded by the sight. His patience would soon be rewarded though, as we shall see.

Villon spent the night with us scenting the house to her specs. She found a comfortable chair and settled down to a quiet night's sleep. In the morning, coffee was made, the food and water bowls were replenished, and we were ready to begin our routine. Wolfie waited at the door, tail wagging in anticipation of its opening and the beginning of a new day. Villon was right behind him and I brought up the rear. Outside we found five little kittens romping and playing on the porch, waiting for mamma cat to come out. When she did, there was an eruption with kittens dashing in and out of corners, Wolfie barking at the commotion and Villon running down the steps to get away from it all. It went on that way every day for a while. Each morning we found our little friends waiting for us. The kittens were now used to Wolfie's barking and paid him no heed at all; they weren't leaving. They would follow us on our walks down to the brook or up the mountain road, working hard to keep up. We were their pack and the world was a wonderful place. That pretty picture soon faded as each of them left to find their own place in the world. But Villon stayed. Once she established herself as a member of the household, she brought forward the symbiotic benefits of our relationship. Especially for Wolfie! Villon was now comfortable enough with us to spend nights outside where her nocturnal skills excelled, and she knew best.

Each morning Villon would set outside the door four or five mice neatly stacked in a pyramid. She would sit beside her trophies waiting to show us her magnificent bounty. Wolfie, barking, leaping in the air in anticipation of the door opening, would go nuts. He'd grab a mouse and run down the porch stairs. He would toss it in the air, dance around it as though he were stalking his prey, pounce upon it, then sit and enjoy his quarry. When he was done, it was back to the porch for more. Villon sat with a smug superior air about her. She invited me to join in the feast, purring, scenting my leg. She didn't know that I didn't eat mice. Wolfie gladly took up the slack. Villon took the last mouse for herself, went to the corner and had her breakfast. I could hear the cracking and the masticating of the skull as I read the day's news. She knew she was top cat. Wolfie would now wait politely until she finished eating from his bowl. He was in awe of her prowess, as was I. In the hierarchy, she was an alpha and Wolfie was happy to accept that as long as the morning treats kept coming.

Villon was "in like Flynn. She was solidly part of the family now and had established her place in our new social order. When on our morning walks, we would take over the road. Wolfie in the lead, me in the center, and Villon bringing up the rear. Like scientists, we would examine all the evidence left on the road from the night before. They were better at it than I was; their sense of smell made reading the road an open book. We all enjoyed this pack behavior. I think I speak for all of us when I say that we felt proud and powerful. The birds along the road would yell their warning calls, passing the message on, letting the other birds in the area know there was a fearsome cat with an awesome pack coming down the road. Folks driving by would smile and wave, enjoying the sight of our merry little band of urchins.

There were no other cats in the area, so Villon had about a ten-acre hunting territory. She intimately knew every acre and covered her territory every day. When she went out into the fields, we knew she would return with something good to eat. I always got a kick watching her march off to work, shoulders hunched and dead serious. No weekends, no holidays or overtime for Villon. She had to do what she had to do; that's all there was to it. Wolfie sat at the fence waiting for her to return, though now he was like the lion king waiting to be fed by his pride. Villon paid no mind to the lazy lug.

We lived that way for a decade. All of us thriving in the life we had created for ourselves. We were all growing older though and over time the world changes. New people moved into the area and brought with them their cats and dogs and kids. Huge cats, the size of bobcats, now prowled Villon's killing fields. Villon was small in comparison to the newcomers. I always figured she was the runt of the litter, although one that made good. Yet another reason to respect Villon. Sometimes she would come home battle weary and scarred. Late at night I could hear her defending her porch, taking on all comers. She fought like a Spartan at Thermopylae. No one got past Villon. Wolfie had similar problems with our newcomers. At first, he was happy to see the new dogs and wanted to play with them, but they wanted to establish their dominance, which confused him. He'd had no competition over the years and had few skills with which to handle that new type of aggression. Wolfie soon figured them out, and treated them like the assholes they were. They could come to the property line but not one paw further.

I didn't care for the changes myself. A house just up the road became a Section 8 rental property with a steady flow of occupants. Tricycles were left on the road, the garbage cans were overflowing and there was a lot of loud arguing. Coming from a blue-collar neighborhood, Jackie Gleason and the honeymooner types were familiar to me, but these guys would make Tennessee Williams blush. One lady had a screech so shrill she could make the Banshees run for cover. They kind of made a voyeur of me for a while, but I soon grew tired of it when often the arguing carried on into the night. Winters were much quieter because they had to keep their doors closed. All that ugliness seemed so out of place in such a beautiful landscape. One day, after a foot or so of new snow, my blower got a flat tire. It was stuck in the snow! I couldn't move it. There it stayed in my driveway while the snow fell, covering it until it began to look like a snowman. A friend came by and finished clearing the driveway but that was it. I was moving to Florida!

I left Wolfie and Villon at the house with my roommate Eileen. She had known them as long as I had so I knew they were in good hands. It would make life difficult if I were to take Wolfie and Villon with me. Being cramped in an over packed jeep for long periods of time would not fly. Even temperaments as steady as theirs would soon become taxed. Better to find us a place, then go back and get them. I would start looking in Hobe Sound, an area I was familiar with. After a month of searching, I found a place in Vero Beach. I was able to get the lease down to six months but there was a caveat—NO PETS! I needed a place to live so I accepted, figuring I would use it as a base to find a proper home for us to live. I found a permanent place in Vero that was pet friendly and where we could all live together. We were all set. Then Wolfie became ill with Lymphoma. The veterinarian's prognosis was not very good. When Wolfie began to experience pain, moaning at night, weak and lethargic, we had to have him put down. I made the trip to New York, picked up Villon and we drove in silence to our new home in Florida. The sense of loss was profound—for both of us.

Villon was at least thirteen years old. I told her that this was her forever home, but that adjustments had to be made. The condo association did not permit pets wandering about on their own; even cats. It would have been a great place for Wolfie, with dog runs and such, but I would have to put a harness and leash on Villon when we took our walks. That would have made a funny picture; but it was not to be.

The ibis and the rabbits, the squirrels and the birds, all have breakfast on our front lawn. On the cul de sac where we live, the Sandhill Cranes walk around like they own the place. You have to get out of your car to shoo the ducks off the road. All of these critters have no fear whatsoever. Villon the huntress, if she roamed freely, would create havoc in the shire! She was going to have to learn to become an inside cat, which she did. It all worked out. She was an old momma cat by then and didn't have the energy or the ambition she'd once had. She scented the house to her specs, investigated every nook and cranny and chose several spots to call her own. Villon was never destructive, never messed in the house and was always amenable to the house rules. It was like she understood the parameters, agreed, and went with the flow. She never asked to go outside or bolted through the door when it was left open. She seemed content to be the lady of the house. Where she once had acres to roam and make her own, she retired and downsized to preside over this small house and sometimes me. Leaving her gopher hole in the heart of Pangea, Chat Villon went on to become a queen in tropical   Florida.

ONE ACT PLAYS

THE BAT

List of Characters

<u>Jason Traveler:</u> Successful entrepreneur and venture capitalist. He is in his late forties, trying to retire.

<u>Martin Epstein:</u> Semi-retired lawyer, Jewish with a Brooklyn accent. He is Jason's neighbor.

<u>Evelyn Epstein:</u> Tall woman, toned with an energetic personality. Martins wife.

<u>Residents of the community:</u> Three women – four men.

<u>Sargent Kowalski:</u> Seasoned veteran, late fifties, looking to his pension. His uniform and demeanor are relaxed and laid back.

<u>Officer O'Brian:</u> Fit, thirty years old, with one year on the job. Uniform buttoned to the chin. He is eager to serve and protect.

<u>Officer Davis:</u> Veteran police officer, friend of Kowalski.

<u>Officer DeAngelis:</u> Young Italian officer with a lot of personality.

<u>EMS officer:</u> with three crewmen.

<u>Newsgirl:</u> with cameraman.

<u>Protester #1:</u> Male mid-twenties committed to his beliefs.

<u>Protester#2:</u> Wife of protester #1, she looks like husband.

<u>EPA:</u> Agent Folger is prissy, full of hubris, believes he is empowered by an omnipotent Government.

<u>Animal Control-AC:</u> Captain Kessler, late forties with a few too many pounds, a follower by nature.

(The scene takes place in a gated community in Vero Beach Fl. A quiet sleepy shire, with palm trees, lakes and waterfowl wandering about. This is the home of Jason Traveler, a recently retired venture capitalist. While watering his front lawn one evening, he has become the target of an attack by bats. Spraying them with the hose, he tries to keep them away, but one of them attacks from behind and lodges itself in his hair. He tries to brush it away, only to get resistance and hisses from the bat. He cannot see the bat, but he imagines it having razor sharp teeth. (Talking to himself)

<u>Jason:</u> Suppose it has rabies!

(He paces back and forth, talking to himself,)
I'm going to need help. Who do you call when you have a bat in your hair? 911, I guess. At least they'll be able to direct my call to someone who knows about these things.

(He takes his phone from his pocket, fumbling while trying to dial. He throws the hose down and starts over again. (Speaking to the bat,)

Your days are numbered buddy! *(the bat hisses)*

Hello . . . Hello . . . 911? . . . yes, I have an emergency. I have a bat in my hair and it won't leave . . .yes . . . yes, a bat. The kind that flies around at night . . . how do I know where it came from? *(the bat chirps)* "I am being cooperative . . . five or six of them . . . I know there are penalties for making false claims . . . *(bat squeals)* There! Can you hear it? . . . that's the bat! He is yelling at you from the top of my head. Finally! . . . My name is Jason Traveler, I live at 2575 Banyan Place . . . it's in the Malibu subdivision.... Yes . . . yes, please send the car. I will be waiting in front of the house. Yes . . . yes . . . goodbye and thank you. *(He puts the phone in his pocket and starts pacing again. Talking to the bat)*

You're going to have to find a new home, my furry little

friend *(the bat hisses)*. I should call Martin and get him over here. *(he reaches for his phone and searches through his contacts.)*

Martin . . . Martin . . . oh here it is . . . *(he dials, the phone rings and Martin picks up.)*

Jason: Hello Martin, Jason here . . . listen Martin, you have to come over, right away . . . I'll tell you when you get here . . . its, sort of an emergency . . . Ok . . . Ok! . . . I have a bat stuck to my head and I can't get rid of it . . . can you give me a hand? . . . Good . . . good, come right over. (the bat hisses as Jason paces back and forth in front of his house)

(Martin arrives and approaches Jason cautiously. He stands nose to nose with Jason as he examines the bat. He circles Jason studying the bat from all angles.)

Martin: This is a handsome bat . . . *(getting closer as the bat squeals)* look at those ears! . . . and he has very broad shoulders.

Jason: How do you know it's a He?

Martin: I can tell by the hair above his eyes. Just look at those bushy eyebrows! Don't ask me how I know this . . . I just do.

Jason: Martin, the bat is on the top of my head . . . I can't see him!

Martin: Well then, take my word for it. This is a unique bat.

Jason: Martin, you're talking crazy man. Where's Evelyn?

(Martin is still examining the bat and is getting too close. Jason backs up as Martin advances.)

Martin: Wonder why he chose you?

Jason: Because . . . I was there?

Martin: No, no! . . . (wagging *his finger at Jason*) he could have chosen anybody; but he chose you.

(Jason continues pacing, frustrated and anxious)

Jason: I just called 911 and told them I had a bat in my hair . . . the operator, she told me I could be prosecuted for making prank calls and interfering in police business.

Martin: What did you say to her?

Jason: I told her it was a genuine emergency, and that I needed an ambulance to take me to whoever in this world removes bats from people's heads.

Martin: What did she say?

Jason: Their sending a patrol car out. *(They both are pacing, thinking.)*

Martin: *(clapping his hands together)* That's it! . . . this means something . . . The two of you are connected somehow . . . you have a history, and he's trying to tell you something!

Jason: What are you a psychic now. You're as batty as this bat is! (the bat chirps)

Martin: You're the one with a bat in the belfry.

Jason: I'm surprised you don't see the seriousness of this Martin . . . where's Evelyn? . . . It could turn out badly you know . . . the bat is either sick or crazy or both . . . he could have disease . . . maybe he hates people. (the bat hissssses)

Martin: I think he has a message for you.

(Evelyn joins them on the lawn, and they stop pacing.)

Jason: Finally! Some sanity!

Martin: I will remind you once again that you are the one with a bat in the belfry.

Evelyn: What's that on your head? It's moving! ha, ha, it's a bat . . . where did you find it . . . Martin, why didn't you tell me Jason had a bat stuck to his head . . . this is classic . . .where's my cell phone . . . this is going to make me legend on Facebook. *(circling Jason, taking pictures. The bat chirps)*

Martin: They have a history.

Evelyn: You mean like sex? Is that what this is! Weird sex! I see why you didn't want to tell me. I'm still going to post it on Facebook though, I'll just leave out the sex part.

203

Martin: No, not sex, he has a message for Jason. They have a past history and the bat is here to make it right. Evelyn, he called 911 for an ambulance and they told him he was crazy and was making crank calls.

Evelyn: I should make a follow up call, make sure they take it seriously. What do you call something like this? (dialing)He's not a vampire is he? The bat I mean. (*Martin shakes his head*) Too bad, I could have used that.

Hello, I would like to report an incident. Yes . . . 2575 Banyan place, it's in the Malibu subdivision . . . no one is injured . . . well do animal attacks count . . . then it's an emergency . . . an attack by bats, one of which is attached to the gentleman's head. Jason Traveler . . . he is very upset, he's pacing . . . he thinks the bat may have disease . . . Jason, he says you should sit down and stay calm . . . he won't sit down and refuses to be calm . . . thank you very much, we will be waiting.

Jason: Thank you Evelyn, that will probably help.

Evelyn: Hey, anytime you have a bat nesting in your hair, just give us a call.

Martin: We're here for you buddy.

Evelyn: (*flipping through the pictures on her phone*) These are precious . . . I should download them to my PC before posting them . . . just one more! . . . don't move . . . this is great! . . . that is one handsome bat. (*the bat squeals excitedly*)

Martin: I told him . . . he wouldn't listen (the bat chirps) . . . he can't see the bat because it's on his head.

Evelyn: (*walking away, staring at her phone*) Have him look in the car mirror . . . Great pic! I dare anyone to say my posts are dull now. Be right back.

Martin: You want to see the bat? (*taking Jason's arm*) Right this way. (*leading him to Jason's SUV*). I think an introduction is in order. Look into the mirror...Bat, this is Jason Traveler, your host for this occasion *(bat chirps)*. Jason, this is the bat who has travelled all this way to befriend you.

Jason: He looks like a hog with big ears. *(Looking into the car mirror at different angles to study the bat)*. A Hog Homunculus, or should I say the homunculus of a hog? *(the bat squeals and hisses)*

Martin: That could get tricky . . . I'd go with homunculus of a hog.

Jason: Seriously?

Martin: Is there anything you'd like to tell him while you have the opportunity Jason?

Jason: Why, did I do something to the bat that I have to apologize for?

Martin: Well, maybe he wasn't a bat at the time when the 'issue' took place. Don't look at him as a bat, see him as he was all those years ago.

Jason: Say what? Oh . . . excuse me while I search the Akashic Record for someone I knew several lives ago, who is now a bat. OK, be right back. *(a police siren is heard)* . . . Ahhh the Calvary has arrived! Martin, put a lid on it will ya. If anyone heard us talking like this, they'd be calling for the straight jackets. Officers! Thank you for coming out.

Sargent Kowalski: Good evening Sir, I am Sargent Kowalski, and this is officer O'Brian.

Officer O'Brian: Evening Sir.

Sargent Kowalski: We're here, responding to a call of an assault with a bat.

Jason: No, no . . . I have been assaulted by a bat . . . your dispatcher got it wrong. Can't you see it on my head? *(pointing to his head)*

Officer O'Brian: It's not our job to judge fashion Sir.

Jason: That's all well and good officer but this is not fashion. I

205

need transport to a place where they remove bats from people's heads.

Martin: *(to Jason)* I don't think your helping . . . let me explain *(speaking to the officers)*. Officers, my neighbor here has been attacked by a wild animal, sorry bat, and he needs your bat removal taskforce immediately. I have known this gentleman for many years and will vouch for him. He is an upstanding member of the community.

Officer O'Brian: Sir, all of our citizens receive our complete attention.

Martin: Yes, yes, I understand . . . I'm just asking that you keep an open mind about this, as there are unusual circumstances.

Sargent Kowalski: Officer O'Brian, look up the code for the incident and call it in. Say that the officers have arrived at the scene and are investigating.

Officer O'Brian: Got it!

Sargent Kowalski: (to Jason) Protocol sir. Now let's start from the beginning. You say the perp attacked you and lodged itself in your hair.

Jason: Correct.

Sargent Kowalski: And this was done against your will. The bat was not there by invitation.

Jason: Ahhhh coorrecct, Sargent, could you please just take me to a hospital.

Sargent Kowalski: Sorry sir . . . information is key to your police department doing its job properly.

Officer O'Brian: *(scrolling through a tablet for code)* Sargent I can't find the codes that apply to this situation.

Sargent Kowalski: *(joining O'Brian)* There must be something we can use.... otherwise no EMS. Here! Take this one . . . go with assault and battery. That will get the ball rolling and we can put this one to bed. Things are not right here. This guy's friend over there thinks the bat has a message to deliver.

Officer O'Brian: We still have to follow up Sarge--

Sargent Kowalski: The sooner we get started the better. And O'Brian . . . remember that you are wearing a body camera. Anything you say or do can be used against you in a court of law.

Officer O'Brian: That's what I tell the Perps!

Sargent Kowalski: Well, as an officer of the law, you are guilty until proven innocent. Even then, the media has to approve of the verdict or you will be shadowed by it for your entire career. Make the call O'Brian, I will finish interviewing the batman.

Office O'Brian: (*preening himself*) How do I look? . . . you know, in case we get on the news.

(The Sargent shaking his head joins Jason to complete their interview. Passersby have begun to gather down stage, asking questions and theorizing about what might have happened.)

Woman#1: It's a sign from God, that's for sure.

Woman#2: Or it could be hygiene. He could be exuding some kind of odor that makes the bat crazy.

Woman#1: It's a message about hell and damnation.

Man#1: They were a stealth group with military training. They were in and out before anyone knew what was happening. I didn't even see them. Did you Bob?

Man#2: No, I didn't see or hear a thing. That's how good they were. The wife and I sat right over there while it happened. What did they get away with anyway?

Man#1: The TV I guess, they always go for the TV. Look . . . EMS is here. That means battery as well as breaking and entering. It could have happened to any one of us. (Four EMS workers enter stage left carrying stretchers, oxygen tanks, IV stands. The lead guy, approaches officer Kowalski carrying a clipboard.)

EMS: Evening Sargent . . . how many victims?

Officer Kowalski: Only one . . . this is Mr. Traveler.

EMS: Sir

Jason: Evening

Martin: Good to see you!

EMS: Where is the victim?

Officer Kowalski: Mr. Traveler is the victim. He has a bat in his hair, and the bat won't let go.

EMS: Oh! . . . I thought it was one of those buns the martial arts people wear on top of their heads . . . *(the bat chirps. EMS officer speaking to his men)* . . . Hold off guys . . . leave the stretcher, put the rest away.

Martin: He liked that.

EMS: Who? . . . liked what?

Martin: The bat . . . He liked what you said.

EMS: How do you know it's a he?

Martin: Don't ask. I just know.

EMS: Sir, we have to establish the correct gender pronoun to use . . . it's regulations. We could lose our jobs calling someone by the wrong gender pronoun . . . .and with the lawsuits and all! *(shaking his head)* it is a nightmare!

(A siren is heard off stage. A second police car has arrived. Radio talk is heard, Officer Bill Davis an old classmate of Sargent Kowalski enters)

Officer Davis: Sorry Eddie. Our dispatcher made the first call on this case, so the jurisdiction here is ours. We will be taking

208

the lead.

Sargent Kowalski: *(with a broad smile)* Mr. Traveler meet Officer Davis.

Jason: Officer *(shaking his hand)* good to see you . . . are you here to take me to the hospital?

Office Davis: No sir, were here to investigate several beatings with a bat . . . five or six I'm told.

Sargent Kowalski: Bill, the bat is on his head. Our guy got it mixed up as well.

Office Davis: What the hell? . . . I thought it was some kind of weird hair do.

Jason: Good Lord! *(pacing)*will no one take this seriously! *(imploring the heavens)* "My kingdom for an ambulance!"

Officer Davis: Is this guy right in the head? What's he talking about? . . . Kingdom?

Martin: He's quoting Shakespeare.

Officer Davis: And you are?

Martin: Martin Epstein, I'm his neighbor.

Sargent Kowalski: Mr. Epstein claims our victim knew the perp in another life.

Officer Davis: Whaaa . . . Ah . . . OK . . . sure *(winks at Kowalski)* makes sense to me! . . . that's why he grabbed hold of the victim's hair and won't let go. Ex-wife maybe?

(The bat screeches, Officer Davis looks puzzled at the bats response. An officer in riot gear comes on stage ready for action.)

Officer Davis: Stand down DeAngelis, the crime scene has been secured. It seems our bats have wings.

Officer DeAngelis: Drones again?

Officer Davis: Take off your helmet DeAngelis. Look . . .*(he takes off his helmet to get a good look at the bat, examining it closely. The bat hisses)*

Officer DeAngelis: Huh! Bejesus! Where in hell did that come from? *(the bat screeches as DeAngelis examines him)* what are we gonna' do with this one?

Martin: I don't think he liked that officer.

Both officers: Who? . . . liked what?

Martin: The hell comment. This fellow is from the past, maybe even a relative. Its insensitive to associate him with the minions of hell. *(ignoring Martin, they continue)*

Officer Davis: *(examining the bat; the bat hisses)* I don't know what were gonna' do yet . . . I'm not sure . . . get back into uniform and tell EMS to wait while I figure out how to explain this to dispatch. I'll call this in myself.

Officer Kowalski: *(smiling)* OK, and with that my partner and I will bid you adieu. Remember your sensitivity training . . . you could say something insensitive and traumatize someone for life.

Officer Davis: Very funny Kowalski . . . you know, you did arrive on the scene first . . . in the old days, the first officer on the scene always took charge. I wouldn't mind if you--

Officer Kowalski: No, No, No, we have to follow the regulations . . . isn't that why you were demoted . . . for not following regulations?

Officer Davis: You know dam well the new chief was making an example of me.

Officer Kowalski: OK . . . sorry Bill, that was out of line. I couldn't pass up the opportunity for a good dig. O'Brian, pack up, were leaving the sensitive and caring officer Davis in charge here. Mr. Traveler it has been a pleasure.

Officer Davis: DeAngelis, on second thought call dispatch. Say that the officers have arrived at the scene and are investigating.

(The crowd has grown, and so has the speculation and analysis of what might have happened. Evelyn returns)

Evelyn: Jason this has gone viral! In one hours' time you have become famous; right across the globe! There is a contest going on to name the bat. It started in France and has spread across Europe. Fourteen thousand entries so far. A GoFundMe page has begun to collect money to study the relationship between you and your bat friend here. The International Society of Chiropterologist will be sending a delegate to study the situation.

Martin: Evelyn, that's wonderful!

Jason: Wonderful! wonderful for Evelyn. *(bat chirps)*

Evelyn: By the end of the week you will be more famous than you ever were in business.

Jason: I don't want to be famous! I just want this bat removed from my head.*(bat hisses)*

Martin: Not so good Jason *(waving his finger)* . . . this may be bigger than you think. There is a meaningful symbiosis going on here.

Officer Davis: Gotta go! . . . DeAngelis, time to start interviewing witnesses. *(approaching him to speak privately)* I'm going to call the Lieutenant and see if we can't get some help here. Maybe we can pass this off to Animal Control.

Jason: Officer Davis, can you please let EMS take me to the hospital?

Officer Davis: Were working on it Mr. Traveler. I'm still trying to establish jurisdiction . . . then we will be able to move forward . . . please be patient.

Jason: How can I be patient when I have a bat clutching my skull! (bat hisses)

<u>Officer Davis:</u> Please Mr. Traveler . . . (*walking away, talking into his phone*) Yes Lieutenant . . . Davis here. Lieutenant, we have responded to a rather peculiar call. I think it might be more of a case for Animal Control, rather than Vero Beach P.D. It's not assault and battery as reported, it's an assault by a bat . . . you've heard about it? . . . the media? No they haven't arrived yet . . . yes, yes, turn over jurisdiction to EPA and Animal Control . . . DeAngelis . . . yes, yes a good man. What? Tell him to tell jokes on the police line? . . . oh yes, of course, good for P.R. Thanks Lieutenant . . . a full report . . . yes, thank you.

(*DeAngelis has rolled out police tape to cordon off the area. The passersby have gathered behind the tape.*)

<u>Man#1:</u> Cyrus Johnson called the news people to report on this, but I'm not so sure it's about assault anymore.
<u>Man#2:</u> (*nodding in agreement*) It's beginning to look that way.
<u>Woman#1:</u> The Lord works in mysterious ways!
<u>Woman#2:</u> I still say it's about odor.
<u>Woman#3:</u> This could become an epidemic! What with climate change and loss of habitat confusing the bats, all this could be the beginning of the end they're talking about on T.V. What if the bats start eating our brains? . . . then what?
<u>Man#3:</u> Bats eat bugs . . . they don't eat people.
<u>Woman #3:</u> I blame this on the republicans--
<u>Man#3:</u> Of course you do--
<u>Man#1:</u> There's a safe zone down the street. Go on . . . keep walking!
<u>Man#2:</u> Heard it all before!

(*A man passes by and enters the group*)

212

Man#4: Hey, how are ya? I just got an alert on my phone saying there has been an assault down here. What's going on?

Man#1: They're investigating now. Looks more like an animal incident than an assault if you ask me.

Officer Davis: Officer DeAngelis can you step over here please. I just spoke with the lieutenant. The EPA and Animal Control people are coming by to take over. They will have jurisdiction. And one more thing Bobby. The lieutenant wants you to work the police line. You know, tell them jokes, make them laugh. He says it would be good for our PR.

Officer DeAngelis: Anything for the Lieutenant! (*DeAngelis approaches the police line*)

People, people, everything's fine . . . hey, have you heard the one about the Rabbi and the Priest who go into a bar?

Martin: Jason, you are being swept away by destiny.

Jason: I want my life back!

Martin: Jason, your being perversely persistent in your resistance to these events. Think about how the bat must feel? (*bat chirps*) You could at least try. (*chirp*)

(*laughter is heard coming from the police line*)

Jason: I don't want to try . . . I want to say goodbye . . . to the bat and the whole crowd over there. Perversely persistent? . . . that's kind of strong isn't it?

Evelyn: That is kind of strong Martin.

Martin: OK . . . your resistance is perplexing . . . either way, you're not helping.

Jason: Well then, why don't you take care of the bat if you care so much. You assume the responsibility for housing this bat. (*bat chirps*)

Martin: I'm working on it!

(*A TV news truck has arrived and set up at the scene*)

News girl: Good evening everyone, this is Page Arlington reporting to you from a scene where multiple attacks have taken place in this otherwise sleepy and bucolic community. Five or six marauders with baseball bats, have attacked the owner of this home while he was watering his lawn. Police and medical teams are on the scene . . .

Jason: (*pointing to the news truck and crew*) That's just great! (*sarcastically*) Just what I need; a news truck parked outside my house. (*bat chirps*)

Evelyn: Jason, you can't buy this kind of publicity.

Jason: Evelyn, I moved here to avoid this kind of publicity . . . this is exactly what I have been trying to get away from. Thanks to the bat, now every inventor, every start-up company will be beating on my door, making a pitch for their "sure to succeed" business or invention.

Martin: It's not the bats fault.

Jason: Noooo . . . it's your wife's fault!

(*more laughter from the police line*)

Evelyn: I guess it is my fault. I'm sorry Jason. I really needed something good for my Facebook page. Everyone was commenting on what a dull life I have, and I needed a tid-bit to give the page a boost. I had no idea it would blow-up like this. I was trying to help you as well, and I guess it kind of backfired.

News girl: We have an update ladies and gentlemen . . . it seems our preliminary reports were incorrect. There has been an assault . . . but by a bat. I mean, the flying mouse kind of bat. The assailant attached itself to the victim's hair and has refused to let go.

Evelyn: Martin, (*reading from her phone*) the animal rights people are sending a representative here to insure the rights and well-being of the bat. There is concern on Facebook for the bat's welfare.

Martin: I know . . . I called them.

Evelyn: Martin isn't this complicated enough without your--

Martin: It will all work out Evelyn . . . you'll see.

Evelyn: We should tell Jason--

Martin: Just don't tell him that I'm the one who called the animal rights people.

News girl: It is touching to see in action, the sense of community the people of Malibu Subdivision have. Friends and neighbors have all pitched in to help in what has now become a very complicated situation. As you can see, off to my right, the good men folk of Malibu are directing and diverting traffic to keep the streets open, so that our emergency services can get in and out. The ladies are offering water and information to those who have come to see for themselves, firsthand, what now has the attention of the entire world. Hold on Jeff, I see some protestors have arrived at the police line. They are carrying signs. Let me get a little closer . . . 'Animals have the same rights we do' reads one, and another reads 'We demand equal rights for bats', clearly there is concern for the bat involved in this case. This is Page Arlington, reporting live, Vero beach FL. Back to you in the studio Jeff.

(Evelyn has told Jason the new news)

Jason: Yet another player in our little fable! *(pacing)* This is turning into a full-blown drama . . . maybe a tragedy *(bat screeches . . . talking to the bat)* The finale is at hand my furry little friend . . . La comedia finita! Leave while you can!

Martin: Jason . . . your upsetting him.

News girl: Back again Jeff with an update as to the identity of the homeowner and person of interest in this historic case. He is none other than Jason Traveler, the controversial financier and venture capitalist who dominated the news cycle just two short years ago, with accounts of misogyny, money laundering, lewd and offensive speech, and of course his torrid affair with actress Caroline Mac Duff.

<u>Woman #1:</u> I always knew the devil was working in that household.

<u>Woman#2:</u> Nah! . . . it's all about the olfactory, the nose brain and all of that. The world is organized by odor.

<u>Man#1:</u> I heard the newsgirl say he is involved with the Hollywood crowd.

<u>Man#2:</u> Then this could not have happened to a more deserving fellow.

<u>Man#3:</u> It's probably just a publicity stunt, and by the looks of it they have succeeded!

(*A helicopter hovers above the scene*)

<u>News girl:</u> Good evening everyone, this is Page Arlington on location in Vero Beach FL. where a bat and a buyout specialist have come together in the most unusual circumstances. I have here with me Evelyn Epstein, neighbor and good friend to Jason Traveler . . . Evelyn what can you tell us about what has taken place here.

<u>Evelyn:</u> Good evening Page, thanks for having me. Well . . . Jason was watering his lawn when he was attacked by several bats, one of which grabbed his hair and never let go . . . we came to help him, my husband and I, but we didn't have a clue as to what to do. That's when I posted it to Facebook, and what has become of that post is incredible.

<u>News girl:</u> So, you were the first to post it on Facebook?

216

<u>Evelyn:</u> Correct

<u>News girl:</u> And the world has responded to the plight of this bat, who in the hands of a notorious carpetbagger, has an uncertain future.

<u>Evelyn:</u> Well . . . I wouldn't say Jason is a carpetbagger--

<u>News girl:</u> And as an update for our viewing audience, the EPA and Animal Control have arrived on the scene. Finally, the government is exercising control over what has become an international incident.

(Kowalski and O'Brian have returned and approach Officer Davis)

<u>Officer Davis:</u> Well, look what the cat dragged in!

<u>Officer Kowalski:</u> The lieutenant called me personally on the car radio . . . said you might be needing help with crowd control.

<u>Officer Davis:</u> The EPA and Animal Control people have arrived, and we will be turning over jurisdiction to them. We are here for support only. Hopefully we will be able to wrap this up before the end of our shift. DeAngelis is over on the line telling jokes. The lieutenant says it's good for PR.

(Laughter is heard coming from the police line)

<u>Officer O'Brian:</u> I know some jokes.

<u>Officer Davis:</u> Well then, why don't you join DeAngelis on the line? *(O'Brien turning to Kowalski, straightening his tie)*

<u>Officer O'Brian:</u> How do I look? *(Preening himself, slicking back his hair)*

<u>Sargent Kowalski:</u> You're ready for prime time. O'Brian, remember the body camera.

<u>Officer O'Brian:</u> Got it Sarge. *(O'Brian saunters off to join*

DeAngelis on the line)
Evening folks! 'Why did the chicken cross the road?'

<u>News girl:</u> Jeff, more protesters have arrived on the scene. The street has become very crowded in the wake of this historic event (*approaching the protesters*) Sir, I see your sign reads "Bat lives matter." Can you tell us a little bit about what brought you here this evening and what it is you are supporting?

<u>Male protester:</u> Yes, of course, and thank you for having me. Facebook told us to come. We are here to demand justice for the bat and to end the subjugation of the people of the earth by the 'Imperialist capitalist'.

<u>Woman protester:</u> We were having dinner when the message came across my tablet.

<u>Male protester:</u> And on my cellphone. We dropped everything and came to resist the 'Fascist'. It's not so much about what we support, we haven't got word yet as to what that is, so for now it's about what we are against.

<u>Woman protester:</u> Our community center has created a safe place and we dropped off our baby to join the people demanding justice.

<u>News girl:</u> So, you're here, saving the future for your baby! Do you have a boy or a girl?

<u>Woman protester:</u> Our baby has a penis, but that doesn't necessarily mean he's a boy. We don't allow gender pronouns that will enslave our child. The children are our future. They mean everything to us.

<u>Male protester:</u> Who did you leave the baby with at the safe center?

<u>Woman protester:</u> The baby was in the highchair while I was getting ready to go. I didn't go to the safe center. I thought you took care of that!

Male protester: I was busy texting the location of the protest to the group.

Newsgirl: So, your genderless baby is at home in the highchair, and here you are sacrificing your dinner to make a better world for all of us.

(*The protesters exit abruptly*)

News girl: Ladies and gentlemen, the police have asked us to move and to make room for the Federal authorities. We will relocate and continue with our live report from Vero Beach Fl. Back to you in the studio Jeff.

(*Jason, Evelyn, and Martin, talking amongst themselves, are approached by the officers of the EPA and Animal Control*)

EPA: Sir, my name is Ian Folger. I am with the Environmental Protection Agency, and this is Captain Kessler of Animal Control. This is an interesting situation Mr. Traveler. We don't get many like this.

Martin: This is a special case! . . . Hi, I'm Martin Epstein, the next-door neighbor. I have been working on this case since the beginning.

AC: This case? From the beginning?

EPA: Mr. Epstein these are matters best left to the trained, professional represenitives of the government. You need not concern yourself any further with this matter.

Martin: Do you speak the bat language? (*bat chirps*)

AC: No, and I very much doubt you do either. (*bat hisses*)

Martin: There is more than meets the eye here. I have been studying the bat and I believe I may have opened a line of communication with him.

EPA: (*studying the bat, getting in Jasons face*) This is a Florida

219

Bonneted Bat. It is a protected species in the state of Florida.

Martin: I know, I love those ears (*bat chirps*) and look at those eyebrows! (*chirps again*)

Jason: Will someone kindly remove this creature from my head! (*bat screeches*)

Martin: I don't think he likes being referred to as a 'creature' Jason.

AC: This bat is also on the U.S. governments list of endangered species. If it is nesting, it cannot be disturbed.

Jason: Let me get this straight . . . you're saying that if this bat is nesting it cannot be removed from my head?

EPA: Not without EPA approval.

Jason: That's crazy!

EPA: Mr. Traveler, calm down. You can be sure we will do what is best.

Martin: Gentlemen! (*waving his arms in the air*) it is all moot. I think I may have found a way to communicate with the bat. By asking a series of questions, using the groupings of sounds I have collected, I believe we may be able to better understand why the bat is here and what his intentions are.

AC: Bats don't talk.

Martin: But they do communicate.

AC: With each other (*a little annoyed*)

Martin: Until now!

Jason: It has been uncanny how the bat comments at what seems to be the appropriate time, like he was putting his two cents in.

AC: Bats don't comment on things.

Jason: Whatever you want to call it, the bat has been putting his two cents in all along.

Officer Davis: I've noticed that.

Officer Kowalski: I have as well.

EPA: OK . . . let's stay focused here--

Jason: Hold on agent Folger! . . . Martin are you saying you have found a way to communicate with this thing? *(bat hisses)* I mean, don't joke around, because otherwise, I have to live with this son of a bitch sitting on my head. *(bat hisses)* You say it's male with big bushy eyebrows. If he's male, he can't be nesting.

Martin: Exactly! . . . he is here for another reason.

Jason: *(pacing)* What am I talking about. I sound as crazy as they do. . . . OK, OK, Martin even if you could, (hesitantly) or when you do communicate with this bat, what would come of it?

Martin: I will find out what's going on.

Jason: And?

Martin: We'll see if we can remedy this situation. I think my first impression, that it was all about a past life was wrong. I think he is here for reasons that are not clear yet.

EPA: So, you admit you are wrong!

Martin: No, not at all.

AC: How do you know it's a male?

Martin: Look at him, look at those shoulders--

Jason: Can we move on please!

Martin: Sorry Jason . . . anyway, I have been studying the bats responses--

EPA: It is important that we establish the bats sex, so we know how to proceed . . . how do you know its male without examining its body parts.

Martin: The same way I know your male without examining your body parts.

Officer Kowalski: You never know, who's to say--

Jason: Gentlemen please . . . Martin continue.

Martin: I have been studying the bat, and it seems he

understands what we are saying, but he is limited in his responses. For instance, if I were to call him a flying rat, he would screech like hell. *(bat screeches. Martin speaking to the bat)* I said IF I were to call you a flying rat, *(bat screeches)* OK, fair enough . . . I'll find another metaphor.

AC: Are you talking to the bat?

Martin: Of course, and the more we talk the more I understand. Our little talks have become mostly telepathic though.

AC: (to EPA) Aren't there regulations covering this agent Folger?

EPA: Regulation #147 might apply here--

Jason: Hello! Before we bring out the handcuffs could we let him finish. *(bat chirps)*

Evelyn: The little guy's timing is awfully good. *(bat chirps)*

Martin: See! . . . that chirp means he is in total agreement. *(chirp)* Now should he disagree you will hear a hiss(bat chirps. To the bat) oh yes, of course . . . if he strongly disagrees you will hear a long-drawn-out hiss. (chirp)

EPA: *(speaking to AC)* He really believes he is talking with the bat.

AC: This is getting out of control . . . is he allowed to talk to the bat?

EPA: I'm not sure, I'm going to check on that. Officer Davis please ask EMS to standby. Mr. Epstein may be needing transport to the hospital for a checkup.

Jason: What about MEEEEEEEE!

Officer Kowalski: *(to Evelyn)* You know, I've noticed too, that the bat seems to know what's going on. How does your husband know all this stuff?

Evelyn: Martin knows a lot of things.

EPA:(shaking his head) Davis, tell EMS to make plenty of

room . . . it may get crowded in there.

Jason: Martin, before they call out the National Gard, finish what you were saying. Something tells me you've got a plan.

Martin: I think I may. (*moving off to the side*) Step into my office.

(Jason and Martin break away to talk. A helicopter is heard hovering above, there is laughter on the police line and EPA, AC and Officer Davis talk amongst themselves.)

Martin: I have put together a series of yes or no questions that might give us a picture of what's going on here.

Jason: Like what?

Martin: Like . . .Did you come here to see Jason? . . . Are you nesting? . . . Do you plan on staying? . . . or . . . Do you have a name? Between that and our newly developed telepathy, we might get somewhere.

Jason: OK . . . I'm as crazy as you are, but let's get started.

(Martin pulls a notebook from his back pocket)

Martin: Step into my laboratory. . . . (*bat chirps*)

EPA: (*getting off the phone with his office*) There are no regulations regarding talking to bats. I've asked them to write one, though it won't be ready for a couple of hours. Regulation #147 doesn't apply to this situation either.

AC: What is #147 anyway?

EPA: Interference with or hindrance of an ongoing EPA investigation.

AC: That could apply to almost anything. "Show me the man, and I will find you a crime" kind of thing.

EPA: It really worked well in Dallas last year. After the Ferguson Mo. mess, we found a fast food chain that openly criticized the EPA in an op-ed in the local newspaper. They said the only thing we were any good at is forcing caloric counts on menus. We used Reg#147, and they are out of business.

AC: That's beautiful! Wish we had #147 at animal control. My kind of organization.

Officer Davis: What? Making people do and say things they don't want to do or say?

AC: It's for their own good. For everybody's good.

Officer Davis: How do you know?

AC: The regulations say so.

(We pick up Jason and Martin in the middle of their conversation)

Martin: And listen to this…He was living in a bat house, in a tree, beside a big picture window. He could see the big screen TV in the living room. Every night, for months, he would watch Batman and Robin on the television. He was so consumed with the show he began to neglect his bug gathering duties. He was getting thin in the face. The other bats assailed him with accusations of laziness and sloth. He decided it was time to move on and become the superhero he was meant to be. But! . . . he needed a Robin…that's where you came in.

Jason: So the bat needed a Robin to fulfill his television fantasy and *That's* why I have helicopters hovering over my house.

Martin: Pretty much.

Jason: Why does that not seem outrageous?

Martin: I don't know

Jason: Welcome to the twilight zone!

Martin: Initially he thought you would make a good Robin. He has since changed his mind. He says you're a flake.

Jason: Well now…isn't that the pot calling the kettle . . . listen to me (*hands in the air*) I'm defending myself.

Martin: You shouldn't take it personal.

224

Jason: You are absolutely right! I agree 100%. Maybe his echolocator needs a tune-up. Maybe I'm not up to the task of playing Robin to his batman . . . just get this thing out of my hair and out of my life. *(bat screeches)*

Martin: Jason . . . you want out of this? . . . because if you do, we have a plan.

Jason: You and the bat?

Martin: Yes

(Jason and Martin take a few steps backwards, not to be overheard.)

Martin: We have come to an agreement. He admits to having made a mistake in choosing you for a host. He will have his echo-locator checked as you have suggested, and he is willing to do his part to rectify the situation.

Jason: *(sarcastically)* Puckish little fellow isn't he?

Martin: *(annoyed)* Jason!

Jason: Alright, alright, I'll go along, "Thank you bat" *(bat chirps)*. So what's next? *(rubbing his hands)* what's the plan?

Martin: Well, he has agreed to make a transfer should we be able to guarantee certain conditions.

Jason: Really! *(being haughty and sarcastic)* And what would these conditions be? Transfer to what?

Martin: I am to build a perch for him, which I will strap to my shoulder and we will make the transfer that way.

Jason: Why doesn't he just fly away?

Martin: He wants to continue with his plan. *(chirp)* He says he's not going to let a little snafu like a badly calibrated echo-locator interfere with his mission.

Jason: Remind him he's supposed to fly over buildings, not into them.

Martin: Jason--

Jason: And what about the politburo over there? What are they going to say?

Martin: They can't say a thing. The bat can do and go wherever he pleases. There are no regulations governing the behavior of bats. The regulations are for the humans that come in contact with them. (*chirp*)

Jason: And what's in it for you? Are you working for him? you sound like his lawyer!

Martin: Research . . . I'm doing this for the research opportunity. And I am a lawyer, so it should not be surprising that I sound like one.

Jason: OK . . . Ok, go on. What other demands has the bat made?

Martin: He wants a bat house in the carport, out of the sun. No bug lights, he wants his larder full.
The condo must be sufficient--

Jason: Did you say *Condo?*

Martin: Yes, and a three-story condo at that. We both feel that you should help and contribute with the cost of his maintance.

Jason: So, you want me to pay child support for the bat?

Martin: It's only fair Jason. *(bat chirps)*

Jason: And what is it going to cost me?

Martin: Well the food is taken care of. There is no electricity, cooling or heating bills. I guess just the cost of construction, maybe a little paint now and then.

Jason: Just so long as he doesn't ask for a maid and room service. Did you say th*ree story Condo?*

Martin: Yes…He is expecting that his celebrity will attract a good many *"Chicks"* as he calls them, and he will be needing suitable accommodations for them.

Jason: So, you want me to subsidize a *Bat Brothel!* *(bat squeals)*

Martin: Bats are poly amorous.

Jason: Have you talked to Evelyn about this?

226

Martin: We wanted to run it by you first.
Jason: Well! She's going to love your new "We"

(Evelyn overhears her name and joins Jason and Martin. The EPA and AC watch closely.)

EPA: We'd better keep an eye-out with these people . . . they look like their planning something.
AC: Maybe plotting their escape.
Jason: *(greeting Evelyn)* Evelyn! come meet *Bat and Robin*.
Evelyn: Sounds like ice cream . . . you guys sharing?
Martin: Sharing yes, but not ice cream.
Evelyn: I hope this is not going to get kinky?
Martin: Evelyn, we have a unique opportunity here. I could become the world's leading Chiroptologist.
Evelyn: Since when have you wanted to be the world's leading Chiroptologist. And what the hell is a Chiroptologist anyway?
Jason: A bat expert--*(interjecting)*
Martin: Ever since I met Bat. He needs a partner and I have agreed. He has seen every episode of Batman and Robin--
Evelyn: The TV show?
Martin: And he wants to be a superhero.
Evelyn: Well I'll be . . . you're kidding right?
Jason: (to Evelyn) And he'll be moving in with you!
News girl: Jeff, we seem to have come to a standstill here in Vero Beach while we await word from the government regarding this complex case. The crowd has thinned, the information stream is slow, and only the steadfast folks who have been here from the beginning are left. We are all wondering if this incident will be resolved at all this evening.
AC: When are we going to get our new regs, so we can do

something about this?

EPA: I've just called the bureau. There is a delay . . . the reg writers are in sensitivity training and can't be disturbed.

AC: What are they being sensitive too?

EPA: They are chasing their dragon tails. Walking, talking, and breathing can become stressful, so we have a lady come in during the week to train us to go about our jobs playfully. We put on our imaginary dragon tails and try to catch them as we circle the room. Then after a good game of Candyland we're completely refreshed and ready to go to work.

AC: Sounds like good training.

EPA: Just another example of how the EPA loves us and wants us to be happy.

Evelyn: Well, if we're going to do this thing, let's get this show on the road.

What's our first move?

Martin: You and Jason keep everyone busy while I go to the house to build the transfer perch.

I have it all planned out, so it won't take long.

Evelyn: I love it when your being clever.

Martin: (smiling) That's why I do it. (*Martin steps away and in a loud voice*)

Oh!!!my bladders going to burst! (*He heads for his house*)

News girl: Ladies and gentlemen, one of the key players in this drama has just left screaming that his bladder was bursting. Could this be because of his contact with the bat? Is that why the EPA is here? To stop an epidemic before it can spread?

Man#1: I always knew it! . . . they're after our internal organs.

Jason: (*To Evelyn*) My turn! (*approaching the group at the line*) Hello! . . . No one's bladder is bursting due to the bat. The gentleman had to pee is all....and let us hope he made it to

228

the bathroom in time.

(*EPA and AC block Jason's way*)

EPA: Mr. Traveler, if you wouldn't mind stepping back.
News girl: Jeff, the EPA officer has just stopped Mr. Traveler from approaching the crowd. He is being quarantined close to the house. Jeff, that was the closest look we have had of the bat, and I can say it was something.
Jeff (off stage) What did he look like Page?
News girl: A bat.
Jason: Don't worry Evelyn, it'll be OK. He won't be living in the house or anything. I'm sure it won't be long before they both tire of their little adventures.
Evelyn: If you're so amenable to the bat why is he leaving?
Jason: It was his choice. Evidently, I'm not on the same wavelength. The bat admitted he made a mistake. Martin is a perfect fit. Besides, he's going to be the world's foremost Chiroptologist.
Evelyn: That's what I'm afraid of.
(*Martin returns, crossing stage to join Jason and Evelyn*)
Martin: I'm back!
EPA: Hold on Mr. Epstein . . . (*blocking Martins way*) what's that you have in your hand? . . . You're not planning anything are you Mr. Epstein?
Martin: Well hello there Agent Folger. Planning? . . . nah…why this is a gift for my new friend. (*Bat chirps, EPA and AC look at each other perplexed. Martin walks around Agent Folger and addresses Evelyn*) Darling, would you be so kind as to do the honors of hitching up my harness?
Evelyn: I would be delighted!
AC: Can he do that?

EPA: I don't know.

Evelyn: *(Attaching the bungee cords around Martins back)* Humm . . . this is a switch.

I guess you're going to find out what it's like to wear a harness every day.

Jason: *(seeing Martin hitched up)* That's incredible! You're a regular MacGyver! . . . Bat, are you paying attention? *(bat chirps)* How did you do this?

Martin: I used a paper towel holder. I took out the sleeve from the roll and wrapped it with contact paper that had a forest motif, put the two together and Voila!

Jason: Brilliant!

Evelyn: *(Evelyn stepping around to get a look at Martin. She is laughing)* You look like a pirate!

Martin:*(staring intently at Evelyn)* You're turning me on--

Evelyn: Not in front of the bat!

Jason: Bat! . . . Behold, your limo has arrived. *(squeal)* Martin, don't you and the bat have some business you want to attend to?

EPA: Mr. Epstein I'm going to have to ask you to cease and desist. Mr. Traveler, could you step back please.

Martin: Stop what? Standing here? You want me to sit?

EPA: Your interfering with an official EPA investigation.

AC: Yah . . . that's regulation 147! (to EPA) I thought you said 147 doesn't apply?

EPA: He doesn't know that.

Newsgirl:*(To her camera man)* I think we're spinning our wheels with this story. There's nothing happening here, lets pack it in. I'll call the office and let them know we're heading for the studio *(They pack up and exit stage)*.

Martin:*(talking with the bat)* OK, I'll tell them. Don't worry, they won't tell a soul. *(to Jason and Evelyn)* He wants me to tell that his name is to be Afflatus. It is part of his new identity. You are not to tell anyone though. It could blow his cover.

(*EPA, AC and Davis talk amongst themselves*)

Man#1: I think I'll call it a night . . . I'll check back in the morning . . . Beverly, we should order out...it's getting late. How about pizza?

Woman#1: We had pizza two nights ago.

Man#2: Night Ben . . . Sonia. I guess we should be going too Carol, it'll be getting dark soon.

Woman #2: Guess so . . . what happened here anyway . . . was all this about anything?

Officer DeAngelis: Wait . . . wait!

Officer O'Brian: We've got more material!

Martin: Afflatus, I think it's time to . . . of course not! I don't care for Ozzie Osborne either . . . He won't be allowed anywhere near the house, I promise. . . . Yes it is gross . . . not to worry, I've got your back.

EPA: Mr. Traveler, Mr. Epstein----

Martin: As a guest of Mr. Travelers, I have a right to be here.

Jason: And Mr. Epstein has agreed to entertain my verbose little roommate.

AC: What's he talking about?

EPA: I don't know.

Jason: Let's go bat . . . the world is waiting for its first ever "Furry Superhero"

(*The bat squeals and leaps onto the perch on Martins shoulder. They both stare intently at EPA*)

Martin: You have no authority here, and besides that, you can't tell a bat how to live. It's out of your jurisdiction. (*bat squeals*)

Officer Davis: DeAngelis roll up the police line and put things away.

Officer Kowalski: You too O'Brian, then wait in the car for us.

EPA: *(to AC)* He's right . . . I can't tell the bat what to do. I can tell them what to do, but I can't tell the bat what to do.

(EMS approaches and whispers something to AC)

AC: I think you can go. . . . We're almost through here. Job well done guy's!

EMS: OK guys, lets load up and get out of here.

EPA: How am I going to explain this back at the office.

AC: That you were outsmarted by a bat?

EPA: Don't be ridiculous . . . it was Traveler and Epstein not the bat.

AC: Are you sure?

Officer Davis: Agent Folger, I guess you won't be needing us any longer, everyone's gone.

EPA: Yes... thank you Officer Davis.

Officer Kowalski: That's a wrap! . . . see you at the tavern Bill

Officer Davis: Right, see you there. Order me a double!

EPA: What am I supposed to tell them at the office . . . I need my dragon tail.

AC: Can I come along? (*He puts his arm around a sunken and sullen agent Folger as they exit the stage*)

Martin: Afflatus meet Mrs. Robin. She is the nuts and bolts of this operation. (*chirp*)

Evelyn: Very happy to meet you Afflatus.

Martin: Well Jason, delivered as promised, you've got your life back.

Jason: Thank you, thank you, thank you. It seemed like forever. I was beginning to lose it.

Martin: Well everyone is gone, and things are back to normal . . . well sort of. (*to the bat*) Yes . . . yes . . . Afflatus says forever is anchored in the present.

Evelyn: What's that mean?

Jason: Too deep for me.

Martin: (*to the bat*) Makes sense to me. . . . I know, you have to go to work . . . not to worry, I've got it all planned . . . we'll have the condo ready for you in the morning. In the meantime, the robin house should be comfy. Jason, we're going to say good night.

Jason: Thank you guys, I couldn't have done it without you.

Evelyn: Goodnight Jason. (*bat chirps, they walk home arm in arm*) Humm . . . I can't wait to get my hands on my dashingly clever pirate. Take me to your cabin captain! (*grabbing Martins butt*)

Martin: Evelyn, look at the effect Afflatus has had on us already. I can see that "This is the beginning of a beautiful relationship." (*to bat*) No . . . Casablanca . . . Humphrey Bogart and Claude Raines.... I'm already working on it . . . we can put a cell phone in the condo and you can watch movies on it... we'll put it on Jason's bill. (*They exit the stage. Jason picks up the garden house and continues to water his lawn. The sun is setting behind him.*)

Jason: (*Smiling*) So this is what it's like not have a bat on your head.

The lights fade as the curtain falls

THE NINTH RING

OF SOCMED WELTSCHMERZ

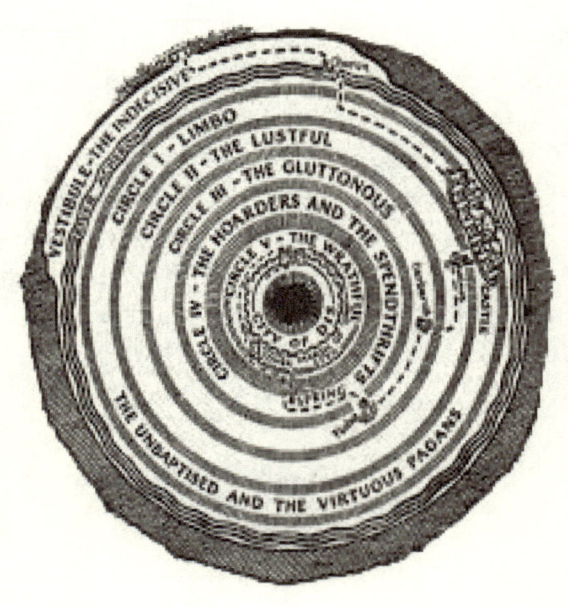

On an elevated subway platform Elvis and Jacob are nondescript amongst the growing crowd. It is the morning rush hour and people anxiously await the next train. Elvis is tall, thin, mid-thirties with long hair and horn-rimmed glasses. A bit of a know-it-all. Jacob is a well-respected stout afician-american gentleman with a beard. He and Elvis have been partners for several years. The train enters the station, comes to a stop, and the doors open. Elvis and Jacob step into the subway car being pushed forward by the crowd. They each grab a hanging strap, not bothering to sit in the available seats in front of them.

Elvis: It's a little more than an hour to Chambers Street, not a bad ride if there are no delays. How do you like living in the Bronx so far?

Jacob: The wife and kids love living in their own house. They're are making new friends and settling into their new schools. Work on the house is coming along. I have to schlep back to Brooklyn to play softball with my friends, but, the season is coming to an end and I will deal with it come spring. Maybe next year I 'll drive.

Elvis: How'd the team do this year?

Jacob: We finished at seventh place

Elvis: (laughing) Better than last year!

The doors close and the train slowly pulls out of the station. An elderly lady forces herself between them, smiles, and takes a seat.

Jacob: Hey, you should have seen this contractors face when I told him I would be back on Monday with my partner Elvis. (laughing) I have never seen a man look so worried so quick!

A train running in the opposite direction passes by and drowns them out. The door at the end of the subway car opens and a man, bible in hand in full voice sermonizes as he walks through the car.

Preacher: "Where do we lie, city dwellers of contemporary delusions? Unholy fixations of money and leisure! I'll tell you! In hollow cities of steel gray, ourselves the hierarchy, the knights and the knaves. The sinners and the saved, the virtuous and the depraved! Troglodytes in cities of steel gray! Pray often people! pray hard. The kingdom of God is at hand." He *opens the car door and disappears into the roar of the subway.*

Jacob: That brother should be on the stage . . . with a voice like that he--

Elvis: Liked the message too. (Jacob looks stunned) Not the hell and damnation stuff, but the knights and knaves, sinners and the saved...he had that down. I don't agree with him, but it was well put together and he certainly knew how to deliver it. Nice to hear another point of view. I get tired of the left-right bullshit.

Jacob: You still writing that book . . . ahh . . . Sokmed . . . sochmed German something.

Elvis: Socmed Weltschmerz . . .The Ninth Ring.

Jacob: Oh yah, that was it. . . . You're gonna sell a lot of books with a title like that. (laughing heartily) Everyone I know will be lining up at the stores to get Sokmed Something Something for sure.

Elvis; Yah, I know . . . but what can I do, it is what it is.

Jacob: You can start by writing about something people care about like, Sex — Murder — Betrayal. Something they can sink their teeth into and read themselves to sleep with.

Elvis: I know, I know, you're right. Maybe after I finish this

236

project, I'll take your advice. It's just that the Orwellian shadows behind social media today, stick in my craw. Five thousand years of trial and error produced this system we live under. Thousands of years of living under dictators, theocracies and militant city states; and when there was a void, in stepped the nomadic hoards. It took the enlightenment, and the discovery of a new continent, where its ideas could be put to work, that allowed men to live with dignity and govern themselves. We became the beacon of the entire world. All of these ideas were pushed forward and spread across the globe by the new merchant class. That's right . . . the mercantile class helped too.

Jacob: Can't leave them out! (sarcastically) I guess that's one for the capitalist! Am I going to get another history lesson?

Elvis: Nah... just a reminder. Without the exchange of goods and ideas along the silk road and throughout the Mediterranean, we would still be in caves. The merchants have pushed the world forward. From the fertile crescent, then across the Levant, agriculture spread. The first cities were built with trade routes connecting them. The surplus led to monumental building projects and the organization of labor. Within a couple of hundred years the Egyptians were building the pyramids. The Nile valley produced a surplus of grain with which they could trade and exchange for the goods they didn't produce. The coffers of the treasury swelled, and schools and libraries and temples were built.

Jacob: Sounds like a history lesson to me.

The door between cars open with a thunderous roar. A frail woman in her thirties enters the car. She is carrying a cardboard sign that reads 'Please Help'.

Woman: Good morning everyone . . . sorry to interrupt you but we are in need of help. I have been diagnosed with AIDS and have lost my job. I have two kids at home, and we are going to be evicted come the end of this month. Anything you can spare, anything at all, would be greatly appreciated and would help us until social services kicks in. Thank you and God bless." *She is halfway through the car when the door opens again and a group of kids in their early teens enter. There are four of them. One of them carries a plastic pail, another a kitchen pot and the smallest of the troupe, a tambourine and penny whistle. The fourth young man removes his cap, holds it over his heart and addresses the people in the subway car.*

Young man: Ladies and Gentlemen! You are about to be entertained! We hope you will enjoy our little performance . . . and if you'll just step back and give us a little room, we can begin!

The kids beat on their pails, pots and tambourines while the fourth began his break dance. He did flips and turns, spins about the pole in what is sometimes rather complicated rhythms. He finishes with a somersault and a split. The subway riders clap and reach in their pockets for change.

Young man: Thank you, thank you!

Using his hat as a basket, he walks through the car collecting the donations. Together, the troupe bows and disappears into the roar of the subway.

Elvis: That was good, I enjoyed that . . . only in NY--
Jacob: They should be in school!
Elvis: I agree . . . If they took that energy and organization and used it to build a future, there would be no stopping them. I still enjoyed it. You know, you perform that act twenty times or so and you've done a day's work!

238

Jacob: They should be in school. We both know you have to know how to do something to get by in this world Elvis.

Elvis: Your beginning to sound like me.

The train stops at Fordham Road and a crowd enters the car forcing everyone closer together.

Jacob: So what's with this Ninth Ring? What's that part about?

Elvis: Dante, the ninth ring of the inferno is where the Ghibelline and Guelps are condemned to. Much like the two parties today, their hell is the ceaseless debate fueling anger and hate. All going nowhere, nonstop. For eternity.

Jacob: (laughing) Sounds like a bad marriage . . . an earthly kind of hell . . . ah, maybe not so funny.

Elvis: And this took place during medieval times! The vitriol that was floating around then was not that different from what we see today. The Ghibelline and Guelps that occupy the ninth ring are the shadows of the mindless Manchurian zombies we see today, repeating the same mantras in the same word order, over and over again. And of course, if you repeat something often enough, and worldwide mind you, it becomes a Meme. A year later people are saying "Of course it's true! Everybody knows that." That's where Socmed comes in. Clever little Socmed is designing the dichotomy-- separating the sides--giving them the talking points to throw at each other--like spears.

Jacob: I hope you mean all the parties . . . I hear the same type of diatribes coming from the conservatives.

Elvis: Absolutely buddy! My interest is in the Herd/Mob mentality and what fuels it. If Socmed designs the stage . . . provides the dichotomy . . . writes the script for each of the players, who do you think is in control?

Jacob: The electrician! And I hope he's union!

Elvis is about to speak when a train passing in the other direction roars on by and Elvis is silenced . . . Jacob smiles in relief.

Elvis: Every airport, train station, bar room and dentist office are broadcasting the same state sponsored paradigms. Hell, you can't even eat a hamburger at a fast food joint without CNN telling you how to view the world.

Jacob: People need to know what's going on.

Elvis: And who is it that determines what we are to know and what our takeaway should be?

Jacob: The news people . . . the people reporting.

Elvis: Ah contraire! CNN, FOX, MSNBC all get their feeds from the same places. If you listen you will hear "as reported by AP or UPI"

Jacob: Yah, I've heard that . . . So? . . . That's where the reporters are.

Elvis: BBC, France24, RAI, RT are all run and funded by the state. They all propagate the same news feed. The same world view, different sides of the issue maybe, but that's part of it. It's like choosing your hamburgers . . . one is flame broiled and the other has a special sauce. We are told by each of them, that theirs is the best . . . lots of pictures . . . lots of words . . . you're still getting a hamburger!

Jacob: That's where we are different! Twitter, Facebook, Fox and all the others are independent of the government.

Elvis: Are you sure?

Jacob; They are all owned by corporations, not the government!

Elvis: OK . . . sure I don't know either

Jacob: But I do know! I just told ya . . . come on Elvis!

Elvis: OK . . . I said I didn't know. It just seems to me that it wouldn't take much to write up some paperwork and documents saying such and such belongs to such and such. They give these guys a ceremonial title, some money and send them on their way till needed.

Jacob: My partner is becoming a conspiracy theorist!

Elvis; I know it sounds that way sometimes. *As* you know, my goal is to become an "expert ancient alien theorist" (*smiling sarcastically*)

Jacob: Yah . . . I won't be forgetting that one too soon . . . what exactly do they do?

Elvis: Mostly talk about things they can't prove. They sift through history to see what doesn't line up and then present it as a could be.

Jacob: Nice work if you can find it!

Elvis: Yah! Have fun! (*seriously*) Somebody's got to do it!

Jacob: Onward! The aliens are depending on you . . . stay focused Elvis!

Elvis: Stay focused Elvis!

An elderly lady with a shopping cart pushes her way between Jacob and Elvis and takes a seat. She turns her head to follow each as they speak, listening to their conversation.

Elvis; And the newspapers?

Jacob: Corporations as well . . . not owned by the state.

Elvis: Does it really matter who owns it?

Jacob: You just made a big deal of state sponsored media--

Elvis: What I mean is that it's not the primary issue--

Jacob: Then what is the issue?

Elvis: The fact is that they all have the same agenda. Left-- right. Up--down, whatever! They're all selling the same product.

Jacob: And that is?

Elvis: Totalitarianism! plain and simple. Socialism and all the free stuff that comes with it are just the carrots being used to bribe you into giving up your freedom. Nothing is free. There is a tradeoff. In exchange for free stuff, you give the state the authority to control and manage your life in its entirety. To make decisions for you, because the state knows what's best. The state becomes a surrogate parent and you are obligated to obey.

Jacob: I like socialism Elvis. Any system that benefits the majority of people over the wealthy few, works for me!

Elvis: The welfare state is indentured slavery.

Jacob: Socialism is an opportunity to see that justice is applied equally across the board, that all people are afforded the same opportunities on a fair playing field regardless of their religion or ethnicity.

Elvis: That's a crock of shit!

Jacob: It's not a crock of shit!

Elvis: It always look good on paper. But let me ask you, where are you gonna find the people to carry out this grand plan? It's never worked before. Matter of fact, it has turned out to be disastrous and horrifically bloody at that!

Jacob: It will be different this time. We've learned from our mistakes.

Elvis: That's what they say after every coup--

Jacob: Worked in Europe!

Elvis: No it didn't. Greece, Italy, Spain are all on the verge of economic collapse . . . the EU has been disastrous for Europe. If you're a proud German, you are a Nazi . . . if you're French and love your culture, you are a racist. Brussels has put into place policies that deliberately undermine national identity, believing that everyone will merge into a new culture and will live happily ever after; when they all have the same stuff.

Jacob: Some countries have done well. Germany is strong. The French economy is healthy, and England has done pretty good with the EU.

Elvis: (laughing) That must be why they are leaving!

A middle age woman from the Caribbean, with a Gucci Bag, stands to get ready to exit the train at the next stop. Elvis steps aside to allow her to pass and she speaks to Elvis with serious concern.

Caribbean Lady: If you got Zombies . . . you got trouble! I know . . . my country is full of dem. Back home, der so many you can't go out at night! *(speaking to Elvis's eye's)* You talk 'bout dem. You be da first dey come for . . . dey gonna get ya if they want ya. *(the doors open, everyone stands aside to let her pass and she disappears through the subway doors)*

Elvis: I wasn't expecting that!

Jacob: (laughing) She thought you were talking about real zombies.

Elvis: I was—

Jacob: No . . . the ones that kill people--

Elvis: I was! Would you like me to recite the "Litany of mass graves?"

Jacob: That won't be necessary, thank you.

Elvis: Thank you . . . that would ruin this beautiful day.

Jacob: (sarcastically) You're on a crowded subway train during the morning rush hour--

Elvis: That's how I know it's a beautiful day!

Jacob: Okay . . . Ok, never mind. I still say the people, the media, Brussels or whoever, don't have the power you say they do.

Elvis: They can create a flash mob in a matter of hours. They define their targets and send the mob to vilify and ostracize anyone who disagrees with the party. Hopefully they don't turn into a lynch mob. You can't blame the cell phones, don't blame them, they are inanimate objects, you have to look elsewhere.

Jacob: Sounds kind of extreme Elvis.

Elvis: The mobs of the French revolution come to mind . . . throw in some Bolshevik thugs, a little Pol Pot and you have a "coup d' etat stew"

Jacob: That's not gonna happen here Elvis!

Elvis: Yah sure . . . like it could never happen in the land of Beethoven--

The lady with the shopping cart gets up to ready herself to exit the train. She lets Elvis know what she thinks of their little conversation.

Lady with shopping cart: Your too smart for your own good . . . you think too much. You may be right, but no good will come from it! *(She exits the train at 59th St. as pan flute music is being played on the platform. There has been a delay and the train doors remain open)*

Conductor: Ladies and gentlemen, there is a police action at 42nd st. We should be moving shortly. Thank you for your patience and have a good day.

Jacob: (laughing) You're a big hit today on the subway today Elvis!

Elvis: I think she was talking about politics in general, and I agree with her.

Jacob: Seems you agree with everyone . . . except me of course.

Elvis: I agree with you too . . . 'cept the totalitarian part.

Conductor: Stand clear of the closing doors.

Elvis: What kinda car do you drive?

Jacob: I know where you're going with this! . . . We drive a hybrid.

Elvis: A state sponsored product--

Jacob: We were more than happy to buy a commonsense vehicle. We're also looking at solar panels for the house. If it makes sense and is good for us all in the long run, who cares if the state sponsored it or not. It means their doing their job!

Elvis: So your OK with the government telling you what's good to eat, what products to buy, what light bulbs to use? What your expectations should be, and what it takes to be a good person.

Jacob: Sure! Why not, if it works?

Elvis: Okay, why not? It's your choice.

The train pulls into Grand Central Station. The doors open to the thunderous roar of conga drums creating a wall of sound. The conductor can barely be heard over the drumming.

Conductor: Ladies and Gentlemen, you can connect here for the A-C-E and D lines--

Jacob: Ah! the drummers are back!

Elvis: Sounds like there's a dozen of them--

Conductor: Stand clear of the closing doors.

Jacob: *(crouching to look through the windows)* Looks like eight, maybe nine, I see an empty drum station.

Elvis: They could drive the subway rats running for the hills with that din!

The subway doors attempt to close several times with a bell ringing at each attempt. A passenger behind Elvis is awoken abruptly and lets out a yell.

Passenger: Whoh! Whats goin on? Where am--

The passenger looks around, smiles apologetically, arranges his newspaper in his lap and closes his eyes to go back to sleep.

Conductor: Stand clear of the closing doors.
The doors close and the train continues.
Elvis: Like I was saying. Brussels and the AP have way too much influence. In Berlin, London, New Orleans or New York, the newspapers all print the same article.
Jacob: It's a large organization with resources. The Times and the Post can't have reporters everywhere!
Elvis: That's so . . . but that's a hell of a lot of power the editors at the AP have. They can decide who the good guys and bad guys are. What the right and wrong of the situation is and how we should view it. People all over the world are getting the same information, the same point of view. Scares the hell out of me.
Jacob: The old lady was right Elvis; you think too much.
Elvis: Yep, I walk right down that road and into the ninth ring.
Jacob:(sarcastically) It'll be alright . . . not to worry. We always seem to muddle through.
Elvis: Actually, there's something even more sinister eating at me. I don't believe that we are wired for the type of social organization that a republic like ours necessitates. It all looks good on paper, but where you gonna find the people to make it so. If our behavior is rooted in our DNA, and modified by the environment, it very well might be that the baseline herd instinct is stronger than any reasoning we might employ. That instinct is so strong that the herd will follow its leaders over a cliff and into oblivion. The need to mimic and merge with the group is compulsive. Just try *not* to stand and do the wave at a concert or salute the flag at a union meeting. The need for acceptance by the group is compelling. Even for the

246

rebellious. I'm thinking that there's a lot of oxytocin floating around when we're in groups and we revel in it.

Jacob: I don't feel a lot of oxytocin 'floatin round' when I'm riding the subway! And it gets crowded sometimes. (laughing) "Where is the love" (mimicking the pop song)

Elvis: Good point! Now were talkin . . . gonna look into that . . . Why it works in certain groups and not in others?

Jacob: Don't get tangled up, we'll be getting off soon. Sounds like you've got some of that Weltschmerz Elvis. You've got yourself all depressed because the general population don't live up to your expectations. Well, gotta tell ya brother . . . BOO HOO . . . get over it . . . find something to do.

Elvis: That's why I talk to you about these things . . . you pick up what I miss. Seriously though, I think this idea that men can govern themselves might be just as much a pipe dream as everyone getting along when they have the same stuff. Maybe we don't even want it. We just like to pretend that we're all individuals and are making choices freely. With a two-party system like ours, where we have to choose between a big mac and a whopper . . . that is not much of a choice. Were still getting a hamburger!

Jacob: That's funny--

Elvis: I 've begun to question the whole concept of individuality too. It's like . . . instead of seeing people, I'm seeing limbic systems functioning as a group. When I look at the neurobiology of it, it's hard to see Elvis as a unique entity. Elvis evaporates into a series of neuro responses programmed by his DNA--

Jacob: Have we changed subjects? What happened to the social media bit?

Elvis: Yeah, were getting off at the next stop . . . We'll save that for tomorrow morning.

Jacob: Oh boy--

Elvis: In the Orwellian world it was required that you engage with the media every day to receive your bit of big brothers love . . . today, we are willing spend hours absorbing the message and pay for it dearly! We're paying for our own training!

Elvis and Jacob stand in front of the doors as the train slows down and enters the station.

Elvis: This contractor didn't really think you were talking about the dead Elvis did he?

Jacob: Don't know, I just left it at that. "Elvis is coming tomorrow" you should have seen his face!

The doors open and Jacob leaves the train, Elvis follows him.

Elvis: As intended! . . . Mom had a devilish sense of humor.
The subway doors close.
The lights fade as the curtain falls

www.ingramcontent.com/pod-product-compliance
Lightning Source LLC
Chambersburg PA
CBHW052047240626
47153CB00006B/2244